HIGHLANDER'S LOVE

Called by a Highlander Book Four

MARIAH STONE

Stone Publishing

This is a work of fiction. Names, characters, places, and incidents either are the products of the author's imagination or are used fictitiously. Any resemblance to actual persons, living or dead, businesses, companies, events, or locales is entirely coincidental.

© 2020 Mariah Stone. All rights reserved.

Cover design by Qamber Designs and Media

All rights reserved. This book or parts thereof may not be reproduced in any form, stored in any retrieval system, or transmitted in any form by any means—electronic, mechanical, photocopy, recording, or otherwise—without prior written permission of the publisher. For permission requests, contact the publisher at http:\\mariahstone.com

GET A FREE MARIAH STONE BOOK!

Join Mariah's mailing list to be the first to know of new releases, free books, special prices, and other author giveaways.

freehistoricalromancebooks.com

ALSO BY MARIAH STONE

MARIAH'S TIME TRAVEL ROMANCE SERIES

- CALLED BY A HIGHLANDER
- CALLED BY A VIKING
- CALLED BY A PIRATE
- FATED

MARIAH'S REGENCY ROMANCE SERIES

- DUKES AND SECRETS

VIEW ALL OF MARIAH'S BOOKS IN READING ORDER

Scan the QR code for the complete list of Mariah's ebooks, paperbacks, and audiobooks in reading order.

But to see her was to love her;
 Love but her, and love forever.
 — Robert Burns

PROLOGUE

Lands near Loch Awe, 1295

A WOMAN'S SCREAM PIERCED THE AIR.

"Whoa!" Owen Cambel pulled on his horse's reins. He'd soon arrive at Innis Chonnel Castle, his clan's seat. He knew he shouldn't stop at all, given what he was carrying, but he couldn't ignore the scream.

Birds chirped in the woods around him, leaves rustled in the wind, a woodpecker tapped. It smelled like pines and wildflowers, wet earth and moss. Nothing indicated danger.

"Ahhh! Help!" There it was again. A woman needed aid.

Where was she? He put his hand on his claymore and clicked his tongue to get the horse to carry on slowly down the path.

"Get off me!" a woman screamed from somewhere ahead of him.

His father's words echoed in his head. *All ye're good at is finding distractions and chasing skirts. Why canna ye take responsibility? Why canna ye be a leader like yer brothers?*

But the woman was clearly in danger. Owen couldn't live with himself if he didn't help someone when they needed it. His heart beat hard as he spurred the horse on and rode faster. One hand held the reins, and he clenched the handle of his sword with the other. Between the trees to his left, movement caught his eye. A man crushed a young lass against a tree, moving his hands up and down her body. She tried to push him away and writhed in an attempt to free herself.

Owen pulled his horse to a stop. "Let her go!"

The man turned and walked towards Owen, taking out a dagger. His biceps bulged under his sleeves, his chest as broad as a barrel. How could Owen defeat a man like this alone? He wasn't a small lad at sixteen, but the man clearly exceeded him in size and strength. Pulse beating in his ears, he jumped off the horse and unsheathed his claymore.

"Are ye going to fight me with a dagger?" Owen asked.

"Shut up, pup," the man said.

He launched himself at Owen and thrust the dagger, but Owen hadn't trained with swords since the age of eight for nothing. He ducked and deflected the weapon. It fell into the grass, leaving the man empty-handed.

His face reddened, and instead of looking for his weapon, he threw himself at Owen like a furious bull. Owen stepped out of the way, not willing to harm an unarmed man, and his attacker fell forward onto the grass. He put his sword at the man's throat and stilled, panting.

"I dinna wish to kill ye," Owen said. "Who is he to ye, lass?"

"I dinna ken him," she said. "He took my silver and wanted...more."

"Give it back to her," Owen said.

"I will give ye nothin'," the man growled through his teeth.

Owen pressed the edge of the claymore closer to the man's neck. "Ye will, or ye'll die."

The man reached into the purse that hung on his belt. He removed a leather pouch and tossed it on the ground.

"Good," Owen said. "Now leave."

The man threw a malicious glance at Owen, turned around, and walked into the woods without looking back. When Owen couldn't see him anymore, he put his claymore into its sheath. The lass sat by the tree, shaking. He picked up her purse and the man's dagger and brought them to her.

"Take yer silver and this for protection."

Owen's chest puffed. Not only did he carry a very important gift for King John Balliol from the MacDougalls, but he'd also saved a beautiful lass. With trembling hands, she took the purse and the dagger. Her blond hair was in disarray, her cheeks were flushed, and her eyes were wide and wet. She didn't look any older than him and was so pretty, so vulnerable, so defenseless.

"Thank ye," she said.

He sank down to squat before her. "What is yer name?"

"Aileene."

Her torn dress and undertunic showed more skin on her chest than was modest, and Owen tried not to stare.

"Do ye live nearby?" Owen said.

"The village is a fair walk away."

"Someone waits for ye? A husband, mayhap? I can take ye home."

He needed to be careful riding alone with enough gold to buy an estate, but who would presume a youth like him was carrying a sack of gold? And the lass clearly needed help...

"I'm nae marrit." She rubbed her ankle under the dress. "I dinna think I can move yet."

"I'll make a fire to warm ye, and ye can have my bread and cheese for the road."

But what about the gold? Shouldn't he take it to Innis Chonnel first? A pretty smile bloomed on her face.

No, the best way to hide something was to put it in plain sight, right? And he felt needed, appreciated, important.

"When ye feel better, I will take ye wherever ye want," he added.

"Ye have a heart of gold, lord," she said.

She called him *lord*... Warmth spread in Owen's chest. At his age, he hadn't done anything yet to deserve the name. Aye, his grandfather was the chief of his clan and a close ally of King John Balliol, and his father was a great warrior, and so were his brothers. Clan Cambel were proud descendants of Diarmid the Boar, a great hero from legends. And yet it was the first time in Owen's life that he'd felt important.

Would he hear the same respect in his father's voice once he delivered the package?

Owen made a fire and kept an eye out for Aileene's attacker. The man could return with another weapon or with some friends, but Owen doubted it. The man would probably assume Owen had continued on his way and so had Aileene. Owen had had his fair share of adventures with servant girls and willing farmers' daughters, but this lass... No one had ever looked at him with such admiration and gratitude.

He was the joker in the family, irresponsible and left to his own devices. He had been surprised when the MacDougalls gave him the sack of gold he now had hidden among other pouches on his horse's back. But he was honored. Finally, he had a chance to prove his worth to his clan.

King John Balliol was a guest at Innis Chonnel. Owen couldn't wait to see his father's astonished face, as well as his brothers'. Craig and Domhnall would surely be surprised. Mayhap his life had turned around today. Mayhap his father would finally agree to take him into battle.

Aileene sat by the fire, massaging her ankle. Owen gave her a piece of bread and cheese.

"Thank ye," she said as she took them from him. Their hands touched, and her eyes lingered on him. Her gaze moved down his tunic and even farther south to the front of his breeches. Was she really suggesting something? She'd just been attacked. Was she really ready?

Aileene looked away and bit into the bread and cheese.

"I want to thank ye," she said. "I need the silver to buy a potion for my sick father. Ye may have saved his life as well."

Owen shrugged. "Nae need to thank me."

She took a bottle out of her basket. "I make delicious berry wine and am on my way to trade it in the neighboring village. I'd love for ye to have a bottle. Would ye like some?"

"Aye." Owen grinned. "I never refuse a fine wine."

She smiled back, dimples forming in her cheeks. She removed the cork and handed the bottle to him.

"*Sláinte*," he said and sipped. The wine was sweet and not very strong, and Owen drank more, suddenly thirsty. They shared the bottle and the food and chatted. Aileene was a lovely woman, and Owen sensed she was enjoying his company. She kept throwing those lingering glances at him, and he knew what they meant. He was all for it, but he also didn't want to take advantage of her.

His head was pleasantly spinning from the wine and her company. She kept rubbing her ankle, wincing from time to time.

"Do ye ken anything about healing?" she said. "My ankle ails me."

Owen licked his lips, his mouth dry. "I can look at it if ye want?"

"Would ye?"

"Aye, but are ye certain? 'Tis nae proper... And that man..."

"I trust ye."

She leaned back and stretched her leg out to him. He sat closer, his groin already starting to warm as he imagined her smooth skin against his fingers. He took her foot in his hands and pushed the edge of her skirt up, revealing a delicate white ankle. There was a shallow scratch there, and he covered it with his hand. He massaged the foot gently. Her soft skin against his rough palms set fire burning in his blood.

He swallowed and looked up at her face. Her lips were

parted, and from under her lashes, her eyes were dark with desire.

"There's nothing ye can do against my will, because I'm willing for anything."

Owen cursed under his breath. Even if there'd been an army of angry, barrel-chested men here now, he couldn't stop.

He put her leg back on the ground and crawled up to her. He kissed her, and she answered back. God's bones, he wanted her. He'd never lusted for any lass like this in his life. His mind filled with fog that smelled like berry wine, sweet female skin, and grass...

∼

Owen woke with a jolt and sat up. The woods were dark around him, his fire already out. His head was killing him, every pulsation of blood in his temples bringing pain. He looked around. Where had Aileene gone? His breeches were still down, and his cock was still hard and ready to go. Did he not finish?

"Aileene?" Owen called, rubbing his face. Mayhap she'd gone to relieve herself.

Owen closed his breeches over the uncomfortable erection and stood up. Everything swayed and swam.

"Aileene?" he repeated.

Her basket was gone. Should he feel hurt she'd left without saying goodbye? How had he fallen asleep like that? How had it gotten so dark so quickly?

He looked at his horse, and his back chilled.

The purse with the gold was gone.

It took his drowsy mind a moment to make the connection. She must have taken it. And she'd left. How would he find her in this darkness, with his head feeling like a banner swaying on the wind?

This was bad. This was worse than anything he'd ever done. Worse than stealing his brother's clothes when they were bathing. Worse than drinking half a cask of *uisge* and accidentally hitting the estate's best-producing ram while practicing archery in the dark. Worse than taking the virginity of the Mackintosh's daughter. He might still need to marry the lass if the truth ever came out.

What a fool he was. What a fool! And why the hell had his cock not calmed down yet? That had never happened before. He didn't feel aroused in the slightest.

He should never trust himself to make good decisions. He should have known she'd steal from him. Mayhap the entire attack had been a plot?

He'd never find her now.

He'd best make his way back home and accept the shame he knew awaited him...and his family.

CHAPTER 1

Mallyne Farm near Inverlochy village, 2020

AMBER HEARD STEPS OUTSIDE THE FRONT DOOR AND RAISED her head.

"Amber Ryan, stop worrying." Her aunt shook her head and took a sip of her coffee. "It's only Rob. He went to feed the cows."

Amber sighed and poked her porridge with a spoon. She'd been here for a week. She should've gotten used to Rob, Aunt Christel's son, feeding the cows and sheep first thing in the morning. And she should've started liking porridge. Where was a peanut butter and jelly sandwich when she needed it?

At least her aunt had good coffee. Her mug sat on the checkered tablecloth steaming with a comforting aroma. The rustic kitchen was bathed in sunlight, but it was still cool, even in summer. Old Scottish farmhouses were probably never warm.

Or maybe Amber was just too used to the summer heat in Afghanistan. The thought sent a shiver through her, and she glanced at the door again. She was safe for now. No one was coming for her.

Yet.

"I should leave you guys soon," Amber said. "I need to keep moving. Sooner or later, the police or someone will come here with questions."

"Aye. Well"—Aunt Christel shook her curly red hair—"you know that neither Rob nor I will say a word."

Amber reached out and squeezed her hand. "Thank you, it means so much that you believe me."

Aunt Christel squeezed her hand back. "I knew your father, lass. He was my cousin, and I spent every summer with him for eighteen years. And I know he didn't raise a murderer. People easily use a gentle soul like you. So, aye, I believe you were set up."

Amber released a shaky breath. It felt good to know that even though the government thought she was a murderer, she had people in her life who were on her side. Unfortunately, that wouldn't keep her from a death sentence or life in prison.

Aunt Christel took another sip and studied Amber with her soft brown eyes. "But, sweetheart, you're not a coward. You can't live on the run your whole life. What's the point? You can't have any friends. Can't marry. Can't have children. Always looking over your shoulder, seeing shadows."

Amber fingered a white porcelain flower at the base of the cup handle. She knew her aunt was right. Amber had joined the army because she wanted to see the world, fight for her country, and protect innocent people from terrorists.

She wasn't the type to cower from a fight, so why was she behaving like a coward now? Growing up, she hadn't been afraid to take the blame for her three older brothers' small sins, such as broken vases or scratches on the car. That had been her way of protecting them. But instead of appreciating her sacrifice, they'd treated her like a doormat.

"I know, Aunt Christel, you're right. My mom raised me to be a good girl. To go to church. To live an honest life. Dad is probably turning in his grave watching me hide like this and not seek justice. Everything inside is screaming at me to stand up and fight and prove I didn't commit that murder."

"Aye. So why don't you?"

Amber brought the cup to her mouth with a shaking hand, coffee threatening to spill on the tablecloth. She took a sip, her favorite drink tasteless against her tongue.

"I'd be a naive little girl if I trusted the system. Major Jackson is using me as a scapegoat. He managed to smuggle drugs from Afghanistan to America for years. So imagine how many people in the military he must have in his pocket. And now that he murdered a US officer, he'll be even more ruthless." She shook her head. "No. I cannot take him on alone."

"Perhaps nae. But why don't you ask your brothers to help? Jonathan was in the military, too. He knows people, doesn't he?"

"Right." Amber snorted. "Jonathan doesn't want anything to do with me. He sold our house after Dad died, and everyone lives their own lives."

Amber had still been a teenager when their mom had died, and the family had started to fall apart. After their dad's death two years ago, they'd stopped meeting for Thanksgiving and Christmas. Kyle was a kick-ass lawyer in New York. Daniel was in San Francisco last time Amber had heard, still trying to sell his sculptures.

"But still," Aunt Christel said, "if you ask for help... Kin is kin."

"Maybe that's how it is in Scotland. And I can't thank you enough for helping me. But if I went to Jonathan for help, he'd be the first to rat me out to the authorities."

Aunt Christel covered Amber's hand with her own, and Amber squeezed it back, her caramel skin looking even darker compared to her aunt's pasty complexion.

"Surely, nae, dear?" Aunt Christel said.

Amber sighed. "He wouldn't risk his ass for me. He has the

right connections in the military, I'm sure, but he also has two kids and a wife and a beautiful house."

"But—"

"Police! Police!" Rob cried.

Everything moved in slow motion. There was the distant rustle of car tires. The front door swung wide, and Rob stood in the doorway, his silhouette black against the sun. "Police!" he shouted.

Amber jumped to her feet, jostling the table, and the coffee mugs and porridge flew off from the impact.

Aunt Christel cried, "Back door!"

Amber ran, her feet heavy, as though she were moving through a swamp. It was like she was trapped in one of those nightmares where she couldn't get away from a killer.

The hallway flashed by, and she reached the old door. Unlocked, thank God! She raced out past the barn, into a field of oats. Her ragged breathing was louder than anything in her ears. Where was she running? Where should she go?

Away. She'd hide and wait nearby for a while and then come back to Aunt Christel's to get her things. Then she'd leave. Go to the woods. Somewhere. Anywhere.

She wouldn't be punished for something she hadn't done.

Behind her, cars revved. She glanced back. They were coming right through the field after her. Amber gasped, adrenaline spiking.

Before her was a grove of trees. They wouldn't be able to get through in their vehicles. She sped up. Thank God she jogged every day and did combat training. She still wouldn't be able to win a footrace against cars.

She flew into the grove. It took her eyes a moment to adjust to the shade of the trees after being in the sunny field. She ran through the trees for a while before she had to stop and catch her breath, her lungs desperately expanding to get more air. She looked around. Thirty feet or so in front of her, an asphalt road ran from left to right, and across it, in the distance, stood a castle. Right, the ruined castle her aunt had told her about. Behind it was River Lochy.

The cars chasing her turned. They'd need to take quite a detour to get on the road.

She ran again, across the empty road, then down the ditch on its other side, almost twisting her ankle.

She made it past the trees and the bushes to a crumbling wall of the castle. The wall extended between two round towers. There was an arched gate in the middle, and through the courtyard was another small gate. If she could just get there, maybe she could hide in the bushes beyond it or swim across the river. Although it was very broad, she was a good swimmer...

She ran inside the square courtyard. On every corner was a round tower. A red-haired woman stood in the middle, and the scent of lavender and freshly cut grass hit Amber. The woman wore a long green cloak and a dark-green medieval-looking dress.

"Here, lass," he said and the woman gestured towards the entrance at one of the towers. "They'll have a hard time finding ye here."

Amber stopped and bent forward. She put her hands on her knees and panted. Her lungs ached and burned, and a piercing pain pulsated in her side.

"Who are you?" she asked.

"I'm Sìneag. I ken ye're in trouble. Trust me. Ye dinna have much time. They're coming."

Tires screeched against the asphalt. Voices.

"Arghhh!" Amber cried in desperation.

Her pulse thumped. She must be insane to trust a stranger, but there was no way she'd make it to the river in time. They could easily catch up to her on the other side anyway. "Come on! Show me."

Sìneag nodded and ran first. They raced through a doorway and into the tomb-like darkness of the tower. Sìneag went quickly down the crumbling stairs into complete blackness. Amber clutched at the wall, barely seeing anything. Rocks rolled from under her feet. Her shoes slipped, and she almost fell. Finally, she slid to a stop when the stairs reached the uneven ground. When her eyes adjusted to the darkness, she saw Sìneag's shape standing there, waiting for her.

"Come, lass, a little farther," she said.

A heavy feeling settled in Amber's stomach. She felt like Little Red Riding Hood being called deeper into the woods by the wolf. She looked up. Somewhere up there, people were looking for her, people who wanted her to be punished for a crime she didn't commit. She supposed going farther under a ruined castle to save herself didn't sound like such a bad idea compared to being caught by them.

It got darker and darker. The scent of wet stone, earth, and mold got stronger. Water dripped somewhere.

Sìneag took Amber by the hand. The woman's palm was cool and soft. "Come here. I ken this place. We'll sit here and wait. Sooner or later, they'll be gone. Then ye go out. Aye?"

She tugged Amber a few steps to her left and down. Amber put out her hand and found a cold, rough stone wall. She slid her hand down as she sat on the ground. Her breath rushed in and out quickly, and she tried to slow it down.

"How do you know this place?" Amber whispered.

"Ah, I ken it well. Have been here many times. There's a rock that interests me."

Amber almost asked about the rock, but adrenaline was pumping through her blood. Any minute, they could find her. She listened for the sound of any steps or voices, but so far, everything was quiet.

"Why did you help me?" Amber asked softly. "How do you know I didn't escape from prison or haven't stolen something? Are you not wondering why the police are after me? Did you see in my eyes that I have a heart of gold or something?"

Sìneag chuckled. "Aye. Something like that. I supposed ye canna tell me what ye're really running from?"

Amber sighed. "It's best you don't know. You may be an accomplice by hiding a criminal."

"Oh, aye?" Sìneag sounded strangely excited.

"I'm not. But the government and the army think I am."

"Poor lass. I may have an escape for ye, somewhere yer government will never reach ye."

Amber grimaced, and she was glad that Sìneag couldn't see her. This was weird. Who was this woman, and why was she trying to save a complete stranger from the police?

"I'm sorry, Sìneag. I'm grateful for your help, but don't worry about me. I'll find a way."

Sìneag was quiet for a moment. "Ye will."

Amber didn't answer. The sound of dripping water echoed off the rocky walls, disturbing the silence of the underground area. Was this what it sounded like in a grave?

The good news was that she couldn't hear the police. They weren't looking for her in the ruins. Not yet.

"Do ye want to hear a story while we wait?" Sìneag asked.

A story? It was an odd thing to do while waiting to be captured by the police, but maybe it would keep Sìneag from asking any personal questions. And it might help Amber to distract herself.

"Yes, please," Amber said.

"Well, ye canna see it, but we're sitting right by that ancient rock I mentioned."

As she said that, something began glowing to Amber's left, and she jerked away.

Sìneag laughed. "Aye, that's it. Do ye see the carving glowing?"

Amber watched in disbelief as the glow grew brighter. It was a picture resembling a child's drawing—a circle made of three waves and a thick line. Next to the lines was a handprint etched right into the rock.

"What the hell is that?" Amber asked.

"Ye wilna believe me. None of ye mortals do at first. But 'tis ancient Pictish magic. It opens a tunnel through time."

Amber didn't know whether to laugh or run. "A what?"

"A tunnel through time. Those who go through the tunnel meet the person they're destined to be with."

The hell?

"And there's someone for ye, too, Amber."

Amber frowned. "How do you know my name?"

"If I told ye I'm a Highland faerie who loves matchmaking, even if the couple is separated by time, would ye believe me?"

This was sounding more and more ridiculous. "No."

She laughed. "'Tis what I thought. But there is a man ye're destined to be happy with, and he lives more than seven hundred years in the past."

Feet pounded outside and neared the entrance. Cold crept down Amber's spine.

Sìneag turned to her and took her hands. With the glow from the rock, Amber could distinguish her face. Sìneag's eyes were wide and worried.

"Just remember, ye need to look for Owen Cambel."

Someone was coming down the stairs. A man swore, something heavy fell, and more f-bombs followed.

"Go through the tunnel, Amber," Sìneag insisted. "It's either that or prison."

Go through a tunnel in time to seven hundred years in the past?

A flashlight beam jumped across the wall.

"Don't move!" a man called. "Police!"

Amber's heart beat violently against her ribs.

"Put yer hand in the print, and think of Owen," Sìneag said.

A gun clicked. "I'm armed. Do not move."

I must be crazy.

But this was it. Either she would be taken now, or she could try this one last thing. It was completely loony, but what could it hurt? Maybe it would open a revolving door or lead into a secret room.

She turned and placed her palm in the handprint.

Owen, she thought, feeling foolish. *Owen.*

A vibration went through her, similar to the buzz of a hair clipper. Her hand fell through the rock as though it were empty air. Her body followed. She tumbled, headfirst, her body spinning. Her stomach flipped, bile rising. She waved her arms, trying to grab on to something.

She screamed as she fell into darkness.

And then it consumed her.

CHAPTER 2

Inverlochy Castle, August 1308

THE CRACK OF WOOD BREAKING BLASTED THE AIR AND HALTED Owen in his tracks. The courtyard stilled. Archers on the walls stopped shooting. Assuming defensive positions, the warriors at the gates tensed and bent their knees.

Through the massive gates, the iron head of a battering ram protruded like a curious monster. Splinters and shards of wood decorated the hole around it. There were cheers and cries of victory from outside the gates.

Owen exchanged a look with Kenneth Mackenzie, the current constable of the castle appointed by Robert the Bruce. Kenneth's eyebrows were knit together, and his mouth formed a thin line in his beard.

"Hold the gates!" Kenneth called. "Swordsmen, draw yer claymores! Every man to the gates!"

Owen and Kenneth elbowed their way to the front row of the

warriors and stared the ram in the face. It moved back from the hole. Men shouldered the gates. More warriors descended from the towers, filling the courtyard. There were at least seven hundred English outside the castle walls, and inside, barely a hundred Scots.

"For the King of Scotland!" Kenneth cried. "For freedom! For yer wives and children! Hold the line! Dinna let a single Sassenach pass by!"

The Highlanders cheered back in a single roar.

"*Cruachan!*" Owen cried, but he was alone in calling the war cry of clan Cambel, though many echoed battle cries of their own clans.

If Owen had Craig, Ian, and Domhnall by his side, and his father and uncle, it would be different. His heart didn't beat with the anticipation of a victory, and it didn't jump with the eagerness of a battle to come.

No. This time, he had a dark, sinking premonition in his gut. There were too many Sassenachs. They had a battering ram and had been so strategic about the siege. The man who led them knew what he was doing.

While the Bruce was in the east dealing with the Comyns and the Earl of Badenoch, the English had decided to regain positions they'd lost. They were right about it being a good time to attack. With the Bruce and so many men away, the castle's defenses were weak.

The second hit of the ram shattered another piece of the gate. Highlanders stepped back instinctively.

"Prepare!" Kenneth cried. "Shields! Hold!"

Moments later, the ram hit again, and the gates burst open.

The swarm of English warriors poured in with a victorious roar. They hit the first line of Scots with a teeth-shattering impact. Swords poked from above and in between the shields. The English pressed, and the Highlander lines drew back.

The first victims among the Highlanders fell as sharp blades found their marks.

"Hold!" Kenneth yelled. "*Tulach Ard!*" he called his clan's war cry.

"*Tulach Ard!*" echoed his warriors.

But they couldn't hold. The pressure was too great. Within moments, the Highlanders' lines were scattered, and a wave of well-armed English cut through them.

∽

AMBER CAME TO AWARENESS SLOWLY. HER BODY FELT FLOATY and ached all over. She lay on a cold surface, and the air smelled like wood, iron, and wet stone. It was quiet, but not as quiet as it had been under the ruins. There was no sound of water dripping.

Were those the echoes of voices from somewhere outside?

Amber opened her eyes. Light came from a single torch in a sconce on the far side of the space. Real fire, not electricity.

Hmm.

She pushed herself up and sat. Sìneag was nowhere to be seen.

'Tis ancient Pictish magic. It opens a tunnel through time.

Yeah, right. Pictish magic my ass. Though, she had experienced the strangest sensation of falling through the stone. But that could have been anything. Maybe Sìneag had hypnotized her or something.

At least there were no police here.

Amber looked around, and her body chilled. Thanks to the light, she could see she was in a large space that looked like a cave. It had rough stone walls and a vault-like ceiling. Wooden planks, crates, barrels, and sacks were lined along the walls. The floor was a mixture of rough rock and earth. Was it the same floor she and Sìneag had sat on in complete darkness?

The allegedly magical rock sat by her side. It wasn't glowing now. Should she try to touch it again? No. The disorientating sensation of falling through a stone still pulled at her gut.

She stood up and looked around. The torch illuminated a

massive door that looked more like a gate, with heavy iron hardware and hinges. Well, that was weird. She was pretty sure there'd been no doors of any kind under the ruins.

Weird but interesting. Amber had always loved adventure novels and stories, and she felt like she was in the middle of one—a terrifying one—now. She knew it might be dangerous to venture out, but she couldn't cower down here forever. How long had she even been here?

She'd be careful, of course, and watch for the police, but so far, there was no sign of them. As she walked slowly towards the door, her shoes thumped quietly against the ground. The door smelled faintly of tar and iron. Listening, ear to the wooden surface, she heard no sounds coming from the other side. She gripped the heavy, round handle, as big as a saucer, and its coldness burned her skin. She pulled it, and the door moved.

Peering through the slit that formed between the door and the frame, she saw another storeroom with more casks, barrels, crates, and sacks, all illuminated by several torches. Stairs led to the upper floor. The room was round, its walls solid and made of rock and mortar.

The stairs had just been ruins before, but they looked almost new now.

What the hell was going on? Had Sìneag's words been true? Had Amber fallen through time to when the castle was still whole...*seven hundred years ago?*

No, that was crazy.

She had to get out of here before she started believing in faeries and magic toadstools. Climbing the stairs, she noticed how solid the smooth stones were under her feet.

She opened yet another door and froze, stunned.

No ruins, crumbling rocks, or darkness. Like the one downstairs, this room was round and illuminated by five torches. Another flight of circular stairs ascended from the room...and a tall, sturdy-looking door appeared to lead outside. Along the walls were swords, shields, bows, and arrows, as well as leather armor and chain mail. This room smelled acrid, like animal fat, and iron, and...blood? Shadows cast by the torches flickered like the gnashing teeth of a giant dragon. The small hairs on the back of Amber's neck stood.

As though she truly was hypnotized, she walked towards the heavy door and became aware of voices, grunts, and the clash of metal on the other side.

She laid her hand on the massive handle. *Don't do it!* a logical, careful part of her screamed.

But she'd already pulled at the handle, and the door moved. She stepped back to let it open and walked out. Cool air brushed against her heated cheeks. The scent of blood and spilled guts hit her.

What have I gotten myself into this time?

The castle wasn't in ruins now. It stood whole. The towers rose high into the sky, not crumbled stumps anymore. The courtyard was a battlefield. Men in armor swung swords at one another, hacking flesh, piercing bones. Some fell, wounded or dead. The ground was saturated with blood. The gates were busted open.

RUN!!!

A man in armor stared at her, his face distorted in a grimace of surprise and battle rage. He lifted his sword and launched himself straight at her.

CHAPTER 3

Owen slashed a warrior's neck, turned, and cut through another man's side. Battle rage took him, turning him into a whirling, cutting, thrusting being.

But no matter how many warriors he killed, more were coming. There was no end. His ears filled with the cries, groans, and ringing of metal against metal. His breath loud, his muscles taut with the strain, he kicked, and fought, and wet the ground with enemy blood.

And then he stopped in his tracks. By the eastern tower, someone with no weapon fought an English warrior.

A woman?

Owen ran closer, wiping the sweat from his eyes to make sure he was seeing it right. She had kicked the man's sword from his hands and used her legs and arms in an elegant, graceful way he'd never seen before. She whirled and kicked her boot into the man's face, and he fell backward. He propped himself on one elbow and reached for his sword, but she stepped on his arm. She leaned down and delivered a punch like a battle-hardened warrior. The Englishman fell back and lay still.

She straightened and looked around, and all the breath left Owen's body. She looked like she came from another world. She was tall and graceful in a predatory way, but her big eyes were wide. Her voluminous hair fell in small curls around her face, making her also look innocent. Her skin was dark, the color of brown honey, and she was so beautiful it hurt to look at her. He'd never seen anyone who looked like her...

But he didn't have time to dwell on it.

A familiar face flashed in his peripheral vision. Kenneth Mackenzie was down on one knee, holding his stomach as a giant English knight raised his blade for a death blow.

"Arrrghhh!" Owen darted forward and smashed into the knight. He pulled out his dagger and stabbed the Englishman through the slit in his helmet. The man fell in a heap of metal and flesh.

Kenneth lay on the ground with his hands clutching his stomach. Owen sank to his knees by his side. He'd seen enough injuries to know the gaping, bleeding wound was fatal.

If only he hadn't been distracted by the woman, maybe he could have saved Kenneth.

"Cambel," Kenneth whispered. "Good. Ye're here. No one is more qualified than ye to take charge now. Save Inverlochy."

Owen swallowed hard.

"Ye dinna ken what ye're talking about," he rasped. "I canna—"

Owen's chest tightened. He couldn't make this wish come true, no matter how much he'd wanted to. He was the worst man to trust with responsibility.

"Surely someone else can," Owen said. "Someone from yer clan... Angus? Or Raghnall?"

"If nae ye, 'tis lost." Kenneth closed his eyes briefly. "No time. My sword, Owen. I wish to die with my sword in my hands."

"Aye..."

That, he could do. Pain tore the back of his throat as he found the blade and put Kenneth's bloody hands around the hilt.

Kenneth looked at him. "For freedom. For Scotland. For me. Show them..."

His words trailed off, and he stilled. The vein on his neck stopped pulsing, and his eyes glazed over.

Owen crossed himself and lowered his head. Kenneth's death was on his hands. If he hadn't allowed himself to get distracted by that beautiful woman... What was she doing here in the middle of a battle? She didn't belong here.

His throat tightened.

Take charge, Owen...

He rose and looked around. Clearly, the Highlanders were losing. Each Scot fought two or three English at a time.

He should call "*Cruachan!*" He should cry out something that would lift their spirits. He should do something to change the situation...

His brother Craig was a leader. His father was. So was his cousin Ian. Owen was a jester who was good only at failing things. His arms hung helplessly.

This was clearly a lost cause. The battle was over.

A female grunt made him look up. The woman was fighting a knight who could crush her under the weight of his full armor. Owen raced towards them, his heart thumping, and met the knight's sword with his own. He pushed against the man with all his might, and the warrior fell.

The woman glared at him, her nostrils flaring, her full lips pressed tightly. Small droplets of sweat ran down her forehead. She was so pretty and dark and furious, like a goddess of war.

He needed to get her out of here, but how? The secret tunnel! Then he'd come back and help his fellow Scots.

Before the knight could stand up, Owen grabbed the woman's elbow and tugged her into the tower after him. "Come. Quickly."

She gasped, but the knight was already rising to his feet. Owen shut the door behind them and bolted it. Then he rushed down into the underground storeroom, pulling the strange woman behind him.

～

Amber fumed as the warrior dragged her down the stairs. Freeing her elbow was impossible, like trying to escape a metal vise. Another man who'd decided to be a hero and take charge of her, as if she couldn't survive without him.

She'd had the situation under control. How dare he!

As soon as her feet touched the stone floor of the underground storeroom, she jerked her elbow from his grasp. His blond hair glowed golden in the torchlight. The flames made his handsome face covered in dried blood, bruises, and cuts look devilish. His green gaze pierced her, the intensity in his eyes all-consuming. Standing now among barrels, casks, and chests, she suddenly became aware that he held a bloody sword in his hand and was almost twice as large as she was.

What did he want? Was this a trap?

Damn her curiosity, damn that woman, Sineag, and damn this guy.

She took a step back. "You try to lay one finger on me, and you'll be missing it."

He blinked, his eyebrows snapping together.

"I'm nae going to hurt ye, lass," he said.

"Why did you drag me in here? What do you want from me?"

His confused frown deepened. "What do I want?" He scoffed. "A little thank ye, mayhap? I just saved yer life. Believe it or nae, I am trying to help ye. Even if me being distracted by ye cost a great warrior his life…"

She gasped. And now *he* was blaming her for something? "I didn't need your help."

His jaw muscles worked under his short blond stubble. He narrowed his eyes, and fire played in them. Something light and feathery tickled her insides as he stared her down with that intense glare.

"Ye didna need my help, did ye?" He shook his head, marched towards the door at the other side of the room, and opened it. "Quickly now, so that I can return to the battle."

Her face fell. "Quickly where?"

"There's a secret tunnel. It'll lead ye out of the castle."

There was a pounding on the door of the ground floor. Then loud thumps as though someone was trying to break through. Amber's heart raced a hundred miles per hour.

"Ye need to go, lass," the Highlander said. "They're about to burst in."

The door above cracked, and the pounding became stronger. He was right, they were about to break through. Just like back in the other Inverlochy—the old ruins of Inverlochy, not this castle that stood undamaged and tall and full of freaking men in armor.

She could try to use the rock... The trouble was, even if all this time travel was true—which, as ludicrous as it sounded, appeared to be insanely real—she couldn't go back to where she'd come from. On the other side of that rock were men and women in uniform ready to put her in shackles for something she hadn't done.

She had to take her chances on this side of the rock.

A loud *crash* and the sound of many feet came from upstairs. The man grabbed a torch from the wall, took her by the hand, and tugged her after him.

"We must hurry!" They went through another heavy door into the back room, where she'd first opened her eyes. The Highlander locked the door behind him.

He ran past the Pictish rock to the end of the cave-like room, towards a small pyramid of casks stacked on top of one another.

"Good man, Kenneth, for blocking the tunnel," Owen said. "But 'tis our only way out now. Help me remove them."

He threw the casks off, and Amber helped as footsteps

pounded down the stairs. The last cask revealed a large, flat, round rock. The Highlander hooked his fingers under it and lifted. A dark opening with stairs appeared.

Amber swallowed.

"Go. The tunnel leads to the other side of the moat."

Amber took the torch from his hand. Was she insane? Maybe. But back in her normal life, she knew she'd end up in prison, possibly even get the death penalty.

Here...who knew?

She was still free, and no one was accusing her of anything or calling her a murderer—except this guy who'd blamed her for distracting him. No surprises there. Men were always pointing fingers at her.

She stepped down into the tunnel, and cold, earthy air enveloped her. The English were now at the second door and beating rhythmically against it. Amber walked to the very bottom of the tunnel. It was so low, she had to double over to walk forward. Roots hung from the ceiling, and the walls and the floor were a combination of rock and wet soil. Water dripped from somewhere. Breathing here was almost like drinking muddy water.

The Highlander descended after her, and she heard the soft *thump* of the lid close. The sounds from outside disappeared, and a strange silence reigned.

She didn't want to think that a whole castle stood above her, several feet of rock and soil.

Forward.

Just like she'd learned in Afghanistan; look ahead and don't overthink it.

They walked for what felt like an eternity. Her back ached, and her thighs burned. The guy behind her breathed heavily, that and their steps and the crackling of the torch were the only sounds in this tomb.

Finally, Amber saw steps before her.

"This is it?" she said.

"Aye. Must be."

She nodded and carefully climbed the stairs. She gave him the torch and pushed the lid at the top of the tunnel open until it fell with a loud *crash*.

Thirty pairs of eyes glared at her. Men in armor stood on all sides, swords pointed at her head. The English.

"Back! Back!" she cried to the guy behind her.

Too late.

The closest man leaned down, grabbed her by the collar, and pulled her up. The Highlander burst out of the tunnel after her, waving his sword and the torch at the same time.

"Grab them!" said someone with an authoritative voice. "They escaped from the castle."

Twenty men rushed forward and pretty much swallowed her companion under their combined weight. Two men grabbed Amber's arms. She thrashed and beat against them, but they held her tightly.

A bald man in his forties wearing heavy armor approached on a horse. He had the piercing gaze of someone in charge. Just like Major Ronald Jackson, the man responsible for all the bad things that had happened to Amber.

"Two Highlanders," he said. "Put them in the cage. I'd like to speak to them later."

"Sir de Bourgh," one of the men holding her said with a sharp nod.

"Take them to Stirling," de Bourgh said.

No! No! Was that another castle? A dungeon? She'd escaped going to prison in her own time only to be put in a medieval one?

They shoved her into a cage attached to a cart pulled by a horse. English warriors put the Highlander in with her and locked the door.

"No! You have the wrong person!" Amber cried.

That would be exactly what she'd be crying to the police. Was this all a nightmare? *Please, let this be a bad dream!* No one believed her—not in either situation.

"Damnation!" The Highlander rose and looked into the distance, holding the cage bars. "Is that the Bruce?"

Amber followed his gaze, and her eyes widened. An army approached the castle. First came the cavalry, after them, infantry. They mowed down the English forces, like a knife cutting through butter. Amber could hear the rumble of hooves even from here. The ground vibrated.

"Sir de Bourgh," the Highlander called. "Ye've already lost. 'Tis the Bruce. Ye'll never win against his forces. He has a history of winning with a few hundred men against thousands."

De Bourgh's face reddened. "Retreat!" he called. "Everyone, retreat!"

The cage started moving, and Amber pressed her face to the bars as Inverlochy Castle faded into the distance.

CHAPTER 4

The cage shook as the cart rolled over the rocky path, making Owen's teeth rattle. His head bumped against the bars, and he sat straighter in the corner.
God's blood.

Again, he'd messed things up. He should have gone through the tunnel first. Instead of trusting the lass, he should have peeked out to check everything was clear before carefully sneaking out of their escape tunnel.

She'd distracted him—again—this magnificent creature who had come out of nowhere and knocked down trained, armored warriors with her half-dance, half-combat performance.

As the woods and mountains passed by, he couldn't stop staring at her. Her brown skin. Her tall, willowy figure with the muscles of a warrior. Her face so bonnie his heart skipped every other beat. She had breathtaking eyes—huge and green with a hazel starburst around each pupil. She bit her full lower lip, and a frown creased her forehead. He ached to reach out and smooth it with his thumb.

And the way she was dressed...

He hadn't dwelled on it in the heat of the battle, but now that he had time to think it over... Something tightened in his stomach. Blue breeches—much like those Amy, Craig's wife, had worn when she'd been found—hugged her long, beautifully sculpted legs. Her short leather overtunic reached the top of her hips. Her shoes had thick soles—something else he'd seen only on Amy.

Women from his time didn't wear things like that. They didn't fight like her, either. And she'd been near the eastern tower, where the Pictish rock was. Owen's heart thumped in his throat.

Was this woman another time traveler?

"What's yer name, lass?" he said.

She looked up at him and hesitated, as though giving up her name would be such a bad thing.

"Amber Ryan." Her face smoothed. "What's yours?"

Amber... What a bonnie name. One he'd never heard, and one that suited her. Warm yet tough. And she had the same accent as Amy and Kate, Ian's beloved, but even more melodic. Almost like she sang the words.

"Owen Cambel."

She went completely still, eyes widening. Then she pursed her lips, gave a nod, and looked at her hands again, avoiding eye contact. But there was nowhere for her to run from here. He'd reclaim her attention. He'd get answers.

"Why were ye in Inverlochy, Amber Ryan?"

She raised her chin. Her gaze was as hard as those amber stones. "I don't think it's any of your business."

"But it verra much is, lass. See, because of ye, we're both now prisoners." He contemplated her. "A woman on the battlefield, distracting warriors... Do ye see why I might be interested?"

"What are you accusing me of?"

"Are ye a spy?"

She scoffed. "As you see, I'm a prisoner, too. And his men almost killed me, in case you didn't notice."

"I did notice," he spat. "In fact, I've noticed too much—" He stopped himself before he could say another word. This was just like thirteen years ago with Aileene. He'd been distracted by a lass in danger and brought disaster to his people.

This time, he'd failed to save Kenneth. If Kenneth were alive, mayhap they could've held the castle until the Bruce arrived.

Take charge... Kenneth had said.

'Tis impossible to give ye any responsibility, his father had always said. *Why canna ye be more like Craig and Domhnall?*

Owen gritted his teeth. "I'm certainly accusing ye of getting us captured."

She threw such a venomous gaze at him, he wondered how he didn't fall dead on the spot.

"Oh, this is perfect. Another guy blaming me for something I didn't do." She shook her head. "What is it about you men? Why do you always feel compelled to find a scapegoat?"

"I'm nae—"

She raised her palm to stop him. "You know what, buddy? If you hadn't dragged me down that tunnel to 'save me'"—she bent her index and middle fingers twice in quick succession. Should he know what that gesture meant?—"we wouldn't be in this situation. I didn't need your help."

A time traveler, a wonderous warrior, an infuriating female... And the most beautiful woman he'd ever seen.

Ah! Distraction.

"What were ye doing in the castle?"

"I don't owe you an explanation."

He was getting tired of her eluding his questions. He'd make her tell the truth—about time travel, about why she was here, and about what she wanted.

"Where do ye come from, lass?"

She looked petrified for a moment. "I don't think you know the place."

"Mayhap I do. Mayhap ye'll be surprised."

She chewed on the inside of her cheek as her eyebrows drew closer together.

When she didn't reply, he pressed. "Tell me. I may be more understanding than ye imagine."

Amber studied him dubiously. "Well, I'm a bit from everywhere, really. Recently, from the Middle East."

"Middle East? Is that the caliphate?"

She nodded. "I suppose that's how you must know it. Yes."

That must explain her complexion. Aye, good. He'd play along while he kept finding things out for himself. "Why do ye speak Gaelic so well?"

A momentary expression of astonishment crossed her face. She touched her lips. "Gaelic?" she said. "I don't..."

"Ye dinna what?"

"Uhm. Nothing. It's an easy tongue to learn, that's all."

The cart rattled and shook as one wheel jerked over a rock. Amber jumped up with the cart, lost her balance, and was thrown at Owen from the impact. She landed with her cheek against his stomach, her torso between his legs. Her long, curly hair looked so seductive spread across his stomach and hips. An immediate image of being naked and that hair falling across his bare skin invaded his mind.

And made him hard.

His cock was pressed against her breasts, the leather of her short coat between them. God almighty, he hoped she didn't feel his reaction. Normally, he'd be already plotting how to get under the lass's skirt. But this one was so different. In every aspect. For one, she wasn't wearing a skirt.

Being locked in a prison cart wasn't the best time to think about this. They were headed to Stirling, the strongest castle in the whole of Scotland. Owen didn't know what de Bourgh had in mind, but he didn't think they'd be welcomed with a feast and entertained as honorable guests. He should be thinking of how to escape, not getting hot and bothered about a lass.

She looked up at him, and he could see a blush even through the brown color of her skin. Her eyes were so huge now. She couldn't look prettier if she tried. She was unique and mysterious, and he craved to know more of her. His hands itched to reach out, pull her higher onto his chest, and kiss her.

"Sorry," she said, breaking the spell.

She clambered back on her hands and knees and crawled away from him to the opposite corner of the cage. It wasn't far. If they stretched out their legs, their toes would touch.

"'Tis all right, Amber," he murmured, feeling empty without her weight on top of him. "I dinna mind ye staying a little longer."

She blinked and pinched her lips together. "Please don't make comments like that." She looked pointedly between his legs. "And if you even think of me in that way or make a move, you will be missing the precious part you obviously can't control. Which doesn't surprise me, by the way."

Owen lost the ability to form words.

She folded her arms over her chest. "And stop with your stupid questions. I'm really not in the mood to give any answers."

That willful tongue of hers. English warriors rode up ahead of the cart and at the back. He doubted they were within earshot, but their presence was as tangible as a smelly goat.

"Be careful, lass," he said. "I am the only friend ye have here."

She lifted her chin. "That remains to be seen."

He grabbed a bar and fingered it. "I saved yer life back there."

"And landed us right in the midst of an enemy. Your enemy, by the way, not mine."

"*Ye* landed us in the midst of the enemy. Nae me. Ye were the one who opened that lid like we were the only two people in Scotland. As though ye *wanted* them to catch us..."

She rubbed the floor of the cart with her boot and pursed her lips. "I didn't want them to catch us. Stop blaming me. What do they want with us, anyway?"

Owen glanced back at the riders. One of them returned a look—an attentive, heavy, careful glance. He was far enough away, but just in case he decided to ride closer, Owen moved across the floor to sit next to Amber. She raised her brows.

"They're taking us to Stirling Castle. 'Tis one of the Sassenach strongholds in the south of Scotland."

"How far?"

"Two or three days of travel, I think."

"And what do you think they want from us?"

"Information, most likely. Mayhap ransom. Probably both."

She sighed. "I suppose that means prison?"

"Aye."

He lowered his head to her, and her scent tickled his nostrils—something clean and flowery and foreign.

"'Tis why we must try to escape before we reach Stirling."

Amber glanced at the guards again, then at Owen. "I suppose that makes us allies. At least for now."

"Aye. 'Tis best we work together, mysterious Amber from the caliphate."

She measured him with a stare.

"Mind your business, Owen Cambel. And I will mind mine."

She even pronounced his clan name like Amy did, with that wee pause between the *M* and the *B*. He liked that.

How mad was he exactly to be thinking what he was thinking? And how mad was he that he wanted to listen to his name coming from her lips again and again? Especially since the worst thing he could do now was lose his head again over a woman while they were being held prisoner.

CHAPTER 5

Amber grasped the bars of the cage and looked around at where they were stopping. The terrain was less hilly. They'd probably left the Highlands and were moving closer to the Lowlands now. There were plenty of opportunities to get lost in the relatively thick woods here.

Owen exchanged a look with her. She hated that she needed to rely on anyone to free herself—especially a man. Especially after what had happened to her in Afghanistan.

But at the moment, she had no choice. There must be some sort of way out of the cage and away from here. Wherever "here" was.

Where was she exactly? She still couldn't fully buy into the idea that she'd traveled through time. Could this be a hallucination or a vivid dream? And where would she go if they managed to escape the English soldiers?

She had no idea. All she knew was that she had to escape. She wouldn't let herself be taken to prison for no reason.

Owen had already checked the giant iron lock on the cage, and so had she. If she'd been from the fifties and wore any hairpins, she could have tried to pick the lock with one. Maybe

Owen knew how to do that, but she couldn't think of anything thin and sturdy enough to do the job.

The soldiers were dismounting and setting up camp. They started making fires and pitching tents. Amber thought that some things never changed, like the look of defeat and sadness on a soldier's face after losing a battle—the grief. She'd known that pain, too.

As the English passed by the cage, they threw curious glances at Owen and Amber, most of them halting for just a moment to ogle her. They were no doubt curious about the way she looked. They might not have seen anyone who looked and dressed like her around here, but that was no reason to stare. Her fists itched to punch the bastards. She felt Owen tense every time they stopped, too.

The air was still bright, but shadows grew longer and everything around them got that golden hue of early evening. Amber crawled to sit next to Owen, and he cocked his head to her.

"If we want to escape," Amber said, "perhaps it's better to wait until most of them are asleep."

Owen nodded. "Aye."

"I'm going to ask to go the toilet now. I won't try anything, just look around. When it's dark, then we can try something."

"Ye want to go where?"

"To the toilet."

Owen just stared at her, confused.

Amber coughed. "To relieve myself."

"Ah." Owen cleared his throat and rubbed the back of his neck.

Was he self-conscious? Amber didn't think he was the type. He seemed to have too much self-confidence, be too self-assured. A man who looked as dreamy as he did was probably used to smooth-talking the ladies.

He looked at her like he knew something about her, something he didn't want to share. It was a reminder not to trust him.

She asked the guard to let her go relieve herself in the woods and two soldiers escorted her to the edge of some bushes. All around the camp, warriors in iron armor bustled about making fires and setting cauldrons over them. Small tents were erected here and there. Some men tended to the wounded, who let out pained yelps and groans. She couldn't see any other prisoners. Sentinels were posted, but they wouldn't see much once it was dark. The woods were thick, and Owen and Amber could disappear quickly if they ran fast enough.

She returned to the cage with a sliver of hope. She sat next to Owen, leaning against the bars like he did, and whispered without looking at him. "Our best chance is to overwhelm a guard at night, get into the woods, and run as fast as we can. The army is stretched along the road like a snake, so it will take them a while to gather some guards to hunt us."

"Aye."

When darkness fell, and mouthwatering aromas of stew reached Amber, she knew it would be time to flee soon. They waited till the men lay down to sleep.

The guard stationed near their cage soon drifted off against a nearby tree.

"Hey," Amber called. "Hey!"

He woke and looked up at her.

"What?" he said with a frown.

"I need to relieve myself."

"Again?" He folded his arms on his chest and huddled. "You just went."

"That was a while ago, and I need to go again. If you don't want to smell piss the whole way to Stirling, let me out."

He grunted, seemingly exasperated, came to the cage, and opened the lock with a big key. As the door opened slightly, Owen grabbed him by the collar and smashed his forehead against the bars. Amber looked around, but no one seemed to have noticed so far. The tents remained silent, and the few sentinels around the campfires didn't move.

The guard moaned, and Owen banged him against the bars again, and he fell like a heavy sack.

"Come," Owen said. "Hurry."

He jumped off the cart and helped Amber down. Her heart drummed in her ears. Half bent and staying low, they hurried away from the camp.

Trees and bushes flashed by in the darkness, and all Amber could hear was her ragged breath loud in her ears.

But then shouts rang from behind them. Their escape had been discovered. *No, not again!*

Amber glanced back. English warriors. Dozens of them.

"Faster!" she cried.

They sped up. Her lungs burned from the strain, her muscles on fire. Faster. She was a fast runner. If only it weren't so damn dark. Her leg hooked on a root, and she fell, facedown.

"Amber!" Owen yelled and stopped to help her up.

They ran again, but the English were catching up, and their cries were louder now.

"Stop!" someone called from behind.

Arrows flew past them, hitting the ground and trees. Someone grabbed her, and she fell, crumpling under the weight of a grown man. Pine needles and twigs stabbed her hands and legs.

"Got her!" the man announced. He reeked of old sweat and alcohol.

Amber wriggled, trying to free herself, but she was already surrounded.

"Got him," another voice came. "Not going anywhere today, you bloody Scot."

Tears of helplessness burned Amber's eyes.

"Let me go!" she yelled. "I'm not even a freaking Highlander!"

"Shut up." The man above her slapped her hard.

Her head burst with pain. He hauled her up and dragged her after him back to the camp. To her right, two men led Owen.

Amber and Owen exchanged an angry, disappointed look. Their guard sat by the cage with a cloth pressed to his forehead.

"Wanted to piss, eh?" he spat as Amber passed by. "Go to hell, you evil bitch. Let the cart stink, you won't leave it again till we reach Stirling."

"I am already in hell," Amber said.

Amber and Owen were shoved back into the cage, and the guard locked the door behind them.

Amber hit the bars. "So close."

"Aye, well, lass. We'll try again."

But his tone wasn't as optimistic as before, and he wore a deep frown.

"No, you won't," said a voice, and Amber turned around.

Sir de Bourgh stood by the cage. Not in armor anymore, he wore a red cloak over a tunic that reached his knees. He had a large sword at his waist. The pommel was decorated with beautiful coiled patterns that gleamed and reflected the firelight.

"You won't escape again," he said, eyeing Amber with curiosity.

He approached the cage and gripped two bars in his hands, staring at her. Amber felt like an animal in the zoo.

"Pray tell, where are you from, dear? I've never seen anyone like you."

A white-hot wave of anger and anxiety hit her. Those eyes again, the lazy authority of a powerful military man.

Owen moved a step closer to him. "Doesna matter, ye pig. She's my wife." Amber looked at him with astonishment. Was he really going to lie to try to protect her? A sweet lightness filled her. "Stop asking yer unnecessary questions, and let us go."

De Bourgh chuckled without taking his eyes off Amber.

"Your wife? And where did you get such a beauty?"

"Dinna look at her like that. Allow yerself one dirty thought, and ye'll be missing yer cock."

De Bourgh looked at Owen, amused. "And how do you plan

to do that from inside a cage, without your sword or your dagger?"

"A Highlander always finds a way."

"Right. Well. I'll keep a watch over my cock. Thanks for the warning. What is your name, brave Highlander?"

"Owen Cambel."

De Bourgh's eyebrows rose. "Cambel? Wonderful. The longest and closest allies of the Bruce. Look at me, lost a castle but perhaps won the whole war. Owen Cambel and his wife... What's your name, dear?"

"Amber," she said begrudgingly.

"What an exotic name. Owen and his wife, Amber, you are in my hands. Once I get started with you, you'll tell me everything. I might yet win this war for King Edward II."

He walked away, whistling a merry tune that sent a chill snaking down her spine.

"I'll be talking to you both soon," he threw across his shoulder.

Owen hit the bars, his face distorted in helpless rage.

"Why do I have a feeling that being your wife might not be a great thing?" Amber said.

Owen glared at her from under furrowed eyebrows. "Because 'tisnt. Now he thinks he has power over me, can blackmail me with ye."

Amber curled her hands into fists. "Then why the hell did you lie?"

"To protect ye, why else?"

"Once again, I do not need your protection! All you've done is put me in more danger."

The look Owen gave her was anguished. Strangely, warmth crept through her stomach in response to that look. Silly her. He shouldn't mean anything to her. She shouldn't trust him and shouldn't rely on him.

But with no one else around on her side, what choice did she have?

CHAPTER 6

T*hree days later...*

DARK, COLD HORROR CREPT INTO OWEN'S MUSCLES AS HE SAW Stirling Castle's walls. They'd been steadily climbing the hill, and finally, Owen could see the cliffs where the castle stood.

He'd never seen a fortress like this one. He'd heard it was impossible to take by siege, and now he knew why. Inverlochy was a child's toy of daub and sticks compared to this castle. The gatehouse consisted of two thick towers. Walls with wooden galleries for archers and defenders loomed taller and thicker than any he'd ever seen. Square towers at the edges of the front wall provided a strategic defense for the castle's most vulnerable spots.

Stirling connected the Highlands and the Lowlands. Whoever controlled the castle, controlled Scotland. And so far, the English did.

"Not for long," Owen muttered to himself through his teeth.

The Bruce was winning. Even the Lowlanders who had previously sworn to Edward were rumored to be taking the Bruce's side. Owen believed that Scotland would be free again, and he was ready to contribute everything he could to make it happen.

The army was slowly passing through the gates. Amber looked up at the sharp spikes along the portcullis.

"Owen," Amber said, her voice small. "Seriously. How do we get out of here?"

Owen's gut twisted. After three days of travel, he was out of ideas.

"I dinna ken yet, lass." He scratched his bristle somberly. "But we will get out. I promise ye."

Or die trying. But he didn't say that.

When inside, they continued their way up and up, past simple houses with thatched roofs, gardens with vegetables, and a small orchard, as well as cows and pigs and chickens. There were several workshops. Eventually, they came to a simple wooden palisade wall with a gate. Behind them loomed a square tower, probably the lord's tower, or donjon.

Owen and Amber exchanged a worried look. With two walls standing between them and freedom, how in the world were they going to escape?

They stopped in the middle of a courtyard at least twice as big as Inverlochy's. Besides the donjon, there was a large building attached to the wall—probably the great hall. A simple village house with a thatched roof had smoke coming out of the chimney, and judging by the aromatic scent of cooked meat and bread that was coming from there, it must be the kitchen. Another stone building was connected to the wooden palisade, perhaps a workshop or the smithy, Owen guessed.

The guard opened their cage, and Owen and Amber descended. It felt good to at least stand on the ground. Owen stretched his legs. The guard tied his hands behind his back, and helplessness weighed on his shoulders. Amber's hands were tied as well, and she jerked them. She looked like a wildcat—cornered and dangerous.

"Move." The guard shoved Owen.

Hating every step he had to take, he walked forward. The lass strolled by his side, somber and wide-eyed. They marched through the entrance into the donjon, and like in Inverlochy, there were stairs leading underground. Only a few torches illuminated the darkness. Unlike in Inverlochy, there wasn't food stored in the room at the bottom of the stairs. Here there was an empty room with three heavy doors, each leading in a different direction and each with guards standing next to them. Owen's skin chilled.

The guards opened the door to the right and pushed Owen and Amber into the shadows behind it. As they passed the door, a musty odor of wet stone and mold hit Owen. A couple of torches illuminated a row of iron cages along the cave-like wall. They passed three, and in one of them, Owen saw a man huddled in the corner. The miasma of excrement and unwashed body made bile rise in his throat.

Someone was rotting in there, and if Owen didn't do something, soon he and Amber would be, too.

Shadows gathered like dark spirits in the corners of the cells as they walked farther into the dungeon. They stopped at the end of the cave-like room, by the final cage. One of the guards unlocked it with a giant key. Metal gnashed as the cell door opened. Amber's eyes widened, desperate and haunted, but the guard shoved her forward. She stumbled and fell, sprawling on the floor.

Anger rose in Owen like a wall of fire. He turned to the guard and slammed his head into the man's nose. The satisfying crack of bone made him smile. The rest of the guards moved to push him into the cell as well, but instead of giving them the satisfaction, he walked into it himself.

"Piss off, ye bastarts," he growled.

One of them locked the door. "You're lucky the lord wants to keep you both untouched. Otherwise, you'd be gathering your teeth from the floor. Now turn around and let me unlock your shackles. And tell your wife, or whoever she is, to do the same."

Their hands were finally free, and the guards left the cave, leaving only one torch just outside their cell. It cast wicked shadows that danced on the floor.

He tried to think of something to lift his and Amber's spirits. But all he could come up with were the things that had gone wrong because of him.

His clan had lost the king's favor. Granted, John Balliol hadn't remained king for long after he'd angered King Edward I of England. Proclaiming Owen had stolen the gold, the MacDougalls had attacked Cambel lands unexpectedly. They'd retaken the lands that the king had given to the Cambels. They'd kidnapped Owen's sister Marjorie, and Alasdair MacDougall had raped her and abused her. In the battle to free her, Owen's grandfather had died. Then the MacDougalls had come after Innis Chonnel and taken the castle, chasing the Cambels away.

It was during that battle that the MacDougalls had wounded and captured Owen's cousin Ian. After that, the Cambels had made Owen's father's castle, Glenkeld, the clan seat, and Uncle Neil and his sons had moved there, too.

Then there was Lachlan...

Last year, Craig had been appointed constable of Inverlochy Castle by the Bruce. Craig had asked Owen to keep an eye on everything while he was gone and had specifically forbidden him to invite anyone from the Inverlochy village in case they might spy for the enemy. But Owen had thought a couple of pretty lasses wouldn't harm anyone. Those lasses had refused to go without chaperons. So their mothers had come, their fathers and brothers. The whole castle had soon swarmed with feasting people. In the chaos, Hamish Dunn, a MacDougall spy, had killed Lachlan, thinking he was killing Craig. The two had looked quite similar, being cousins.

All that was on Owen's conscience. Because he'd been such a

failure. Because he'd been distracted by beautiful women and drinking and rebelling against his father.

But he could perform a small act of kindness now and make sure Amber was all right.

Owen turned to her. "Are ye well, lass?"

She rubbed her wrists. "I'm okay. You?"

He chuckled to himself. He'd heard that strange word—"okay"—from only two people: Amy and Kate.

"Aye, I am *okay*," he said, tasting the word on his tongue.

She walked to the opposite wall and slid down until she was sitting on the floor.

"What now?" she asked.

"Now we wait."

∼

TIME CRAWLED. IN THE OVERWHELMING DARKNESS, WITH only a glimmer of firelight, Amber's mind raced.

Now that she'd been in this medieval reality for several days, she had no doubt she'd traveled in time, just like Sìneag had said. It was insane—and yet it was the only explanation she could think of. Why else was Inverlochy Castle whole now? Why else were men carrying swords, spears, and shields? What else could explain the lack of technology, the thatched buildings, and the people traveling on horseback?

The same questions kept spinning in her head. *How could I have let this happen to me? What possessed me to think time travel was safer than trying to escape the police? And how did I run from being put in prison in* my *time only to land in one in the fourteenth century?*

The biggest question of all was whether she would've been able to clear her name if she'd been brave enough to stand up to Jackson. No. Jackson would've won. She'd grown up being a scapegoat for her brothers. She knew how the world worked.

Owen sat by the opposite wall where the light didn't reach. Only his boot was visible, and it wasn't moving.

"How can you be so calm?" she said.

He didn't reply for a while, and Amber thought he must have fallen asleep. "'Tis nothing we can do to change the situation, lass. So we better save our energy. I wager ye the price of a good horse that we'll need it."

Amber scoffed. "I wish I could be as calm as you. Have you been in prison before?"

She heard a rustle, and Owen suddenly stood before her, tall and imposing. "I havena, nae. Have ye?"

A painful knot formed in her throat. "No."

He studied her with a frown. "Ye should calm down, lass."

Amber rose to her feet and paced the room. She broke out in a sweat, her chest tense and aching, her feet heavy and cold. She rubbed her forehead with a shaking hand.

"I didn't do anything, Owen," she said, and her quiet voice reverberated against the rocky walls. "I shouldn't be here. I'm not even from—"

She had the sense to cut herself off before she said she wasn't even from this century.

"Ye're nae from what?"

There was something in his voice that made her stop and look at him. Something like...

Hope?

No, that couldn't be right. Why hope? What was he hoping she would say?

"I'm not even from around here," she finished. "I have nothing to do with your king or your enemies. Or you. And yet I'm the one paying a price." She shook her head. "It seems injustice and corruption is everywhere."

And in every epoch.

Owen narrowed his eyes. "Did something happen to ye, lass? Some injustice?"

Amber stopped pacing. He watched her coolly. His face, half lit by the light of the torch, was stoic, as though he were at home and not in the icy cold bowels of an enemy castle. He looked like a demigod, with his perfect, gorgeous face, and his golden hair glowing from the light of the torches. Well, he was a warrior after all, facing death was not new to him.

But it was also not new to her.

And yet, somehow, being in this prison was worse than going out on a mission in Afghanistan. At least she'd signed up for that. She'd been empowered.

Here, she was powerless.

Just like in her childhood.

"What happened to me—"

Was she ready to reveal her deepest secret? The whole reason why she'd ended up here in the first place?

No. She couldn't trust him. She couldn't trust anyone. Trusting people had gotten her into this mess.

Never again.

"Injustice is everywhere," she repeated. "Happened to me. Happened to you, I bet. We've all been there."

Owen shifted his weight onto one leg and crossed his arms over his chest.

"Aye. Happened to me, too, lass. And yet I'm the calm one and ye're the one losing yer wits."

"Ah, go to hell. You have no idea."

She shouldn't snap at him. She let out a shaky breath. He wasn't the one from a different time. He couldn't understand what she was going through right now.

Feeling like the ground was sinking under her feet, Amber walked to the wall and leaned on it. The rocks were cool and damp against her hands. Owen came to stand next to her and touched her shoulder. She didn't mind. In fact, warmth spread where his hand lay on her even through her jacket. His concerned face appeared next to hers.

"Lass, ye need to breathe," he said. "Come now, let's do it together. Deep breath in." He sucked in air. "Hold. Deep breath out."

Amber did as he told her. She took in a lungful of cold, moldy air and held it in her lungs for a moment before releasing it. She repeated that over and over. Each time, the tension released a little, until she finally felt like herself again.

She met Owen's eyes. "How do you know about breathing techniques?"

She didn't imagine many medieval Highlanders were knowledgeable about the power of meditation and breathing.

He shrugged. "I ken archery. Ye must stay calm even in the midst of battle. To stay calm, ye breathe."

Amber became aware his hand was still on her shoulder. Soft, pleasant charges of electricity went down her arm and into her chest in waves. Her breathing sped up again, and her ragged heartbeat drummed in her ears. How could a simple touch from a man make her feel like that?

No. It couldn't. She wouldn't let it. She wouldn't make herself powerless against any man. Not again.

Amber shook his hand off her shoulder, and a flicker of hurt passed over his face.

"Thanks for the tip," she said.

He was right about archery, of course. She knew it, too, from shooting guns. She knew it from kung fu. She also did yoga and meditation sometimes. And yet it all escaped her when she was around him.

Owen walked away from her, and with a carefree expression, he stretched out on the cold floor in the middle of the room and put both of his hands behind his head. He stared up at the dark ceiling with a dreamy expression, as though he were cloud watching on a beautiful summer day.

"You certainly look like you've mastered the breathing exercises," Amber said as she sat back down with her back against the wall.

He chuckled. "Aye. There's nothing I can do to change the situation right now. So why waste my breath?"

Amber wished she shared his attitude. "So you know archery?"

"Aye. I do. Not every warrior does, but as a wee lad, I wanted to ken both the sword and the bow."

"Why?"

His shoulders tensed, and his face suddenly lost the carefree cloud-watching expression. "Because my older brothers are all excellent swordsmen. I'm the youngest son and was always left to roam on my own. Archery was a way for me to distinguish myself."

A knot tightened in Amber's throat. Her whole childhood, she'd wanted to be noticed, too. Growing up, her brothers had always been her father's favorites, allowed to do anything they wanted. As a girl, she'd been expected to behave according to the rules and do everything right.

She'd always wanted to break free and travel. It was one of the reasons she'd joined the army.

"How many brothers do you have?" she asked.

"Two. And two sisters. Well, to be precise, Craig and Marjorie are my half brother and half sister."

"I have three brothers, all older."

Owen rolled to his side and propped his head with one arm. The light of the torch was reflected in his golden bristles. "Are they warriors? Yer brothers?"

"One is. Well, he was. He retired."

Jonathan, the eldest, had served in Iraq until retiring because, as he explained officially, his wife had insisted.

"Oh, aye?"

"Well, my father expected his first son to follow in his footsteps. But honestly, I don't think Jonathan ever saw himself being career military like our dad."

"Yer da is a war chief?"

"Something like that. Was. He's dead."

Her father had died of a heart attack. He'd been a US Army colonel, a proud man who'd valued discipline and rules more than anything. He saw very definite futures for each of his children. For his sons: the military, the law, and medicine. His daughter could be a teacher or a stay-at-home mom.

If her father had known her mom had encouraged a spirit of independence and adventure in Amber, he'd have been more careful about allowing Amber to go camping with the Girl Scouts and to parties in high school.

When she'd joined the army, she'd thought she'd kill two birds with one stone. She'd travel and impress her father.

Neither was true. She'd ended up stuck in Afghanistan for the duration of her service. And her dad had still considered her weak.

"Sorry to hear that, lass," Owen said.

"Thank you."

"But ye ken battle, too, dinna ye? What I saw at Inverlochy... I havena seen anybody fight like that."

Despite herself, Amber felt blood rushing to her cheeks. No freaking way! She was blushing. She hated that she reacted to Owen in all these emotional ways.

"Yes. I've seen my share of combat, but it's very different from battles here."

"I dare say. Where did ye learn to fight like that?"

The burning in her face intensified. Surely it wasn't admiration that she heard in his voice? And surely it wasn't that hint of adoration that made her blush like a virgin?

"Home," she said. "It's not a big deal, simple military training, that's all."

It wasn't quite true. Standard military training didn't include martial arts. But she enjoyed kung fu and had taken the classes on her own initiative. It gave her more strength and power, and she loved how graceful it was. Every time she had to use a gun, she cringed internally. Martial arts was a dangerous way of fighting, but it was much more elegant.

"I'd be interested to learn a trick or two," Owen said.

Amber had just opened her mouth to reply that they weren't tricks, and learning would require a long time, when the door at the entrance to the dungeons gnashed, and the heavy steps of several men marched closer and closer.

Owen jumped to his feet, his eyes dark and sharp. With her stomach sinking, Amber rose to her feet as well.

Three guards with torches in their hands stopped before their cell. The light hurt Amber's eyes. One of them reached out to unlock and open the cell door. Owen shifted towards Amber and stood between the guard and her.

"Move, Scot," the guard said. "Sir de Bourgh is expecting your wife."

CHAPTER 7

The door closed behind Amber with a full *thump*, leaving the guards behind it.

She let out a shaky breath as she took in her surroundings. It was another dungeon, not unlike where she and Owen were being held, with thick walls of solid rock, and a domed ceiling.

In the middle stood a massive table with dark stains that made Amber think of blood. Sir de Bourgh sat at the table, a chicken drumstick in his hand. He chewed without taking his eyes off Amber, his smooth skin reflecting the fire in the giant fireplace.

A man stood by his side, tall and slender. An uncooked spaghetti noodle came to mind. Deep creases around his mouth and on his forehead gave his face a sad expression like he knew the day of her death and was unpleased by it.

A cold shiver ran through Amber, despite the room being much warmer than the dungeon where she and Owen were being kept. The shiver turned into an icy wave when she looked at the wall.

An array of instruments hung there—heavy iron handcuffs and cuffs for feet connected by an iron rod, sharp spikes, whips, giant knives and axes, something like a bear trap, and other tools that made the blood thicken in her veins.

High above the table hung a giant cylinder with pins and chains reaching to the floor. By the fireplace, there was a chair with the same dark stains as the table.

This was a torture room.

Amber's throat went as dry as a desert. Horror snaked down her spine. Sweat would have broken through her skin if she'd been sufficiently hydrated. Instead, her head ached as though struck by a huge hammer.

She'd once participated in the extraction of a journalist being held by terrorists in Afghanistan. The man's face had been beaten to a pulp, his ribs had been broken, and there'd been burns on his hands and feet. That was the closest she'd ever come to torture.

Would she experience that firsthand? And why the hell had Sineag sent her here to end up with this psycho?

De Bourgh picked at the chicken bone and smacked his lips. Fat dripped down his palm. The scent of food in the room made sickness rise in Amber's stomach even though she was ravenous.

"I'd invite you to dine with me"—de Bourgh gestured at a chair by his side and an empty plate and cup in front of it—"but it might be wise for you to stay away from food and drink. It all depends on what you decide."

Amber swallowed a painful knot. Fear coiled in the pit of her stomach, but she raised her chin. "What I decide about what?"

"You can tell me everything I want to know about the Bruce and his army while enjoying a meal and an excellent wine. Or I can use some of these"—he motioned around the room—"to get the words out of you."

Blood drained from Amber's face. She needed to get out of here. "I don't know anything."

De Bourgh studied her with his sharp, penetrating eyes for a moment, then he gave a nod and picked up another chicken leg. "I suppose you've made your choice, then."

She could fight her way out. Owen was right, none of them knew kung fu or anything similar. If de Bourgh or the other guy approached her, her body would know what to do. There was no way she'd let them lay a finger on her.

De Bourgh waved with his hand, and the thin man's face turned even sadder. The outsides of his eyebrows sagged, and the ends above his nose met like the sides of a sharp roof.

He walked to Amber, and she bent her knees, assuming a fighting position. The executioner, which was the name she'd given him in her head, stretched his hand out to take her by the shoulder. She grabbed his wrist, moved behind him, and pulled his arm against her body while twisting it. The man grunted, and she dropped to her knees and used her entire body to push him down with her. He panted but remained silent.

Amber looked at de Bourgh. He studied her with a surprised and amused expression, still chewing.

"Let me go, or I break his arm," she said.

"What a clever trick," de Bourgh said. "Well done."

Why wasn't he more concerned? Something sharp pressed against Amber's stomach, and her skin chilled.

"I'm afraid I cannot allow that, milady," the executioner grunted. "You need to let me go, or I will be forced to spill your entrails on the floor."

Despite the pain, despite the impossible position, the man had managed to use his free hand to get his knife out. His long arms were probably what allowed him to reach her stomach. Amber had trained extensively but had used kung fu only once or twice to defend herself. This man was something else. Did the executioner not feel pain? Was he not afraid of it like a normal human being?

The sharp edge of his knife dug deeper into her skin.

"Let him go, Mistress Cambel." De Bourgh tossed the chicken bone on the plate and wiped his hands. "He will kill you without hesitation. His arm is more precious to me than your life."

Amber grunted and let the executioner's arm go. He stood up slowly, watching her with pity in his eyes. She stood up as well, furious with him and with herself for not having another plan.

De Bourgh walked around the table to stand next to her. Compared to the executioner, he looked like a ball next to a golf club.

"Where did you learn that?" de Bourgh asked.

"None of your business."

"Hmm." He slowly looked her over. "And where do your peculiar clothes come from? You're dressed like a man in those breeches, but they're almost like stockings. And this garment..." He reached out and took the collar of her leather jacket between his thumb and index finger. Amber stepped back. "Leather. Hmm. Never seen such rich finishing."

He met her eyes. "You look very outlandish to me, mistress."

"Exactly. I'm not from here. I don't know anything about the Bruce. You're wasting your time with me."

"Not from here. I dare say. Your dark skin. Your clothes. Your strange speech. Where are you from, then?"

"Far away. You have no idea how far."

"Elusive again, are we? Let's see if Jerold Baker here can persuade you to open up."

The executioner grabbed Amber by the elbow, his long knife pointed right at her kidney. Amber muttered an oath, her legs as weak as cooked noodles. Should she lie? Tell him something about the Bruce, some sort of nonsense just to make him stop?

"I hope you realize that your elusiveness plays against you," de Bourgh said. "I don't trust you at all. I know you're hiding something. Something big, something that might be of interest to me. Something that I will find out eventually."

The executioner took her to the giant pole standing in the middle of the room. He placed Amber's hand in a crude iron handcuff attached to the pole, and her insides trembled.

Screw this.

She jerked her wrist away before he could close the iron on her and punched him in the nose. Bone cracked, and blood spilled out of his nostrils. He groaned but still managed to bring the knife to her neck with one hand and grab her wrist in a vise-like grip.

"My profession has hardened me to pain," he said calmly. "Your fighting is futile. You will not win."

He was an agent of death, pale and sad and calm.

"Oh, I don't believe you," she spat. "Everyone is afraid of pain."

"Especially you," he said.

He put the knife away, but before Amber could act and free herself, she was handcuffed. Cold iron bit into her skin.

Anger and helplessness burned through her like a high fever. "Let me go." She tried to yank her hand away, but of course, it was hopeless. Jerold Baker took her other hand in a grip as hard as the iron, and put it in the second handcuff.

She stood now with her back to de Bourgh, powerless and exposed despite being dressed. She could almost feel the sharp tools of torture digging into her skin, wrenching her bones.

Would she survive this?

She hadn't done anything to deserve this. It was completely unfair. And it was all her fault. She never should've gone with Owen. She should've gone back to her time and confronted Jackson, should've believed she would find a way to clear her name. At least no one in the twenty-first century would try to torture her.

Tears burned her eyes and blurred her vision, but she forbade herself to cry. She wouldn't give these two men the satisfaction.

De Bourgh walked to her and stood so that he faced her. "My king, Edward II, has entrusted me to restore England's position in Scotland. To weaken the Bruce. And I think you and your husband are the key."

He walked towards the wall and picked up an instrument. It

looked like a giant pair of tongs with bent edges. On each side of the tongs were two long, sharp claws like those on a hay fork.

"This is called a breast ripper," de Bourgh said, and the floor under Amber's feet shook. "I would hate to mutilate a beautiful woman like yourself."

"Please…" The word escaped her mouth before she could stop herself.

"Hmm." De Bourgh chuckled, satisfied.

"Owen would not be happy, not that his happiness is my concern. Maybe we could use this." He came to stand next to a chair. "This would slowly fry your feet. Jerold Baker knows this one especially well. It's very effective at getting people to answer questions they previously didn't want to answer." He picked up a thick wooden shield and put it between the fireplace and the chair. "Once the skin starts to scald, Jerold Baker puts the shield between the soles and the fire. The promise of sweet relief is usually enough to start anyone talking, even after they've assured me they don't know anything. Just like you."

Amber closed her eyes. Sweat broke out on her skin, drenching her. She could almost smell the burned flesh. Burns like that would eat through her flesh to the bone. She might never be able to walk again.

"Please," Amber said. "You're wasting your time with me. I don't know anything about the Bruce."

She didn't notice a tear until it ran over her lip and into her mouth, salty on her tongue.

"I would gladly release you, Mistress Cambel. I'd hate to punish a woman as beautiful as you. You're a mystery, unlike anyone I've ever seen before. But I cannot afford to fail. The king will restore my lands in the south and my title if I succeed. If I don't, my daughters won't have dowries, and my son won't have an inheritance."

He put the board back and came closer to her, an expression of sympathy on his face.

"For the last time, will you talk? Will you answer my questions?"

Amber exhaled. If her life was over, she might as well meet the end with her head high. She'd had a good life. She'd lived it honestly and always tried to do what was right. She'd known love and had met a handsome warrior who'd made her begin to feel things she hadn't felt in a long time. Maybe ever. She'd traveled back in time, for God's sake. How many people could brag about that?

"Go to hell," she whispered.

De Bourgh gave a slow nod and sighed. "You leave me no choice. Jerold, take off her short coat and her tunic."

Amber closed her eyes. Her cheeks flushed and burned as Jerold Baker cut her leather jacket and her shirt and ripped both off her. Her naked skin prickled sharply as air touched it. She was now in only her bra and jeans.

Silence hung in the room. She opened her eyes and found both men staring at her bra with puzzled expressions.

"That as well, my lord?" Jerold Baker said.

"What is that?" de Bourgh asked.

"Does it matter?" Amber said.

"No," de Bourgh replied. "Remove that, too."

With some sort of giant scissors, Jerold Baker cut her bra, and it fell to the floor.

Another shiver ran through Amber. Would she lose her breasts now?

"Flog her," de Bourgh said.

Flogging...

Fuck.

If she didn't bleed to death from that, an infection would kill her. She wished she knew something about the Bruce to trade for her life.

With a sinking stomach, Amber watched Jerold Baker go to the wall of torture tools and remove a whip. It was like a snake attached to a big stick. Amber's whole body shook, her breath coming in and out in shudders. She locked eyes with Jerold Baker as he walked to stand behind her wearing that same sad expression.

"You will pay for this," she said. "I don't know how. I don't know when. But you will."

Somehow, she knew that if she survived this, Owen wouldn't let this go. He was no one to her, and she was no one to him, but something told her he wouldn't take this lightly.

"We'll see. Begin," de Bourgh said.

A crack echoed in the air behind her, and red-hot pain scorched her bare back. She grunted and sank from the impact. But before she could recover and take a breath, another lash tore her apart. This time, she couldn't stop a scream.

Blows rained down on her, one after another, and soon, the only thing that existed was world-shattering pain.

CHAPTER 8

The door to the dungeon screeched and clunked somewhere in the darkness. Owen jumped to his feet and leaned on the iron bars. A torch lit the hall, then another. Heavy feet pounded against the stone floor as the two lights approached. The dungeon's other inhabitant fussed in his cell by the exit.

"Food. Water. Please," he begged.

Owen's stomach rumbled, too. His lips were parched, and his head ached. He hadn't had a drop to drink in he didn't know how long. He had no idea what time of day it was now. Mayhap it was tomorrow? Mayhap they were still in the same endless day.

His main concern was Amber. His stomach had dropped and his calm and peaceful demeanor had disappeared when they'd taken her, and every moment she was away was agony.

What was de Bourgh doing to her? If he touched one hair on her head, Owen would make him wish he were never born.

He peered into the darkness until his eyes hurt, but he couldn't make out anything beyond the light of the two torches against the blackness.

"Amber?" he said. "Is that ye?"

"Shut up," came a male response.

Owen gripped the iron bars until his fingertips were numb. Finally, they were close enough that he could see a man marching with two torches and behind him—

Icy fingers gripped Owen's core.

Two men carried Amber's limp body.

"Amber!" Owen called.

She didn't move. Some sort of a cloak covered her shoulders.

"She can't hear you." The man with the torches opened the door to the cell.

They carried her inside, her feet dragging over the ground. They placed her on her belly on the bench attached to the wall in the darkest corner of the cell.

"Don't turn her on her back." The guard gave one torch to Owen.

With that, the three of them left. Owen's wide eyes remained fixed on Amber's immobile body.

Jesu, Mary, and Joseph, please, let her be alive.

He wouldn't forgive himself if she died. Wherever he went, trouble and tragedy followed. The feud with the MacDougalls, which had led to the deaths of his grandfather and Lachlan, Marjorie's kidnapping, Ian's...

Even when he was a wee lad, he'd always managed to make a mess of things. Like when the MacKinnons had come to visit Glenkeld. Owen had begged his da to let him go out on the hunt with the men. He was a good shot for a ten-year-old. But his father had barely acknowledged Owen's request. He'd been too busy talking to his guests.

A disgruntled young Owen had fed the hounds so well that morning, they'd been tired and not interested in the hunt. Consequently, an angry boar had almost attacked the MacKinnon chief. It was only Owen's father's excellent aim that had saved the man's life.

Later, when his father realized who was responsible for the mischief, he'd given Owen a hiding with a soft whip that hadn't broken his skin but had stung nonetheless. Unfortunately, it hadn't taught Owen to behave. It had taught him a way to get his father's attention.

But Owen couldn't mess this up. Not when the life of an innocent woman was at stake. Especially since that woman was Amber. He put the torch into a sconce on the wall above the bench and sank to his knees by her side. In the light of the fire, he could see her back rising and falling in small, shallow motions. She was pale, but she looked serene. They hadn't hit her face.

Carefully, he lifted the cloak a little from her shoulder. Bare skin. De Bourgh had undressed her. What else had he done to her? A painful chill went through him, followed by a hot rush of anger.

That bastart... Oh, he will pay. If there's a single bruise on her...

He lifted the cloak higher, until he saw the first cut. It was a lash, red and broad. The skin in the middle of it was broken, and the cut bled.

"Oh, lass," Owen whispered. His fists clenched, fingernails biting into his palm.

He uncovered her back completely and saw a dozen or so long, bleeding cuts.

"Holy Mother of Jesu," he muttered in horror.

He needed to treat her. Wounds like this could be deadly. She could get a fever, especially here in this dirty, moldy underground cell. But he had nothing, not even clean cloth to cover the cuts. And where were her clothes? She needed to stay warm to stay alive.

Owen covered her again and stood. He ran his fingers through his hair and looked around, hoping to find something that would help him. Any warrior knew the basics of how to treat cuts and wounds, so he was ready to help her. But all he had around him was dirt, dust, and rocks.

He sank to his knees again and felt Amber's pulse on her neck. It was weak, but it was there. Had she passed out from pain? A dozen lashes would be tough for a healthy man, and as strong as Amber seemed, she was a woman. And the days on the road weakened her.

He needed to speak to the guard. Plead with de Bourgh to take her to a healer. He could make a deal, trade some insignificant or even false information for Amber's recovery. It had been a brilliant move on de Bourgh's behalf to start the torture with Amber and not Owen. He couldn't stand to see her suffer so.

The door to the dungeon screeched and gnashed again, and he rushed to the bars.

"Please, help," he called to whoever carried a torch towards him. "She needs a healer."

The person first stopped by the other prisoner. Owen heard a metallic *clang* and some liquid being poured, then came the noise of a hungry man gulping food down. Then the light came towards Owen.

Soon, he could distinguish the features of a guard. He was short and hunched over with a crooked back. He looked about fifty years old and wore a simple cap on his bald head. He had a large nose, a protruding lower jaw, and small, deeply set eyes that made him resemble a hound.

No, this man wasn't a guard. As far as Owen could see, he was unarmed. He must be a warden.

The man put the torch into a sconce by the grating and then removed a large purse from behind his back. He fished out a waterskin and he tossed it into the cell through a gap in the bars. Then he took out a loaf of bread and did the same. It landed right on the floor, in the dirt, but Owen's mouth watered at the sight of it.

Nae, he had more important things to think about.

"Please help," he said. "My wife is badly injured. She'll die if she isna treated. Can ye take me to de Bourgh? Or bring a healer here?"

The man looked sharply at him, his furry brows knotting together.

"Where're ye from, lad?" he said, his Highland accent even thicker than Owen's.

"Argyll. Loch Awe."

"A Cambel?"

"Aye. Owen Cambel."

The man grunted. He looked back into the darkness he had come from.

"My name is Muireach," he said. "I'm from Kintail myself."

A thread of hope moved in Owen's chest. "Mackenzie land," he said.

"Aye."

Owen swallowed. Whose side was Muireach on? The Sassenachs had taken Stirling from the Scots at the beginning of the war, so if Muireach worked in the castle, he could be on the English side, like the MacDougalls. But he was a Highlander. The Bruce had spent some time during the winter of 1306–1307 in Eilean Donan Castle, the seat of the Mackenzie clan. Was it possible Muireach was still a supporter of the Bruce? Owen had to be very careful now.

"Are ye a Mackenzie?" Owen said.

"Aye. From my mother's side. Came to Stirling as a young'un. But I'm a Highlander to the bone."

Owen looked for a twitch, for a hitch in his breathing, for something that would tell him if Muireach was lying. There was nothing.

"My wife and I were taken prisoner at Inverlochy," Owen said. "De Bourgh tried to take the castle back from King Robert the Bruce. He tortured her." He gestured at Amber, and Muireach looked over to where she lay in the cell. "I'm afraid if she doesn't get treated, she'll die."

Muireach didn't respond. He seemed indifferent. Owen was beginning to lose hope.

"Ye must be careful who ye talk to," Muireach said. He scoffed, took the torch, and walked away.

"Wait!" Owen called. "Please, help her. She's an innocent

woman. She has nothing to do with the Bruce or the English. My family will reward ye if ye help us... Muireach!"

But the hunchback didn't turn, he only sped up. Owen gripped the iron grating and shook it. Would Muireach tell de Bourgh that Owen had tried to bribe him? Would de Bourgh punish Owen or Amber? Had he just made things worse?

The heavy door to the dungeons rattled and closed. Owen cursed and kicked the loaf of bread. It bounced against the wall and fell on the floor again. He shouldn't have done that. It was their only food, and he and Amber both needed strength. He picked up the bread and ate a bit of it. It was hard, stale, and tasted moldy. But it was food.

He picked up the waterskin and sniffed. Water. He drank hurriedly, only now realizing how thirsty he was. He could easily finish it all, but he had to leave something for Amber. She'd wake up eventually, and she'd need food and water more than him so she could recover. Hell, she'd need all the help she could get.

Owen went to sit on the floor by her side. Gently, he stroked her curly hair. It was a little wiry but soft to the touch. He studied her face. God, she was beautiful. Those big, slightly slanted eyes with long, curly eyelashes. The full and kissable lips, her wide mouth... He wanted to make her smile. She had an elegant neck he craved to kiss.

"Please, live," he whispered. "Ye must live."

"I wish I were dead," she croaked.

Owen sat straighter. "Lass?"

Her lashes fluttered, and she opened one eye.

"Jesus," she said. "My back is on fire. Did the son of a bitch peel off my skin?"

"Nae. But I will peel off his."

"It wasn't de Bourgh who flogged me. He has a man for that."

"Both of them, then."

"I don't remember anything after the first several lashes. I think I passed out."

"Ye have about a dozen as far as I can tell."

"How bad?"

Owen inhaled sharply. "'Tis nae good, lass. They all bleed. And I dinna have anything to help ye."

Amber closed her eye and swallowed. "Well, damn."

"I have water and bread, though. Here, try to drink." Owen held the waterskin to her mouth and tilted it. Amber drank some and then coughed.

"God, I'd give my arm for some Advil," she muttered.

Ad— What? That must be something from her time. But that wasn't important right now.

"Shush. Save yer strength. Eat." He broke off a piece of bread and brought it to her mouth. She moved her arm under the cloak but hissed, winced, and stopped. Then she bit into the piece and chewed slowly.

"That's awful," she said through a mouthful.

"Aye. When we get out of here, I'll make ye my famous field stew. It tastes only a little bit better than this."

A weak smile lit up her face. Owen's breath disappeared from his body at how beautiful she was.

"You said 'when' we get out of here... Do you still believe we will?"

He didn't know what he believed. But he had to make sure they had hope. Or there wouldn't be a point to any of this.

"Aye," he said. "I swear to ye, we will get out."

The door to the dungeon rattled again, and there was the sound of steps shuffling through the hall. Owen frowned and peered into the darkness. He didn't want to leave Amber's side in case they had come back for her.

But it was Muireach who stopped in front of the bars and glared at Amber.

"The lass woke up," he said. "Better if she were asleep."

He passed a cloth pouch through the bars and put it on the floor with a dull *clunk*. Owen stood and went to pick it up.

"What's this?" Owen asked.

"Put the salve on her cuts. It'll help her heal and protect

against rot. There's a drink that'll dull her pain. Give it to her first. Put the salve on when she sleeps, or she will scream, and guards will come. There's also a bone needle and catgut thread if her cuts need stitching. Give her more of the drink if ye do, or she'll wake up from the pain. Also, there's some boiled mutton and bannock for her and for ye to keep yer strength up. Ye will need it."

Owen came closer to the bars. He was ready to kiss the old man.

"Thank ye," he said. "Highlander to Highlander. Thank ye."

Muireach faltered. "We both ken who the true king is. 'Tisna the old Edward, and 'tisna his son. I canna do much from Stirling, but I can help a fellow countryman. 'Tis long overdue that the English leave our lands. And God be my witness, I will help ye both escape or die trying."

Owen looked back at Amber. She was smiling.

"I told ye we will get out of here," he said to her.

"But first," Muireach said, "ye must make sure *she* doesna die."

CHAPTER 9

Amber blinked against the fog. Something bothered her, a sensation at her back. Not quite pain, or maybe a distant pain. She was cold. Her head weighed a hundred pounds. Through her blurred vision and the darkness, she noticed someone on their knees by her side.

She shifted her head to look at them, and the movement sent sharp agony ripping through her back.

Owen. With the name, her memories came back. The time travel. Being captured by the English.

The lashing.

She groaned as she remembered the sensation of torn flesh, of fire consuming her skin.

"Lass?" Owen said. "Are ye in pain?"

"A bit."

"Can ye hold on for a wee bit longer? I'm almost finished."

"What are you doing?"

"Stitching ye."

"Oh." The word "stitching" caused an immediate rush of adrenaline, which sharpened all sensations. It felt like red-hot needles pierced her all over. "Is there any more of Muireach's magical potion? It knocked me out good."

"Nae, I'm afraid there isna."

Amber took a deep breath in. "Fine. I'll be fine. Just do it quickly."

"Aye. Dinna move."

She felt a sharp pull at the small of her back and sucked in more air.

"Just a couple more."

Another sting, stronger than the one before. "Ahhh, mother of—" She bit her finger.

"Tell me something about yerself," Owen said. "To distract ye. Something good."

Something good? What was there to tell that was positive? One positive thing was her mother. She'd been the strongest and the kindest woman Amber had ever known. After she'd died of cancer, Amber's stubborn dad had given up on life.

"Mom's fried chicken," Amber said. "That was so good."

Owen chuckled. "Fried chicken does sound verra good. Yer ma did it herself? Ye didna have a cook?"

Oh crap. Yeah, she still needed to pretend she was from this time. Another pinching stitch caught her breath.

"Breathe, Amber," Owen reminded her. "Send yer breath through that pain."

She exhaled through the place in her lower back where it hurt. Surprisingly, that dissolved the pain and relaxed her. She kept inhaling and exhaling.

"No. We didn't have a cook," she said, already regretting telling him the truth, but it was as though her tongue couldn't stop moving. "Did you?"

"Aye, we did. Nae a verra good one. But, aye." He chuckled. "He hated me."

There was another pinch and a pull.

"Uffff," Amber breathed out. "What? How can anyone hate such an angel like you?"

Owen chuckled. "The story involves his daughter, the midsummer night bonfire, and a big raspberry bush."

She shook her head. "You're a man whore, aren't you? I knew it."

She shouldn't call him names like that. But it was as though her filter had taken a vacation. Maybe Muireach's potion was something like a truth serum.

"Dinna fash, lass. 'Twas nae but a kiss. I was fourteen, and she was a year younger."

Thankfully, he wasn't offended. And she was relieved it wasn't a story of seduction. Something dark twisted in her when she thought about Owen and other women.

He chose that moment to put the needle through her again, but the pain was weaker this time.

"That gives me an idea," Amber said. "Let's play a game. Two truths and a lie. Do you know it?"

"Nae. Are ye sure ye can play games, lass?"

"I think I absolutely need to."

"Aye. All right. How does the game go?"

"I tell you two truths about me and one lie, and you need to guess which is the lie."

He cleared his throat. "Do ye play games like that wherever ye come from?"

Amber's head began clearing, and with that, pain grasped her back harder. She also suddenly realized she was completely naked from the waist up. How much of her boobs had he seen? Heat rushed to her cheeks.

"Yeah," she said. "We do."

Had the potion worn off? Would she even be able to come up with a lie?

"Aye, let's play this game of truths and lies."

"Okay. I'll go first."

She was already regretting her choice of game. She'd told him as little as possible about herself, hiding the biggest truth of all—that she was from the future. She needed to be as general as possible.

"I like apples," she said. "Hate romantic comedy. Want to get married."

Ah! So she *could* lie to him. Good. Owen didn't move for a moment, and she could feel his gaze on the back of her head like hot coals.

"What's a romantic comedy?" he said.

Oh shoot. "It's like theater. A story about love, and it's funny," she said, then muttered to herself, "and full of clichés."

"What did ye say?"

"Nothing. Which one's a lie?"

"Why do ye nae want to get marrit?" She could feel him pinch the sides of her skin and pierce her flesh. She sucked in a sharp breath and exhaled slowly through that pain.

"How did you guess?"

"I dinna see ye enjoying a funny show about love, and who doesna like apples?"

She shifted her head and looked back at him. His profile was pure concentration. His lips were tightly pressed in the midst of his scruff, his nostrils were flared, and his brows were drawn together. Despite the pain and fear, the presence of this gorgeous, hunky man made blood rush to her face.

"I said dinna move, lass."

"Bossy much?" She turned her head back and laid it on her hand.

"So why dinna ye want to get marrit?" he said and pierced her again.

She wasn't ready for this pain. "Ahhh!"

The prisoner at the other end of the dungeon screamed, too.

Owen took her free hand and lowered his face to her. "Breathe, lass," he said gently but firmly. His handsome green eyes were right in front of her face, full of concern, and a lock of his blond hair fell across his forehead.

She inhaled and exhaled slowly. "Please tell me you're nearly done."

"One more stitch. Then I'm done. Tell me why ye dinna want

to get marrit. My sister Marjorie didna, either. Did someone abuse ye?" His voice jumped with the last two words.

Bryan had been angry and irritable after he'd started working closely with Major Jackson and had become increasingly controlling in bed. The final straw was when he'd duct-taped her to the bed and spanked her. He'd stopped when she'd asked, and she had agreed to it in the first place. So was it abuse? She didn't think so, but it had been more painful than stimulating.

"Let's just say there are things in my past I wouldn't want anyone to have to deal with."

She couldn't imagine truly trusting anyone enough to get married to them. And in the unlikely event that there existed a man who wouldn't try to control her and blame her for all his faults and problems, how could she ever connect her life with anyone and have children when she could be taken to prison or even sentenced to death at any moment?

Owen hemmed. "Things in yer past," he muttered.

Was he daring to judge her? "Yes, things in my past," she said. "Things you have no idea about."

"Aye. I havna. Because ye dinna tell me."

He slid the needle into her skin again, and she felt every excruciating detail of that pain.

"Mhhhhhh," she released a half scream, half moan into her hand.

He finished quickly and then covered her with the cloak and sat on the floor by her side, crossing his legs.

"'Tis done," he said. "Now my turn for yer game."

Amber exhaled. She didn't have any energy to play anymore, but she needed some distraction from the throbbing, burning mess that was her back.

"Okay, champ. Bring it on."

He looked at her intensely. "My cock was once hard for a whole day. I shot a squirrel in the eye. And ye were born in my time."

His words didn't quite register at first. "What was that last one?" she mumbled.

"Ye were born in my time. Which one is the lie?"

Well, the good news was she didn't feel any pain anymore. Instinctively, she shifted her arm to push herself up and try to sit, but she felt like the stitches would explode at any moment.

Owen glared at her. "I told ye nae to move."

"You know?" she whispered.

"That ye are from the future? Aye. I ken."

Had Muireach's potion caused her to lose her mind? Did it induce hallucinations? She'd accepted the idea that she'd traveled in time, but hearing it from him like it was the most normal thing in the world... Once, in Afghanistan, a bomb exploded next to the Humvee she was in. The butt of her gun had hit her in the solar plexus, and she'd been unable to breathe for a moment. She hadn't been able to hear anything beyond the ringing in her ears. That was how she felt now.

"How do you know?"

"Yer clothes. Yer accent. Yer words. Yer fighting. Everything about ye. I realized it from the beginning."

"But—"

"I ken others who've come from the future. I've heard an accent like yers before. United States of America, aye?"

Blood drained from her face, and cold tingles covered her skin.

"Did you say the United States of America?"

"Aye. I dinna feel at liberty to say who those people are. 'Tis nae my secret to tell."

"So there are more..."

"Aye. There are more."

What was this? This crazy reality where people from the States had traveled back in time to medieval Scotland? Was this her life now?

"And were they all sent by Sìneag?" she asked. "She said she's a Highland faerie, and that she loves matchmaking people through time."

Owen chuckled and shook his head. "The Highlands are full of superstitions and legends. I was raised on those stories. Some people see faeries, kelpies, and magical folk behind every boulder and tree. I dinna. I havena heard of a faerie who matchmakes through time, but I have heard stories of another world—the faerie world. They have a kingdom of sorts that we people canna see. They're invisible to us unless they want to be seen and heard. But 'tis all legends."

Amber bit the inside of her cheek. "Looks like a legend came to life. What about that Pictish magic she talked about?"

Owen shrugged. "Picts were Celtic people who lived before us Scots. They're ancient folk, and I ken only stories of them. Stories of druids, of Beira, the queen of winter, and the great hero Diarmid the Boar. 'Tis told that my clan originates from Diarmid. We Highlanders are a strange people, I suppose. We believe in our Lord Jesu Christ, and yet we dinna build a new house without planting a rowan tree somewhere by the entrance for protection against evil spirits. A groom wouldna get marrit without a blossom of white heather on his bride. A midwife opens all windows and doors in the house during childbirth and she dinna let people sit cross-legged."

He rose to his feet, walked towards the bars, and leaned back against them. "So, aye, I believe ye met a faerie. And I believe ancient Pictish magic sent ye back through time. So ye can stop pretending ye're from the caliphate."

Accusation saturated his voice.

What was he accusing her of? He had no idea what it was like. She scoffed. "Do you suggest I announce to everyone I'm from the future?"

"Nae. But I dinna understand why didna ye go back through the stone while we were still in Inverlochy Castle? Isna it where ye belong?"

"Well, buddy, that's not an option."

"Nae anymore." He gestured around the cell. "But if ye had gone back right away, we wouldna be here."

"Unbelievable. Are you still blaming everything on me?"

She'd been wrong about him. Him stitching her wounds, nursing her, the flirting and lingering gazes—none of that mattered. Underneath it all, he was just like every other man in her life. Looking for a scapegoat to blame for his faults.

And she'd always been the perfect victim.

That was the whole reason she was in this mess. And she'd be a fool not to learn from her mistakes.

"I'm tired," she said.

Guilt flashed across his face. "I dinna blame everything on ye, lass," he said. "Ye're just a shiny distraction I shouldna have been fooled by."

He turned and paced to the other side of the cell.

Good, Amber thought, *he's finally stopped the interrogation.*

But why did it feel like she wanted him to climb on the bench, lie down behind her, and take her in his arms? Why did it feel like his arms would be the safest place on earth?

CHAPTER 10

It must have been about five days after Amber's flogging that Owen heard the pounding of many heavy feet on the dungeon's steps. He hastily shoved the salve back into the pouch and then under the bench. He threw the cloak over Amber's back and stood to face whoever was coming.

During the past few days, or at least what felt like days, he'd taken care of Amber's wounds. Thankfully, they seemed much better. The swelling and the redness had subsided, and there was no pus. Muireach came every day with food and water and new salve, potion, and pieces of cloth.

Three guards stopped in front of the cell, and one of them opened the door.

"Come with us," one of them said to Owen. "Now."

Owen hesitated, not wanting to leave Amber alone.

She opened one eye, still drowsy from the potion. "Go, Owen," she said. "It's okay. I'm not going anywhere."

"It's nae ye going anywhere that I'm worried about," he said. But he knew Muireach would keep an eye on her. Throwing a last glance her way, he walked out. "All right, lads, take me to yer bastart commander."

That earned him a hard smack on the back of his head, and

he grinned. They walked down the hallway of the dungeon, and when they entered the landing area, Owen saw someone tall and dark descending the stairs.

"Owen Cambel?" a strangely familiar voice said.

He knew that voice... "Hamish..."

Hamish stood before him, as tall and menacing as ever. Thin battle scars decorated his face, and his black eyes were unreadable.

Great. Another traitor. The wasp nest was getting bigger.

"What's going on, lads?" Hamish asked.

"Don't know," one of the guards said. "Sir de Bourgh asked for the Highlander. He got nothing out of the wife, so I guess it's this piece of shit's turn now."

A look of confusion flashed on Hamish's face.

"Walk." The guard shoved Owen.

Hamish followed Owen with a deep frown. This wasn't good. Last year, Hamish had infiltrated Inverlochy's troops. He'd pretended to be from the MacKinnon clan while spying for the MacDougalls that whole time. The man was a devil. He'd kept his identity a secret for several weeks and eventually killed Lachlan.

If Hamish discovered that Muireach was helping them, there would be trouble. He'd also interfere with their plan to escape. They needed to be even more careful now.

Owen and the guards walked to the other wing of the dungeon. Several heavy doors lined the hallway. They stopped before one of them, and the guard opened it.

The chamber was clearly made for torture. The image of Amber being lashed right here invaded Owen's mind and brought a painful heaviness to his gut. They must've tied her to the giant pole in the middle of the room and flogged her with a whip hanging on the wall.

There was a massive table with roasted chicken, bread, cheese, and apples. De Bourgh stood by the fireplace with his back to Owen and played a jolly tune on a fife. Another man, probably the Jerold Baker that Amber had told him about, sat and sharpened a long knife, tapping his foot to the rhythm of the song.

Clapping and humming the melody, Owen walked into the room. The two men looked up at him and the music stopped.

Owen leaned on the table and tore off a chicken leg. "Please, dinna stop on my account. I've been locked up in the darkness for what feels like a lifetime. I've missed music and food"—he poured himself some ale from the jug—"and drink."

He gulped the ale and moaned appreciatively.

"Ye have a good cook and some great ale, Sir de Bourgh." He wiped his mouth with the back of his sleeve.

De Bourgh cocked one eyebrow and set the fife aside.

"Please, enjoy it while you can," he said, his voice terse. "I brought you here to see if you'd be more talkative than your wife. How is she, by the way?"

He had the audacity to ask about Amber after what he'd done to her... Scalding waves of fury cascaded through Owen. He tightened his fists to stop himself from grabbing one of those sharp torture instruments and putting it through de Bourgh like a spit through a pig.

This was a good start. He'd disoriented the bastart and thrown him off his game. He couldn't lose the advantage now.

Breathe, he reminded himself. *Breathe.*

"Ye well ken how she is," he said. "And I will talk. Why nae talk while there's music, food, and drink? A good, safe place to sleep. A roof above my head. What's nae to like?"

He took the chair at the head of the table, the one he assumed was de Bourgh's. He tore off a piece of bread and chewed. Hmm, the bastart did have a good cook. De Bourgh's nostrils flared, his lower jaw jutted out, and his lips flattened into a line as thin as a thread.

Good. Owen wanted him mad. He needed to find out how to get out of here, and an angry de Bourgh was much more likely to slip a crucial piece of information.

"'Tis much better food than what yer man brings down to the dungeons." Owen drank some more. "So while I'm enjoying yer hospitality, ask yer questions."

De Bourgh let out a long, loud exhale, almost a growl. Then he straightened his shoulders, lifted his chin, and walked to stand by the table. His eyes darkened, and the expression on his face made Owen's smile fade a little.

De Bourgh snapped his fingers, and Jerold Baker was at Owen's throat in a flash. He was surprisingly strong for such a thin man and lifted Owen up. Something radiated heat next to Owen's throat. Looking down, he saw a glowing rod and broke out in a sweat.

"You think you can be coy with me?" de Bourgh asked, his teeth bared. "You think you can make me forget what matters? You're no guest, and I'm no host. Make no mistake, your life and your wife's life are in my hands. I won't show any mercy. I won't make a mistake. Success here will ensure my children's future, and that is not something I will play with. So if you and your wife want to stay alive, you will answer me."

Owen gave a small nod.

"What is the Bruce planning?" de Bourgh said.

Owen needed to be smart. He needed to say enough so that de Bourgh would believe him, but still not give him anything important.

"He kens about ye and yer plans to take back the Highlands."

De Bourgh narrowed his eyes and shrugged.

"Hmm. I'll bite. How many men does he *really* have? Did he have everyone with him at Inverlochy?"

"I think five thousand." That wasn't true. The Bruce didn't have more than two thousand men, but Owen knew the enemy feared the Bruce and thought he had many more. The skill and cunning of the Highlanders, their knowledge of the territory, and the unexpected moves they made were the Bruce's strength, and Owen wasn't going to let his king down.

De Bourgh pinched his lips in consideration. "Five thousand

is a large force, but there's a difference between an army of trained warriors and simple farmers holding swords for the first time."

"He has knights."

It was true. He did have knights. When the Bruce had returned from the west where he'd been hiding, several Scottish knights had joined him. And the more success he had, the more men followed him.

"The rest are battle-hardened warriors," Owen said.

Another lie. The Bruce accepted anyone who wanted to join him. Most were passionate and dedicated. But they weren't all trained warriors like those in the English army.

De Bourgh narrowed his eyes. They glistened like black glass beads under his eyebrows. "Lies. They cannot be." He nodded to Jerold Baker. "Time to show our Highlander what happens to liars in Stirling."

The red-hot rod came closer to Owen's neck. The burn sent a blinding pain through him and snatched his breath away. But before the rod could dig deeper into his flesh, the door opened.

A tall man with shoulder-length white hair and a short gray beard came in. It was the same man who had given Owen the gold for the king all those years ago.

Chief of the MacDougall clan, John MacDougall of Lorne.

Jerold Baker moved the rod from Owen's face, but the scent of burned flesh and hair lingered in the room. Owen didn't notice the pain anymore. Rage and hatred rose in him like a wall of fire. MacDougall's eyes widened in surprise and then narrowed.

"I see ye're busy crushing Scottish flies, Sir de Bourgh," he said without taking his eyes off Owen. "Canna say I disapprove. I've wanted to crush this filth for a long time."

"Oh, yes, you must know each other," de Bourgh said. "Owen Cambel was just telling me about the Bruce's army."

MacDougall came in and let the door shut behind him. "It wilna be the first time he's betrayed his king."

A low growl escaped Owen's throat. "Ye treacherous pig. Ye well ken 'twas yer betrayal, nae mine. Ye orchestrated the whole thing. Ye have looked for a reason to dishonor my clan in front of the king for years."

"King John Balliol gave part of MacDougall lands to yer clan. What did ye expect?"

"I expected our ally to be honorable and just. But 'tis better this way. We ken yer true nature, and I'm glad we're allies with ye nae more."

"Shut up."

"Aye, try to shut me up. Ye wilna. While ye go lick the arse of the Sassenach king who couldna care less about ye, the true Scottish king is gaining power."

MacDougall marched to Jerold Baker and went to grab the rod, but he winced and laid his hand on his side.

The MacDougalls had attacked Glenkeld when all the Cambel men were away, and Marjorie'd had to fight them off. In that battle, she had wounded John MacDougall when he'd tried to kidnap her son, Colin—MacDougall's grandson.

The injury still clearly paining him, John cursed, took the rod with his other hand, and pointed it at Owen's cheek. The heat burned his skin even without touching it. "The true king, ye say? The true goddamn king who killed my brother-in-law, Red John Comyn. How's that honorable and just, huh, Cambel?"

"Red John Comyn deserved it. He was a traitor. He wanted the English crown to rule Scotland."

De Bourgh cleared his throat. "John, perhaps you can wait until we're done. I need information from him."

But MacDougall only waved de Bourgh off. Owen chuckled. Anything that would postpone the torture was good. MacDougall was wreaking havoc on de Bourgh's plan.

Jerold Baker took the rod from MacDougall's hand and shoved it into a bucket with water. It hissed and steamed.

"And so what if the English crown rules," MacDougall said. "'Tis only for the better. It makes us stronger—"

"We're stronger if we're free," Owen said. "But ye'll never ken true freedom. Once the Bruce is done with ye, all ye will be able to do is flee. Ye'll be licking English arse for the rest of yer life as a fugitive."

"And how do ye imagine the Bruce will do that? MacDougall is the strongest clan in the Highlands. And we have the English army to back us up. He'll never win. He's finished."

"Finished? Ye're the one who's done." Owen laughed right in MacDougall's face. Fury boiled in his stomach. He should stop now before he said something he'd regret. But already the words were bubbling out. "He's coming to take Lorne. That's why he's back. Yer peace treaty is about to expire. He'll take Lorne like he took Badenoch and all other Comyn lands."

MacDougall's face became grim.

Damnation.

I've done it again. I've messed up.

De Bourgh took a long black whip in one hand and slapped the palm of his other hand. "You *will* tell me everything."

"Ye dirty toads," Owen growled.

MacDougall threw his arm back and slammed his fist into Owen's face. Bone-crushing pain exploded in his cheekbone. Another blow landed on his jaw. Jerold Baker held Owen by the shoulders as if he were just a sack of meat.

Owen had to give it to MacDougall, he was still a powerful man, even though he was much older now. The third blow landed on Owen's temple, an expert hit meant to bring real damage.

It plunged Owen into darkness.

He woke up without opening his eyes. De Bourgh's and MacDougall's voices rang in his head as they argued.

They were some distance away, but he was still in the torture chamber. His head ached as though split in two. Bile rose in his stomach. He was lying on something hard.

"He said five thousand men," de Bourgh said.

"Do ye believe him?" MacDougall asked.

"It would certainly explain his rapid success in the east. How he got rid of all the Comyns, how he got the Earl of Ross to sign a peace treaty..."

"Aye. If 'tis true, the situation is worse than I feared. The peace treaty the Bruce signed with us ends in three sennights. I kent he would come for us one day. I didna think it would be so soon."

"Which is why we need to do something drastic."

"Aye. Listen. He has Highlanders who ken the territory well. But so do I. Let's use his weapon against him. Let's surprise him in Lorne. I suggest we repeat the successful strategy we used at the Battle of Dalrigh. We took him by surprise and completely destroyed his forces. I will have my men and yer men hide in the hills by the Pass of Brander. We can use galleys to cross Loch Awe so that he doesna see us coming. We can use the terrain against him—something he'd been doing so well against ye."

Owen's breath caught in his chest. Mayhap he hadn't messed up after all. If he could get this information to the Bruce, they had a real chance to stop de Bourgh and the MacDougalls and turn the tide of the war.

But first he had to get out of here alive.

CHAPTER 11

A weak metallic *clank* woke Amber up. Her heart drummed hard against her rib cage. She listened for footsteps, but none came. Had she imagined the noise?

She'd been so worried about Owen when they took him, but she was too exhausted and had dozed off eventually. What condition would they bring him back in? Would Jerold Baker flog him, too? Worse? How would she be able to care for him if she could barely stand?

She was lying on her side and pushed herself up to sit. The shirt Muireach had brought to her lay on her back and the movement made it slide across and rub against her cuts. Pain radiated through her body, but the cold air was welcomed against her feverish skin. Her jeans were loose now. When was the last time she'd felt full?

She wondered how much time had passed since they took Owen away. She missed her watch, the one her mom had helped her fix.

Amber remembered the scent of her mom's chocolate chip cookies and mint tea. Her melodic Southern accent. Her soft, gentle hands on Amber's forehead when she was ill. Amber had loved the girls' days she and her mom spent together while her dad and brothers played ball.

She remembered her mom washing hair straightener from her hair, and after that, leaning over the kitchen table together, examining the insides of the antique watch spread out on their white tablecloth. They'd read a book on clock mechanics and studied the tiny wheels and barrels with curiosity.

She'd asked her mom why she didn't throw the watch out, but her mom had just held the tweezers in her long fingers and picked up a tiny barrel and set it in its right place.

"I can't bring myself to do that. Your grandfather gave it to me when I married your dad," she'd said, her dark eyes shining from the memory. "He bought it with his first profits from the barber shop he opened in New Orleans. He said it was a family heirloom, and I should give it to my firstborn son." She'd handed the tweezers to Amber, her slightly darker fingers brushing against Amber's. "You try, hon."

"But you haven't given it to Jonathan."

"I did," her mother told her. "That's why it keeps breaking. He has no interest in it. I think it's so fascinating, how it all works, the mechanics of it. I wish I'd followed my dreams and had become an engineer. Don't make my mistakes, Amber. Do what you want to do with your life. Don't allow men to define you."

Amber knew her mother loved her father, but she'd also understood what her mom meant. Her father was a rock, dependable and strong. But he could also be stubborn, controlling, and fixated on his beliefs.

Her mom had given her the family heirloom, and that was where her fascination with mechanics had begun. She'd loved looking at the watch. It had brought her a sense of peace and control, as well as a connection to her mom. When she'd lost it while out on an operation in Afghanistan, she'd been crushed.

Now, not knowing how many days had passed since they'd

been brought here, how many minutes or hours since the guards had taken Owen, made her stomach squeeze with anxiety.

"Who did that to ye, lass?" a male voice rumbled.

Amber's whole body jerked and she spun around. A man stood on the other side of her cell. He was tall and dark with wide shoulders. His face was half hidden in the shadows, but she swore she could see scars disappearing into his beard. He was dressed like a warrior, not unlike the Highlanders she'd seen at Inverlochy, with a long, quilted coat, woolen hose that covered his legs below the knee, and pointy leather shoes. Everything he wore was dark, and a sword handle peeked from behind his shoulder. She couldn't see his eyes, but she felt the weight of his gaze on her.

"Jerold Baker," she replied without thinking.

She realized the cover had slid down completely and her back was exposed. She picked up the cloak and wrapped it around herself.

He came closer to the bars and into the light, revealing his face. The expression of menace there made Amber gulp.

"On whose orders? De Bourgh's?"

"Who else's?"

His face went stony. She should be more careful. She had no idea who this man was or what he wanted. What if he was some sort of overlord or something? Or what if he worked for de Bourgh? Now he'd seen someone was healing her wounds...

Had she just put Muireach, herself, and Owen in more danger?

The door at the end of the hallway clanked and footsteps of several people sounded against the floor. The man looked into the darkness of the hallway.

Owen appeared flanked by two guards. He was walking, thank God!

"Come to gloat, Hamish?" Owen asked.

The man gave him such a heavy glare that Amber was glad she wasn't on the receiving end of it. The guards opened the door, pushed Owen into the cell, then locked it and left. Without saying another word, the man walked past the guards and into the darkness.

Owen's tall frame lingered by the entrance. "He didna do anything to ye, did he?"

Amber shook her head once. "No. But he saw my scars... He saw everything."

Owen stood with his back to her, and she couldn't see his face. He hit the cell bars with his hand. "That snake. He'll tell de Bourgh. He'll ken 'tis Muireach helping us. And if he kens 'tis Muireach..."

Their escape was doomed. A cold, dark feeling of desperation twisted deep in her stomach. What if they never escaped? What if she'd gotten a life sentence after all—one in the Middle Ages?

Amber's eyes burned, but she wouldn't cry. "Are you all right?"

He turned, and the light of the torch fell on him. Amber gasped. His nose was bleeding, and one eye was swollen and closed completely. Something was wrong with his neck. It looked too red and yellow.

"I'm all right, lass. Dinna fash about me." He approached her. "Ye should lie down."

Amber's blood chilled when she saw him up close. "I'm fine. Come here, let me see." She patted the bench next to her. "What happened?"

Owen sat by her side, and Amber turned him so that more light from the torch could fall on him. Her heart clenched. She hated seeing him like this. This strong, kind, caring Highlander.

Warmth spread through her chest as she thought about how he'd tended to her these last few days. He'd relentlessly redressed her wounds and given her Muireach's potion. He'd talked to her to distract her when she'd moaned and cried out in pain. He'd even made her smile.

And the fact that he knew about the time travel... That was

such a relief. She was grateful he was here with her. If not for him, she'd be dead by now.

Without wanting to, she'd started to care about him. And even trust him. That was dangerous. He'd already blamed her for complete nonsense. A man like him, an irresponsible joker, a playboy, would blame her for his problems.

It would've been easier if he thought her crazy and distanced himself from her. But instead, he'd accepted she was a time traveler. Right now, they had a common goal—to escape. But what about later, once they were out of here? Would he betray her then? Abandon her?

Amber thought about Bryan. She'd trusted him. She'd loved him the whole year they'd been together. He was a good guy, kind and caring. But he'd had issues. He'd wanted to control her. Eventually, she'd broken things off.

He couldn't get over their separation. From time to time, when he'd get drunk, he'd come on to her. Like that last time, two weeks ago.

Amber remembered the hot air of the desert and the smell of old beer in the makeshift US Army bar. The half-broken, flickering neon signs, and the chatter of drunken soldiers trying to talk over rock music.

She'd gone with a fellow soldier to have a beer after a long recon mission. Bryan had approached her, and she'd quickly realized he'd had too much to drink, even though he looked calm and collected and wore his kind smile. He'd reached out and brushed his knuckles against her cheek. "Have a drink with me. For old times' sake."

Translation: he wanted to have sex with her again. And maybe get back together.

"You've had enough, Bryan," Amber said. "I'm tired. I'm going to bed."

She turned to walk away, but Bryan caught her by the elbow. "Just one freaking drink, babe. Please."

There was no use trying to reason with him when he was like this.

She already saw violence starting to rise in the depths of his eyes. Amber yanked her elbow from his grasp.

"I said no."

He grabbed her by the shoulders. She pushed him, sending him flying into the crowd. Some people caught him, and the whole bar stood still and looked at her. Most of them were men, and what most of them saw was an altercation. That a woman had attacked a man. They hadn't seen that he'd started it, that it was self-defense. They also hadn't been in the bedroom with him, where his touch left bruises on her breasts and her shoulders, where his bites left traces.

That push had shown him she'd never let him be rough with her again.

But all they'd seen was that she was violent against him.

And a couple of hours later, she'd pay for it.

Would she eventually pay for being open and vulnerable with Owen, too? She had to be careful. She had to remind herself that trusting anyone—especially a man or a system run by men—was stupid. She could only rely on herself. She'd learned that the hard way.

She was tired of being a doormat for men. For once in her life, she wanted a man to value her, to appreciate her.

As she looked into Owen's green eyes, she prayed she wasn't being foolish now. That she could trust him like she trusted herself.

A careful voice at the back of her mind warned her she hadn't known him for long, and that he hadn't had anything else to do other than care for her. What they'd been through together might not mean anything. But mesmerized by his proximity, by the orange fire playing in his one eye that wasn't swollen shut, she brushed that voice away.

"What happened?" she repeated the question, coming back to her senses.

"As ye see, lass, the English and I talked."

She couldn't resist it. She reached out and cupped his jaw, willing the bruise on his cheekbone to go away. His eye widened for a split second in surprise, then he held his breath and leaned into her palm. His skin was warm, and the bristles on his jaw rough. How would it feel to have him brush against her inner thigh with it?

"Your turn for some salve now," she said, clutching the cloak around her shoulders with one hand. "I'll put it on your neck."

He chuckled, but a grimace of pain distorted his face. "I can do it myself. Although I would prefer for ye to do it."

"Then let me."

Amber asked him to look away and quickly put on the shirt. When she was decent, she sank to her knees in front of him, itching to put her hands on his thighs and feel the steel of his warm muscles. She took out the clay box of the salve and opened it. The aromatic herbal cream melted against her fingers. She put a good heap on Owen's burn and gently spread it around. He hissed under his breath, his fingers clenching the bench until his knuckles whitened. Amber took out a fresh cloth and tied it around his neck.

"Is it okay like this?" she asked. "Not too tight?"

"'Tis all right."

"Let me put some on your face."

She scooped more of the salve and spread it against the swollen bruise on his cheekbone. His intense gaze left pleasant tingles on her skin.

"Yer touch makes the pain go away," he said.

Amber's hand lingered on his hot skin. Time froze. She was lost in the green depths of his gaze, in the golden glow of his skin, in his musky, masculine scent.

"I highly doubt that," she said, her voice hoarse.

"Aye, ye have a magic touch, lass. Is yer kiss magical, too?"

A kiss. Amber's breath caught in her throat, and her stomach did cartwheels. She imagined his lips on her. Would he be demanding or gentle? Would he taste as masculine as he smelled?

Her whole body melted like that salve on her fingers.

No. What was she doing? Kissing would only complicate

things. She'd decided not to trust him, not to get involved. She should follow through with her decision.

Amber withdrew her hand and closed the clay box. The air felt hot around her, and her skin broke out in a sweat. She didn't look at Owen, but she sensed his confusion, his disappointment. She put the box away along with the other pieces of clean cloth.

"You should rest," she said.

Right, pretend like he didn't say anything about a kiss. Pretend like you didn't just melt.

"Lass—"

"No. Please. Let's not."

The dungeon door clunked open, and Muireach's shuffling footsteps approached. Then he stood before them on the other side of the bars.

"If ye want to escape, tonight is yer best chance," Muireach said. "MacDougall and de Bourgh just left."

CHAPTER 12

An hour or so later, Muireach brought them English guards' clothes: two clean undergarments and two red tunics with three embroidered golden lions.

Amber gathered the edges of her dirty, bloody undertunic in her hands to pull it up and over her head.

"Turn away," she said.

His mouth suddenly dry, Owen cleared his throat and did as she asked. The images of Amber's naked back and the sides of her breasts burned in his mind. Her back wasn't injured in his imagination. Instead, her dark skin was smooth and glowing and soft as silk. Blood flowed to his cock. What was wrong with him? She was still injured. And she'd very clearly indicated she didn't want anything between them.

How could he be so aroused just because she was taking off her shirt? He let out a long breath and made himself think of something else.

Of the escape.

This was their only chance. If they failed now and got caught, de Bourgh would figure out that Muireach had helped them. And then the poor man wouldn't come out alive.

Owen undressed and put on the English clothes.

"Okay, decent," Amber said, and he turned around.

Even in men's clothing, she looked like a woman with her long, unruly hair, her graceful movements, and her delicate frame.

"Ye still look like a lass," Owen said. "Ye'll draw some attention. There aren't many people here who look like ye. I admire that, but it'll betray us to the English."

She crossed her arms over her chest. "What do you suggest?"

"A cap. Or a helm. A hood, mayhap. Something to put yer face in the shadows."

"He's right, lass," Muireach said from the hallway where he'd waited to give Amber privacy. "The men that guard the dungeon have helms."

"Then we'll need to make sure we get some."

"Are ye both ready?" Muireach asked.

Owen locked his eyes with Amber. She nodded. "Aye," he said. "We are."

Muireach unlocked the cell and opened the door. "God, help us," he muttered as Owen and Amber marched out of their prison. Owen's heart pounded heavily in his chest. They passed by the cell with the half-mad Englishman. He watched them leave but didn't make a sound.

They stopped before the heavy wooden door of the dungeon, but Owen laid his hand on Muireach's before the man could open it. He looked at Amber. "Ye promise to nae fight, lass? Ye might open yer stitches and bleed."

Her jaw muscles played, showing she clearly disagreed with him, but she gave a short nod. "I'll do my best. But honestly, freedom is more important to me than a little bleeding."

"Lass," Owen said as a warning, "if ye do fight, I promise I'll put ye over my knee when this is over."

Her face went blank at that, and even though it was hard to tell in the darkness, he thought he saw her blush.

"All right, all right," Muireach grumbled. "Ye can settle yer marital issues after ye disappear in the air like a child's fart. Wait for my signal."

He walked out, leaving the door open a slit. Owen watched him through it and saw him stop and greet the guards. They glanced briefly at Muireach and then continued talking. One of them was older and sat on a small stool, the other one leaned against the wall leisurely.

Muireach made a sign behind his back with his hand, and Owen opened the door. He stepped on the stone floor without a sound, although he was afraid his thundering heartbeat might alarm the guards. Muireach walked on slowly so the guards would concentrate on him.

Owen reached the man who was standing, grabbed the sword propped against the wall next to him, and stabbed the guard in the back. He grunted and sank to the floor. The second guard watched in astonishment as his comrade fell. He opened his mouth to cry out an alarm, but Muireach rushed forward and pierced his throat with a dagger.

"Aye, ye Sassenach bastart," Muireach growled. "Wanted to do this since the day ye took the castle."

Owen looked back at Amber, who watched everything with a pale face.

"Lass?" he said, worried they were taking too long.

"I'm fine. Let's not waste any time."

But before they could move to take the stairs, the door to the other wing of the dungeon opened. Hamish and five English warriors entered the space.

They froze. Hamish's expression changed from shock to furious determination. His sword glistened in the light of the torches as he drew it from its scabbard. Five more swords appeared.

"You Scottish animals," growled one of the men.

Owen stood protectively between them and Amber, his fingers tightening around the grip of his weapon. Muireach assumed a defensive position, dagger in hand. The air crackled with tension, as though lightning had struck nearby. No one moved.

Hamish glared at Owen with something unreadable in his eyes. Then his eyes darted to Amber, and he nodded to his right. It was such a small twitch, Owen almost didn't notice it.

Hamish whirled and stabbed the Englishman to his left in the chest. The rest of the soldiers stared in shock, so did Owen. The only one who didn't lose his wits was Muireach. Using their surprise to his advantage, Muireach stabbed the soldier closest to him and let out what sounded like a war cry as he jumped forward with impressive agility for a man his age. The soldier raised his sword and deflected the blow.

One of the other men launched himself at Owen, and he finally came out of his stupor and raised his sword. He brought his blade down and it bit into the man's ribs. The guard yelled but managed to strike out, the weapon missing Owen only by the length of a fingernail.

Owen swung his sword again, but he was too slow. The guard blocked it and thrust his own blade towards Owen's neck. Owen didn't have time to deflect, but before the blade met his flesh, a shadow passed behind the man. There was a loud *thud*, and the guard stumbled and fell to the floor. Amber stood with a wooden plank in her hands.

Hamish dealt a deadly blow to the last guard standing, and Owen looked around. Every single English enemy lay dead, blood spreading around them like small, dark lochs. Hamish wiped his blade on a cloth, and Muireach was already walking towards Amber with his bloody dagger still in his hand.

Amber leaned down and removed the helm from one of the guards. She put it on, and it hid her face somewhat, but her long, curly hair stuck out in all directions from underneath it. She quickly shoved the mass under the helm. Owen hoped it would stay there and that the dark night outside would conceal everything else.

He took another one of the helms and put it on. He undid a

guard's belt and cinched the scabbard and sword around his own waist. Muireach helped Amber do the same with another sword and sheath.

"Go," Hamish said. "Quickly."

Owen laid his hand on Amber's shoulder, but before he started up the stairs, he turned to Hamish. "Why did ye help us?"

Hamish sighed and looked at Amber. "I couldna let him hurt her like that anymore." He glanced up towards the stairs. "Now go. I still have a mission to complete in Stirling. But I hope I wilna meet ye on the battleground." Owen turned to follow Amber and Muireach, but Hamish said, "Owen, I am sorry about Lachlan."

Owen drew in a quick, angry breath. This was not the place nor the time to talk about this; though, it did make him feel a little better that Hamish regretted what had happened with Lachlan. He nodded, and then they fled up the stairs to the ground floor of the tower, through a larger door, and farther out into the cool, summer night.

Owen had forgotten how sweet fresh air was, how soothing the chirping of night crickets and the hooting of an owl was. It was liberating to look out into the vast open space and not see thick granite walls.

The yard was empty, and no smoke rose from the kitchen's chimney. The stables and cowshed were quiet. The great hall, too. Down the hill, torches illuminated the wooden palisade and the unforgiving outer curtain walls of the Stirling fortress.

"There are nae guards that I can see by the palisade," Owen said. "But there will be at the gatehouse. We must convince them to let us out."

"Aye," Muireach said. "Let us get the horses."

They went into the stables, and Muireach and Owen worked as quickly as they could to saddle the horses. He'd rather ride double with Amber since she was still recovering and weak, but that would raise suspicions, and they'd be faster on separate mounts.

Two horses were saddled, and Owen began saddling a third.

Muireach frowned. "Three horses?"

"Aye. Ye're coming with us."

"Nae."

Amber touched Muireach's shoulder. "You must. De Bourgh will know you helped us escape. He'll kill you. Come back to the Highlands. Don't die here with no purpose."

Muireach let out a long sigh. "Aye. Ye're right. But it will be more difficult for us to get out of the castle with me. Guards ken I'm the warden and needed here day and night. Why would I suddenly leave in the middle of the night? They'll smell foul play like vultures smell carrion."

"I wilna leave without ye, man," Owen said. "We'll think of something."

Muireach grunted and continued saddling the third horse. When it was ready, they walked back out into the night. Amber's long, strong legs brushed against him as he helped her mount. She looked at the horse as though it were a kelpie, but she didn't say anything. Mayhap she didn't know how to ride, which wasn't surprising, considering she was from the future. Amy grew up on a farm and could ride, but Kate had learned to ride here.

"Everything all right, lass?" Owen said, his hand still on her ankle. "Ye can ride, canna ye?"

"Yep. Yep."

"We'll go slowly until we reach the forest. Then I'll take ye on my horse. I dinna want yer wounds to reopen from hard riding. We dinna want ye to bleed again."

"Okay. I'll try not to bleed to death."

Muireach and Owen mounted, and they slowly rode down the hill. They passed the castle buildings, the dark palisade, and went into the outer yard. The thatched houses were quiet until a dog barked a couple of times from somewhere. Owen put one hand on his sword, but the night fell quiet again, the only noise the soft thumps of the horses' hooves against dry dirt.

Finally, walls as tall as mountains stood before them. The gatehouse had two square towers on either side that loomed over them and seemed to support the black sky. The small windows on the first floor were illuminated from the inside with the golden glow of torches. Owen wondered how many sentinels were up there.

He glanced up and cleared his throat. He needed to do his best impersonation of an English accent. "Open the gates!" he called.

Someone appeared in the window. "Who goes there?"

"William and I have been sent to accompany Muireach on a mission from the commander," he said.

Owen was a good singer and could mimic people well, but he could hear his accent slipping.

The dark figure was silent for a moment. "But the commander left. He never said anything about letting anyone else out."

Owen almost said "aye," but stopped himself. "Yes. But he gave me the mission before he had to go. Open the gates. We must make haste."

"Why must Muireach go? He never leaves the castle."

"It's none of your concern," Owen said angrily.

"It is. He's a Scot."

Owen gritted his teeth. "One of the Bruce's men was caught in Caerlaverock. Muireach knows him and must confirm his identity."

The guard grunted. "Wait there."

The guard moved from the window, and Owen saw two shadows on the wall. The man was probably talking it through with another guard.

Owen rubbed the back of his neck. The swelling had reduced somewhat, and he could already see with both eyes. Thankful for Muireach's salve, he peered into the darkness trying to see what was going on upstairs. His gut stiff, he exchanged a glance with Amber, who sat like a log and held the reins as if they were her last hope.

The shadows in the window disappeared, and after a while, two guards came out of the tower. One of them looked at Owen. Now that the soldier was closer, he could probably see Owen's injured eye and the bruise. Amber turned her face a little to the side and bowed her head. Sweat trickled down Owen's back.

"Got in a fight, I see?" the guard said.

Owen chuckled. "Some people cannot keep their mouths shut when they've had a few mugs of ale."

The guard nodded, looked at Amber, and frowned. "I don't recognize you. William, is it? Are you new?"

"New, yes," she said, doing her best to make her voice sound hoarse and English. "Friend, we must away."

"All right, all right."

The guard finally stepped back, and the two of them proceeded to the gates, lifted three heavy bars, and pulled the gates open.

Owen inhaled deeply and then let out a long breath. There it was, freedom, right in the darkness between those giant, impenetrable doors.

He urged his horse forward gently. He'd send it into a gallop if he could, but he'd promised Amber they'd go slowly. He heard the other horses moving behind him, and his heart thumped in his chest as he listened for any signs of pursuit.

The forest was getting closer. The moon came out from behind the clouds, and he saw the woods before him like a black, frozen sea. Not long now. He looked back. Even in the darkness, he could see Amber's wide eyes and her erect posture. Her horse snorted and shook its head. Amber was making it nervous.

"Just a little longer, lass," Owen said.

"Stop them!" someone cried from the castle. There was the rumble of horse hooves and Owen saw the dark shadows of three...four...five riders galloping down the slope from the gates.

His skin chilled. "Quick!" he yelled. "Forward!" Muireach's horse darted forward.

"How?" Amber cried. "How do I make it gallop?"

Damn, she really didn't know how to ride a horse. "Spur it on with yer heels in its sides!"

The riders were approaching, but he couldn't leave her alone.

"Come, Amber! Do it."

She dug her heels into the horse's sides and it neighed, reared, and dashed forward. Owen followed.

They approached the woods, but the riders were right behind them. Amber rode first, her horse flying now. She didn't have any control over it. *Please dinna throw Amber off.*

He spurred his horse on, allowing it to gallop faster. But the guards were already catching up. Muireach slowed his horse down and came level with Owen.

"I'll hinder them. Ye and Amber go on."

"What? Nae!"

"Aye. 'Tis how I fight for Scotland's freedom. The Bruce must ken about the ambush at the Pass of Brander. 'Tis how he can get rid of the MacDougalls and win this war."

"Nae, Muireach! We can all escape, the three of us."

"Goodbye, Owen Cambel. For Scotland!" He unsheathed his sword, turned his horse, and galloped back towards the riders.

"Stop!" Owen called.

Owen was torn between needing to save Amber and wanting to go after Muireach. But the older man was already too far away. If Owen turned back now, he'd lose sight of Amber, and who knew where her horse would take her, or if it would throw her off its back.

"Damn it, Muireach!" Owen cursed under his breath as his throat tightened painfully and nausea rose in his stomach.

The man had made his choice. And he was right. Owen needed to get the information about the Pass of Brander to the Bruce. It wasn't about his freedom anymore. It was about Scotland's.

He glanced back for the last time. Muireach had stopped three of them. One already lay on the ground, and two were fighting him. Two more riders still chased after Owen and Amber. But they'd slowed down when Muireach attacked and were far behind now. Owen and Amber had a good chance of losing them.

He needed to catch up with her, so he spurred the horse on, leaning close to its mane in an attempt to fuse with its sleek body and dissolve in the wind.

CHAPTER 13

Black trees flashed against the dark gray night, branches hitting her face, grazing her skin, and tearing her clothes.

Please, don't let me die. Please, let all this be a dream...

The last time Amber had prayed like this was when she'd found Bryan in a pool of blood in his barracks in Afghanistan.

That night, she'd prayed for it all to be a nightmare. That life wouldn't fade from his eyes as she held him. That the bullet wound was just a prank—something he'd drunkenly decided would be hilarious.

He whimpered as she held him. "Shh," she said, stroking the side of his head. His blue eyes were wide and held her gaze. "I'll call the medics. You just hold on, okay, Bryan?" She took her phone out, but he grasped her hand with his bloody fingers.

"Listen to me, babe... Major Jackson did this."

Amber frowned and shook her head. She'd always known there was something strange about Major Jackson. The aura of all-consuming power around him, gossip on the base that he held poker nights and always won. Pretty much the whole base owed him money. When they were still in a relationship, Bryan had started weekly outings with

Jackson to a teahouse in Kabul. That was also around the time he became more and more irritable and started being rougher and rougher with her.

Yes, she knew Jackson was a bad man to mess with, but shooting an officer? And yet she could picture it. Jackson, all tall, square-jawed, with shoulders as broad as a tank, with a gun pointing at Bryan.

"Why?" she said through a clenched throat.

"He smuggles Afghani drugs into the US. I helped him because I owed him a lot of money. He owned me. But I just couldn't live with it any longer. Just imagining how many Americans became drug addicts because of me... The guilt was eating me alive. I said I'd report him if he didn't stop. I have proof... Aman Safar..." He swallowed hard. He was so pale. "He'll be back soon. Run and hide, Amber. Run and hide..."

And then he stilled, and his body went slack against her. His eyes glazed over, and she knew he was gone. "Run and hide" were his last words.

And that was what she'd done. Instead of standing up and fighting Jackson. Instead of making sure the drug-smuggling bastard was behind bars.

The thunder of hooves rumbling next to her dragged her out of her memories.

"Dinna fash, lass," Owen called, and relief flooded her in a warm wave. "Just hold on a wee bit longer. They think we're going north to Inverlochy. We'll go east to lose them. It'll all be over soon enough."

She was afraid if she moved the wrong way, she'd lose her balance and fall, so she nodded without looking at Owen. She had no idea what she was doing, and it felt like all that stood between life and death were her fists clenched in the poor horse's rough mane.

Owen took her reins, and by some miracle, both horses turned right and continued their wild ride to the east. Amber didn't know how long they went on like that. An eternity, surely.

Finally, the horses slowed down. Her horse was wet with sweat and smelled like salt air mixed with freshly cut wood.

"I think she's tired," Amber called to Owen, who was still riding by her side.

"Aye. Mine, too. They've galloped a long way."

The horses slowed to a walk, and Amber breathed heavily with the animal.

"God, I can't believe this is over," she said.

They cleared the woods and rode over rolling hills, silver in the moonlight. "Aye. See there?" He pointed somewhere between the hills and Amber saw dark dots and squares. "A village or a small town. We may be able to sleep in an inn tonight."

Amber exhaled. An inn sounded like heaven. She craved a bed and a shower, which wasn't possible, of course. But if there was a bath...

"Really?" she said. "Are you sure they won't find us here?"

"'Tis verra difficult to find tracks at night, and they'll think we're heading north." His face darkened. "Thanks to Muireach, there are just two men after us. 'Tis unlikely they'll find us tonight. They'll have more men on the morrow, but we'll be far away by then. And we'll be much more careful."

Amber's gut squeezed at the thought of Muireach and his brave decision to stay and fight so she and Owen could escape.

"Maybe he managed to get away," she offered, although she realized the hope of that was minimal.

"Mayhap," Owen said, his tone suggesting he didn't hold out much hope, either.

Amber's chest tightened. Still, it was good to talk, to distract herself from the fact that by some miracle, she was still on the horse. Now that the animal walked calmly down the hill, it was much easier to hold on. The village they were approaching looked bigger than she had initially thought.

"How do you think they found out we were gone in the first place?" she asked.

"Mayhap someone saw the dead guards. Or mayhap the mad English prisoner cried bloody murder."

"I can't believe we're out of there. I can't believe I'm alive." She looked back, but the dark forest behind them was quiet.

Owen threw an amused glance at her. "Ye've never ridden a horse, have ye?"

She bit her upper lip. "Nope. In the future, most people don't."

"Why didna ye say anything?"

"I didn't want to slow us down."

"Ye dinna lack courage, lass."

Amber chuckled. His compliment spread through her veins like warm honey, but a voice deep inside her reminded her he was wrong. If she really had courage, she would have chosen to stay and face Major Jackson and the charges against her. She'd have looked for ways to prove her innocence and to put him behind bars for murder and drug smuggling. But the system had let her down, and she didn't have any faith in it.

"I wish you were right," she said. "Unfortunately, all I've been doing recently is running away. Nothing courageous about that."

"Sometimes 'tis all ye can do."

She gave a sound of acknowledgment. He was right, of course. Why was he suddenly so wise?

When they reached the village, it was quiet and dark. The shutters on the windows of the thatched-roof houses were closed. Their horses' hooves thumped softly against the dirt road. Cowsheds and chicken pens stood here and there. They passed by a blacksmith's workshop, a shoemaker... Amber scanned the medieval village with a tightness in her gut, her senses heightened as she looked for signs of the soldiers pursuing them. Finally, they saw a two-story building with a pole and a branch with leaves attached at its end.

"'Tis the sign for a tavern," Owen said.

They stopped at the inn, and Owen dismounted and tied the horses to a stand next to a trough. Both animals drank thirstily. Owen came to stand by her horse, his hair appearing silver in the moonlight. In his medieval tunic and with a sword at his hip, he looked like a prince from a fairy tale. Except his dark and intense gaze screamed rogue.

"Let me help ye down, lass." He stretched out his hands.

Carefully, with her legs shaking, Amber moved one leg over the horse's back and slid down the saddle into the safe haven of his arms. It occurred to her how she went to him without hesitation. His scent enveloped her—the earthy, salty aroma of the horse, and his own manly musk.

His eyes were gray in the eerie light of the night, smoldering, captivating her in a trance. They promised a happily ever after wrapped in a damn good night, sinful and naughty and free.

His lips were right before her, just an inch away. He looked at her mouth like all the happiness in the world was on her lips.

"I heard the horses," a voice said, and they both glanced in the direction of the inn. A man in his fifties stood there dressed in a long tunic, his bare legs glowing white. He had a barrel of a stomach, and a nightcap on his balding head. "Do ye need a room?"

Owen gently let Amber go and stepped back from her. Cold air chilled where his arms and chest has been pressed against her, and she longed for that proximity again.

"Yes," Owen said with an English accent. Right. They were still dressed as Englishmen, and this area was probably occupied by the English, so they needed to keep up the pretense for a while longer. "We need a room, dinner, and a bath. We rode hard on the king's business and long for a good night's sleep—whatever is left of the night."

There'd been a money pouch on one of the guard's belts, so they had something to pay with.

"Aye." The innkeeper's gaze lingered on Amber, and she lowered her head to hide her face. She was still wearing the helm, and her hair was hidden under it, but what if a lock or two got out?

"Come with me," said the innkeeper.

They went through the hall on the ground floor, passing a

bar, tables, and benches. The space smelled like old food and stale alcohol. On the first floor, several doors led to rooms. Theirs was small but homey and smelled like fresh linens, woodsmoke, and lavender. A large fireplace with flames dancing in it gave the room a warm golden glow. A large bed stood at the far end, as well as a bath that looked more like a giant wooden barrel. The room appeared clean enough, and Amber's muscles ached when she saw the bed.

"Ye two don't mind sharing the bed? We dinna have another room free," the innkeeper asked as Owen eyed the bed as though it were a lion he needed to hunt with his bare hands.

Owen cleared his throat. "That will do."

"Hot water is coming. For dinner, I have stew and some bread, cheese, and apples. Ale, mayhap?"

Owen nodded, and the innkeeper left the room. Amber couldn't wait a minute longer. She went straight to the bed and fell on it. After days of lying on the hard, cold bench, it felt like falling into a cloud.

She moaned as her aching muscles relaxed. The lacerations on her back stung a little in a pleasant, healing way, and she didn't mind.

"Oh my God," she said. "Is this stuffed with feathers? Whoever invented mattresses is a genius."

Owen chuckled. "Only noblemen sleep on feather mattresses. This must be simply wool."

There was a knock on the door, and a young woman entered with two clay bowls of stew, a loaf of bread, a small pot of butter, and a piece of cheese. She put the food on a round table in the corner of the room together with a wooden jug of ale and two clay cups. With a curious glance in Amber's direction, she left.

"Come," Owen said. "Eat, lass. Ye need food."

"After everything that happened tonight, I'm not really hungry."

She removed the helm and set it aside. Her scalp ached pleasantly from the freedom. Her muscles throbbed all over, and dried sweat covered every inch of her body.

"Even more reason to eat," Owen said. "Dinna make me come and make ye."

She groaned and shook her head. The next moment, his giant frame loomed over her. He leaned down and took both her hands in his, making her skin buzz from the touch. He pulled her up, and she stood before him, deliciously confined by his strong arms.

He swallowed hard, staring into her eyes with the intensity of a thousand suns. The floor shook under her feet, and she forgot how to breathe. Her knees jittered, and she felt herself losing balance. But he held her safely in place by the elbows.

"Let's eat," Owen said, his voice hoarse. "Come."

He gently led her to the table, and she let him. She didn't think anyone had ever taken care of her like this.

Owen let her sit and took the chair across the table from her. He poured ale in the cups and clunked his with hers. In the dim light of the room, his eyes were the color of grass in the golden hour before sunset. She melted like wax under the heat of his gaze.

They drank, and the ale was sweet and tasted only slightly alcoholic. She hadn't realized how thirsty she was. She took the first spoonful of cold stew without tasting the food. All her attention was on the golden demigod sitting across the table from her. The man who'd saved her life and helped her escape torture in a medieval dungeon. The man whose very presence made her feel supported and cherished, as well as weak and wobbly.

All things she really shouldn't feel towards a Highlander born about seven hundred years earlier than her. But it all felt so right. So good. Like there was hope for her.

Back home, she had no one. Her mom and dad were dead, and her brothers had their own lives. They'd never been close. That's why she hadn't contacted any of them to help when

Jackson framed her for Bryan's murder. But this man cared for her, even though he didn't really know her.

She tore herself a chunk of bread and spread some butter on it, then bit into it.

"I have a question, Owen," she said through a mouthful.

He chewed as well, his square jaw working. He raised his eyebrows in response.

She swallowed. "Why do you care about me? Why are you helping me, going to these lengths to save me?"

"I see a lass in need, I canna leave her in peril. Ye're from another time. Ye need protection."

"Yes, but there's more to it, isn't there? There must be. Tell me the truth."

He leaned back in his chair and crossed his arms over his chest.

"The truth, lass? I dinna think ye're ready to hear the truth."

"I am. I feel like I've lived through more with you than I have with any of my brothers. This past week, or however long it has been, felt like a lifetime. So tell me. Did you help me out of the kindness of your heart? Or is there more?"

He studied her as though contemplating whether to tell her or not. Then he leaned forward over the table and covered her hand with his. The touch went through her like a bolt of electricity, stealing her breath away.

"There's more, lass. I think ye're magnificent."

CHAPTER 14

Amber's large, dark eyes widened.

He chuckled softly and drank from his cup. She was too much of a distraction. He couldn't pass up a woman in distress, and she was an especially rare one. Looking at her now, her smooth skin glowing, fire from the candle dancing in her eyes, he couldn't hold back.

"The moment I saw ye kicking and punching the English knights—ye had no weapon, just yer fists and yer legs... I dinna think I've seen anyone so breathtaking. And that ye're from the future..."

A spasm of emotion tightened his throat, and he couldn't say a word more. The fact that she was from the future made her mysterious. Made her a heroine who'd stepped out of a myth or a ballad or a fairy tale.

It made her magical.

Pretty women were the reason for many troubles in his life. The reason Lachlan had died, the reason his clan had gotten in trouble with the MacDougalls, and the reason they were out of favor with the old king. Every time something bad happened, it was because he'd been distracted by a woman.

Amber was a distraction, too.

But she made him feel like he was finally alive. Like there was no need to chase the next shiny thing, because the dull ache inside him had stopped in her presence. A voice in his head liked to tell him he was worthless, that he brought only ill to his clan, and that he was his father's least favorite son. That his brothers were all great warriors and responsible men who'd rather die than leave their family in danger.

That he was the danger.

That voice was quiet in Amber's presence. She made him feel like he could be more than he'd ever imagined.

Her full lips parted, and he swallowed hard to keep himself from lunging over the table and sealing his lips with hers.

She was so beautiful. So different. Her golden-brown skin glowed like treasure. Her eyes sparkled with curiosity and wonder. Her body called him, all willowy and muscular and feminine.

"What about me being from the future?" she said.

"Ye make me believe in wonders, lass."

Her lips parted in surprise. He didn't hesitate. He stood and covered the distance between them in one step. He lifted her up to have her stand before him and kissed her.

Her lips met his, soft and warm and succulent, like an exquisite wine from a faraway country. Her body, delicate and strong at the same time, pressed against his and ignited fire in his blood. Desire roared through him, and his cock stood hard and throbbing for her.

She responded, kissing him as hungrily as he kissed her. The soft brushes of her lips against his, of her tongue against his, unraveled something within him, peeling him open, exposing his core, raw and pure and vulnerable.

He reached down to the edge of her tunic, but she froze.

"Someone's coming," she whispered against his lips.

Heavy steps sounded on the stairs, and he unwillingly let her go. They both breathed heavily, their gazes locked, the unresolved desire thick and heavy between them.

Someone knocked at the door, and the innkeeper came in with a bucket of steaming water. The girl who had brought food earlier came after him with another bucket. Amber turned away from them and sat down, hunching over the food to conceal her face. There was nothing to do about her long, wavy braid, but he supposed some men had hair like her in his time.

The innkeeper and the girl repeated the journey several times, and soon the bath stood steaming. They threw Amber a few sideways glances, which wasn't good. He knew they'd leave first thing in the morning. No doubt the innkeeper would remember two English warriors, one of whom had unusually long and voluminous hair.

When the two left, Owen locked the door and leaned against it. Amber stood and walked to the middle of the room, her eyes wide.

"Ye should take yer bath first," he said, his cock swelling again just at the thought of Amber undressing. "I'll go to sleep. Wake me up when ye're done."

He walked to the other side of the bed and started undressing. He felt her watching him, her gaze warm and tingling on his skin. Christ, if he could, he would come to her, take her in his arms, and make love to her in that bath. But he couldn't. He couldn't dive into that temptation. He needed to focus.

Besides, she must be exhausted and in pain from the journey.

He got onto the bed and turned around. His whole body ached, his skin sensitive and feeling every scratch of the blanket and the linens against him.

Her clothes rustled as she undressed and dropped them to the floor with the softest of thumps. The image of her naked body flooded his mind—the seductive curve of the small of her back, the sides of her breasts. Owen clenched his fists, attempting to chase those visions away. They made him harder and hotter.

He heard water splashing and knew she must be sitting in the bath. She hissed slightly, probably from the burn of the water against her wounds.

"Actually, can you help me?" she asked. "I can't reach my back. I'm afraid to strain the muscles and tear the stitches."

Owen swallowed hard. *Say nae. Say nae.*

He could lose his head over her. If he gave in to this temptation, what mistake would he make next because of her?

"Owen?"

"Aye, lass, I'll help ye."

Goddamn idiot. Did he not possess any self-control? It was as though his body had a will of its own. His head screamed at him to stay in bed, but he stood and walked to her.

"Don't look, okay?" she said.

Don't look?

"Aye," he said, ogling her.

She sat in the water hugging her knees, her bare back to him. Droplets rolled down her shoulders. He picked up the soap and the washcloth that swam in the water and squeezed it over her back. She hissed as water flowed down her back. The sight of her wounds made him ache all over.

He ran the cloth down her back as gently as he could. The crusts opened up in places and bled a little. Poor lass. At least now he wasn't thinking of how much he wanted to be inside her.

"'Tis done," he said when he'd washed as much as he could without irritating her wounds.

"Thanks." She took the cloth from him without turning around. He imagined how she'd gently run the washcloth over her breasts, her chest, her neck. Then down her stomach, and farther down...

Getting hard again, he looked away and went back to the bed. As he reached it, water spattered loudly on the floor, and without thinking he swung his gaze to the bath.

Big mistake.

Amber stood naked and wet.

Their eyes met.

"Mother of God," he muttered.

He was wrong. She wasn't a heroine from a fairy tale or a legend. She was a goddess. Her skin glowed golden brown. She had full breasts with dark nipples he ached to taste, a small waist, and full hips. Between her thighs was a black triangle of curls. She had long, sculpted legs with powerful muscles.

She was the image of femininity and strength. His pulse beat in his temples like small drums, his cock swelling even more.

"Lass, do ye want my heart to stop?" he said.

She didn't cover herself. She didn't waver. She showed no sign that she wanted him to turn around now. She reached for the fresh cloth that hung on the edge of the tub and wrapped herself in it, leaving only her sculpted shoulders and arms out.

"Don't get any ideas." She climbed out of the tub and walked to the bed. "Hope you enjoyed the show, but nothing is going to happen. Get in while the water is still warm."

She climbed to the other side of the bed and under the blankets. The clean scent of her skin reached him, teasing him, setting his blood to boil. Now that she lay right next to him, with nothing on but a piece of linen, the last thing he wanted was to leave the bed. He longed to reach for her and make her his.

But being with her would cloud his judgment and lead him to lose his head. He couldn't afford any mistakes while the future of Scotland may be in his hands.

"Aye," he said, and using all the restraint he had, he climbed out of bed and went to the tub.

CHAPTER 15

Amber peered from under the blanket at Owen. His powerful back was coiled with muscle and flowed into a gorgeous, round male ass. A beautiful ass she wanted to dig her fingernails in while urging him to plunge deeper into her.

Her back hurt, but her body felt clean and fresh after the warm water. The sight of naked Owen stirred unrest deep within her and impaired her thoughts. Her heart pounded against her rib cage, and her inner muscles clenched.

He got into the tub without looking at her, but as he turned a little, she saw his hard erection. She bit her lip at the size of it. Was he so aroused because of her? The thought of her making him hard ignited her own desire even more.

Owen lowered himself in the bathtub, still with his back to her, and began washing himself. He sank down into the tub until his head was completely under the water and then rose back up. Droplets trickled down his skin, and Amber wanted to lick them off him.

She closed her eyes, willing herself to think of something else, to distract herself from the heat between her legs and the bubbles of excitement in her stomach.

Just go to sleep, she told herself and closed her eyes. But even though she was tired, she couldn't doze off. The sound of splashing kept her thinking of a naked, wet Owen. Of Owen inviting her to join him. Of Owen guiding her to straddle him, kissing her, grabbing her thighs, growling with pleasure.

Then the mattress shifted, and he was in the bed.

Amber stiffened. The brush of the blanket against her skin felt like a caress. It augmented her senses, making the small hairs on her body stand up. She realized their breathing had synced up. The linen blanket tucked between her thighs felt coarse against her skin, and his presence was like a warm force field over her.

"Lass," he whispered. "Are ye asleep?"

She contemplated not responding. If she did reply, she might not be able to resist anything he initiated. But she couldn't help herself. "I'm awake."

"Can I ask ye a question?"

His voice was warm and low and inviting. She opened her eyes and saw he was staring right at her. She sank into the green depths of his eyes. The scent of clean skin, wet hair, and his masculine musk reached her, and it made her want to rub against him like a cat. She could drink in that smell like a well-aged whiskey.

"Sure." She cleared her throat. She itched to reach out and shift the wet strand of hair on his forehead.

"Why did ye travel in time?"

Oh God, could he have asked a more loaded question? It was probably innocent enough for him, but for her...

Could she admit to him what she'd been accused of? And that she'd been a coward and had run away? More importantly, did she trust him to believe in her innocence?

The truth was, she was tired of lying. Tired of pretending, looking for excuses and justifications. She was so relieved he knew about time travel. It felt as though a burden had been lifted off her shoulders. How would it feel to tell him about the worst thing that had ever happened to her?

What if he used that knowledge against her?

No, she stopped herself. No. He wasn't like that. He'd saved her life and taken care of her. He made her feel like miracles existed and he was about to gift her one.

She'd sworn to never trust anyone again, but she truly wanted to trust people. Even though she was afraid, she could start changing that now.

"Do you really want to know?" she said. "It's not a happy story."

"Aye. I'm nae a stranger to sad stories."

Her hand curled in a fist around the pillow, and she tried to relax it. He may never look at her the same way again.

"Okay," she said. "Here goes."

She took a deep breath in and released the angst that clenched her core. Once she said the words out loud, there would be no turning back. There was a big chance Owen wouldn't be able to accept her if he thought she was a coward... or a murderer.

The emotions roiling through her resembled those she'd experienced when she went out on a mission to eliminate terrorists. The sinking feeling in her gut intensified and she was hyperaware of the slightest movement and every change in the air. Every step could be the difference between life and death, but she took that step and waited for a bullet to hit.

"I ran from the police. That's how I ended up traveling back in time."

"The police?"

"Right. I suppose, you don't have police in your time... It's law enforcement. Like, if you break the law, they arrest you and put you in prison until you're tried for the crime you committed."

"Oh. Aye. I understand. They're like a clan chief who makes sure justice is served and punishes thieves and murderers."

"Yes. Except, in my time, there's a whole giant organization that specializes in that. Men and women work for money as police officers."

"Like a chief's warriors."

"Well, yes. I fought a war for my country in Afghanistan." Owen frowned, so she added, "Middle East."

"So ye truly were in the caliphate?"

"Yes."

"And what crime did ye commit, lass?"

She locked her eyes with his. Was he disappointed in her? Afraid to hear the answer?

No. He seemed to study her carefully but calmly. In fact, his tone was casual, as though he were asking what kind of tea she preferred. That should have been reassuring, but instead it bothered her.

Had he committed a crime?

"I didn't," she said. "But I was set up for one. Someone made it look as though I murdered a man."

His face lost the calm, attentive expression and went blank. Amber's chest squeezed, and her limbs chilled. That was it. He'd never look at her in the same way again.

"So yer police think ye murdered someone and are looking for ye to punish ye?"

"Yes. Under martial law, I can get a lifetime in prison, or"—her throat spasmed, and she swallowed—"a death sentence. And there's no way I can prove I didn't do it. I wanted to try. I did want to, but I was so terrified, paralyzed. The man who framed me, Major Jackson, he's too powerful. I'll lose."

Owen covered her hand that lay on the pillow with his own. His palm was a little callused and warm. The touch reassured her and melted the icy tension in her chest.

"Tell me everything, lass."

Amber's mind flooded with memories.

"De Bourgh reminds me of Major Jackson."

Owen's green eyes held an undertone of steel, and his expression grew hard. He pressed his lips into a thin line and didn't say anything.

"Not because of how he looks," Amber said. "But there's this dead coldness about him, this determination to achieve things no matter what. Jackson's smart. And he made my blood chill."

Where de Bourgh was short and bald, Jackson was tall and had a full head of dark hair. He talked loudly and had a wide, charming smile. But underneath that, she'd seen unmistakable cruelty. People were terrified of him, and his willingness to put the lives of local civilians at risk made her ill.

"Strangely, he was the one who allowed me to stay home for a couple of months when my dad died. I didn't expect him to be so compassionate."

"Yer da died?"

"Yeah. Heart attack."

"I'm sorry to hear that, lass."

He didn't look confused. "Do you know what a heart attack is?"

"Nae. But I can get the idea from the name."

"The funeral two years ago was the last time I saw my brothers. We used to see each other on Christmas and Thanksgiving every year, at our parents' house. My mom died several years ago, and my dad was never the same after that. When both our parents were gone, it was as though we didn't have a reason to come together anymore. So I spent the last two years in Afghanistan. That was when I got together with Bryan."

Owen's face tensed.

"What exactly do ye mean by 'got together'? Doesna sound like he marrit ye."

"In the future, we're much more liberal about relationships. He was my boyfriend."

"Yer lover?"

"Yes, but more than that. We spent time together, went on dates, and so on." She chuckled. "As much as you can go on dates in the middle of a desert."

"What are dates?"

"Meeting and spending a nice time together. Going to a restaurant—an inn, I mean, with good food—drinking wine, talking. In your time, I suppose you'd go for a ride with a lady, or for a walk... Bryan and I were together, you know. He was my man, and I was his woman—without being married. That's normal in the future. People don't have to get married to have children and build a life together."

"Sounds like I'd enjoy the future." Owen chuckled.

"Don't you want to get married?"

"Nae." There was something sad and almost bitter flickering on his face. "Marriage isna for me."

Long ago, Amber had assumed she'd get married one day. She'd wanted a family. She'd always thought after the wedding she'd retire from the army and do something else until she got pregnant.

"I don't think marriage is for me, either," she said. "I wanted it before, but not anymore. I'm a fugitive. A criminal. I can't bring children into a world where their mother could be taken away from them at any moment."

"So what happened to that *boyfriend* of yers?" He said the word "boyfriend" through gritted teeth.

"Bryan. We were together for a year, and then we split up. It didn't work out."

Amber chose not to reveal that he'd became a bit too rough with her. She wasn't proud of it and often wondered if it was something in her that had made him be like that.

"We were on the same base, and he wanted to resume the relationship, but I just couldn't. One night, about two weeks ago, we were both at a bar and he came at me hard. He was drunk, and everyone witnessed how I pushed him away."

"A bar?"

"Yeah, like an inn. Where people drink beer and whiskey and wine."

"Uisge?"

She nodded. He pronounced the word differently from "whiskey," although both words were clearly related. It was still amazing to think she could suddenly understand and speak Gaelic. She wished it had been as easy with Dari, the language spoken in Afghanistan.

"Later, I passed by the barracks and heard something... I went inside to check on Bryan and he was—"

Her voice broke and she tensed as she remembered the pool of blood, and the giant red flower that boomed on Bryan's white T-shirt around the bullet in his stomach.

"He was so pale, like a bedsheet. My hands shook so bad, I dropped my phone in the blood. Then I saw the gun lying on the floor." She shook her head. "I was such an idiot. I picked it up. Just like that, my fingerprints were all over it."

Owen didn't ask any questions, although he wouldn't know what a gun was, or a phone, or fingerprints. She was thankful he let her talk it out without interrupting. Telling her story was like letting go of a terrible pain she'd been holding on to.

"He was dying. I wanted to call the medics, but he stopped me, told me Major Jackson had shot him because he was going to expose Jackson for smuggling drugs. And then—"

Her chest spasmed, and she sobbed uncontrollably. The sound was girly and weak, and yet so freeing.

"Then he died," she managed before grief and regret overtook her. She curled into a shaking, weeping ball, and Owen wrapped strong arms around her. She pressed her cheek against his hard chest and wailed. She wailed for Bryan, and for her broken life that would never be the same, and for how helpless she'd been against a powerful man.

Owen stroked her and whispered something to her in Gaelic that she couldn't hear over the sound of her weeping. Soon, her sobs subsided and her body went limp. Owen only held her tighter.

"It's the first time I've cried since it happened," she said.

She felt calmer; the pressure had eased from her now.

"'Tis all right, sweetheart," he whispered against her hair.

Sweetheart... Warmth radiated through her chest. She wiped the tears and looked up at him.

"Jackson came into the barracks and found me holding Bryan, the gun in my hand. He managed to take a picture and said I'd pay for what I'd done. He was about to call the authorities when I realized just how screwed I was. I panicked. I knew I couldn't win against him. So I held the gun on him and tied him to one of the beds. Then I ran. I've been running ever since."

"So much so that ye ran back in time," he murmured.

Amber swallowed hard. She needed to ask him the question that tightened her stomach and made her clench her fists until her fingernails dug into her flesh.

"Do you believe me?"

"Aye," he said without a second of hesitation. "I believe ye, lass. I ken what it is to be wrongly accused of something."

Relief flooded her system like sunlight. And at the same time, something tightened in her chest to the point of ache.

He got her. He'd protected her. He cared for her.

And she cared for him—more than she wanted to, more than she could afford to.

More than she should.

Because the more she cared for him, the more she was going to hurt. No matter how wonderful he'd been to her, he was a man. And sooner or later, something would go wrong, and he would end up blaming her and dragging her down.

CHAPTER 16

Owen held Amber in his arms as she fell asleep. Limp and warm against him, she breathed evenly, her eyelashes fluttering as if she was dreaming about something...something good, Owen hoped.

He was not as lucky. Amber's confession had woken old demons inside him, the demons he was trying to forget.

He needed to keep a cool head to deliver the news of the Pass of Brander to his family and to the Bruce. The outcome of the war could depend on it.

And yet, just like before, when he was given an important task, he had a beautiful woman in trouble who needed him. He didn't trust his own judgment. Amber stirred more feelings than he'd ever felt for anyone. He'd cared about the women he'd bedded, of course. But it had never gone further than a night or a sennight. Then he'd bid them farewell and hoped they had a long and healthy life.

With Amber, he wanted to put a smile on her face every day. He wanted to kill that bastart, Major Jackson. He shared her anger at being treated so unfairly. He knew the burden of a false accusation all too well. As a result, his father had picked him last for battle and hesitated to give him any responsibility. And not just his father—his brothers, too.

Lachlan's death, the feud between the MacDougalls and the Cambels, as well as King John Balliol's lost favor would forever be on Owen's hands and conscience.

All because he'd been distracted by women.

He studied Amber's peaceful face, her lips...so full, so kissable. Her hair was still wet and lay in small curls around her shoulders. He admired her spirit, her bravery, her fighting skills. She was a warrior. He'd never met a female warrior before.

And that she was a fugitive—

He believed she was innocent. Like he wished his clan had believed him with the gold.

She was too kind, and she'd let people use her. She'd been in the wrong place at the wrong time. That was her only fault. He was furious that men like Jackson had used her. Men like John MacDougall and de Bourgh.

He was furious for her and for his own sake. The time would come when he'd use the knowledge he'd gained against those two bastarts and have his revenge.

But for that to happen, he couldn't allow himself to be distracted. For the first time in his life, he vowed he wasn't going to give in to lust. He wouldn't bed Amber. He wouldn't allow his cock to ruin the most important mission of his life.

He woke Amber up when the wood in the fireplace turned into dying coals and the sky behind the shutters began to lighten. The sun would soon rise, and they needed to go.

"Lass," he whispered.

She stirred, and her breasts brushed against his chest, only a thin layer of linen separating them. Under the powerful spell of her body, his cock woke up and hardened. She opened her eyes and looked at him, sleep fogging her gaze.

"We must go," he said.

"What? Why?"

"So that we dinna attract attention. The English might look

for us here today, and if nae today, then on the morrow. We're nae that far from Stirling."

"Right."

She stretched, arching herself into his body. He clenched his jaw and begged God and the faeries to give him strength not to get any harder than he was. She melted into his arms again, and their eyes locked. For the first time since he'd met her, hers were unguarded. There was an openness in her gaze he'd not seen before. She wasn't pretending to be someone from his time. She wasn't hiding. And she wasn't running.

He looked into her soul, and he knew then that he was lost in her. Forever. From this moment, his heart beat for her. He breathed for her. He was in love with her.

For the first time in his life, he was in love.

The feeling sparked a lightness in his chest that expanded in all directions around him. It was like the sun resided right in his heart.

She was the sun.

He lowered his head and kissed her. She didn't fight it, didn't turn away. She kissed him back like it was the most natural thing in the world. The kiss was gentle and soft, loving. There was not a trace of hunger or passion, and yet it spurred the need in his already throbbing erection.

It took all his restraint not to deepen the kiss, not to throw the sheet to the side and cover her delectable body with his kisses.

Ye canna fail, he reminded himself. *Ye canna let yerself fail this time.*

He pulled back. "We must go," he repeated, his voice hoarse.

She nodded. Disappointment flickered across her face and disappeared. They dressed, ate the remnants of their midnight dinner, put some coins on the table, and left. It was chilly outside after the warmth of the room. The edge of the indigo sky glowed golden in the east, and the village had started to wake up. Roosters crowed. A woman left one of the houses and went to a cowshed with an empty bucket. Owen took a lungful of fresh air rich with the scent of grass and morning dew.

"Can ye ride?" Owen asked.

"Yeah. I think so. If I survived yesterday, I think I'll be all right."

He helped her mount, and they rode out of the village, speeding up to a trot once they were out. They continued like that for a while, and when the horses got tired, they slowed to a walk. Owen used the time to help Amber get comfortable on the horse. She'd learned much yesterday by doing, and now he explained to her what they hadn't had time for yesterday.

They traveled through the woods, staying away from the road that went north. Amber seemed calmer, more relaxed and collected.

"I meant to ask you a question last night," she said. "What did you mean when you said you know what it's like to be falsely accused of something?"

Owen looked sharply at her. Ah, he shouldn't have said anything last night. If he told her, she'd know what a failure he really was. Would she be disappointed in him?

She'd shared with him, and he wanted to do the same. He was in love with her, and he craved a connection.

His horse swayed rhythmically as it walked. The woods smelled earthy, like wildflowers and moss, and wind rustled the branches. The sun was high in the sky, its golden rays streaming between the branches.

"It happened on a day like this," he said, his gut tightening. "A sunny, warm summer day. I was a lad of sixteen on my way home from Dunollie, the MacDougall stronghold. Our clans used to be allies, and my brothers and I were each fostered by the MacDougalls for a few months. Their children were fostered with us at Innis Chonnel, our clan seat back then, from time to time, too."

Amber looked confused for a moment, so he explained, "'Tis a Highland thing to do. To tighten the ties between clans, we foster one another's children. Alasdair, John MacDougall's son, was with my family at the time."

Owen's fists clenched around the reins at the thought of what Alasdair had later done to Marjorie. John MacDougall had *allowed* his son to rape and beat her. Had protected him while he did so. Marjorie had been a changed woman since then. Owen and his brothers had trained her in sword fighting, and she'd become a skilled warrior. But she'd vowed she'd never get marrit. A decision he understood.

"King John Balliol was a guest at our house back then, and I was due to go back home. John MacDougall asked me to take a pouch with gold coins as MacDougall's present to the king."

"You were sixteen years old, and he entrusted you with gold?"

Owen chuckled bitterly. "Aye. It seemed strange to me, too. I'm my father's youngest son, and one of the youngest of the cousins. Craig and Domhnall always got all the attention. Even Ian, my cousin, who was fostered with us for years. My da took him more seriously than me. I was often left to my own devices, so I roamed with the village children and did whatever I wanted to do."

He didn't add that his father had never punished him for neglecting his duties because he'd never even noticed. That was when Owen had started to act out. He'd scared the washerwomen with pranks and hidden spices and expensive salt from the cook.

Owen had craved for his da to value him as much as he valued Craig and Domhnall, and to give him responsibility. He'd tried to distinguish himself from his brothers, but by age sixteen, he'd gained a reputation as a young man who liked to have a good time, chase after milkmaids, and make jests. His da simply hadn't trusted him, and it was Owen's own fault.

So when the MacDougall asked him to take the gold, no matter how much his gut had told him something didn't seem right, he'd ignored his instinct and agreed.

"I imagined how proud my da would be once I came in and

gave that gold to the king. How my brothers would look at me differently. How my father would start taking me with him to battles and give me more responsibility."

His nails bit into his palms as he gripped the reins tightly. "I declared I'd guard that gold with my life if need be, but I didna expect any trouble. A young lad like me wouldna attract much attention. I was so terribly wrong."

Amber eyed him with sympathy. "What happened?"

"On my way, I encountered a bonnie lass being attacked. I fought the man and forced him to leave. The lass was shaken, and I stayed to make sure she was all right. We drank wine and, well, let's say she became affectionate. I was a horny lad, and her attention drew me in like honey draws a bear. I couldna resist."

Amber pressed her lips flat and shoved a strand of hair out of her eyes.

"But I fell asleep before anything happened, and when I woke up, she was gone. So was the gold."

"Hell..."

"Aye. I didna even think there was a point to go looking for her. But what was strange... 'Tis embarrassing to admit, so please dinna laugh."

"Okay."

He sighed. His cheeks warmed a little. "My cock wouldna go down."

"What?"

"My cock was as hard as a rock, nae matter what I did."

Amber's lips curved in a smile. She pursed them to stop it from spreading, but a small laugh soon burst out.

"So she gave you Viagra?"

"Uhm..."

"In my time, Viagra is a medicine that allows men to have an erection for a long time. Usually older men or those with problems. You didn't have problems in that area, I take it?"

Owen suppressed a growl. "Nae. I didna."

And he would very much like to show her that he'd never had

any problems in that area, especially not in her presence. In fact, she had a Viagra effect on him.

Their eyes locked, and her lips parted a little, so lush and soft. He started growing hard again.

Damnation. He was still like an adolescent with her, and not a man of twenty-nine.

He shook his head and looked straight ahead. "So I arrived home with a stiff cock and nae gold. I passed by the great hall, didna even greet the king or my da. I went directly to my bedchamber. I didna know it at the time, but Alasdair must have known about the plan all along. 'Twas his job to point out that I didna have the gold and blame me. Aileene and the man who'd 'attacked' her brought the gold to Innis Chonnel secretly, and Alasdair hid it in my bedchamber. 'Twas all planned beforehand. He came into my room with my grandfather Colin, the chief of our clan back then. My da and my brothers and cousin all came in as well. And the king. They all saw my humiliation.

"And when I told them about the stolen gold, Alasdair pointed at a sack under my bed. 'Twas the same sack that had been stolen from me in the woods."

Amber shook her head. "Someone set you up."

She believed him... Relief flooded him. "Aye. Alasdair blamed me for stealing the gold."

"Why did the MacDougalls betray your clan?"

"King Balliol gave a part of their lands to our clan for good service. They wanted us to fall out of his good graces and take their lands back. But what they did started a feud. 'Twas the beginning of the end. 'Twas a trap, and I fell right into it."

"Not just you, your family, too. Did they believe Alasdair, or did they believe you?"

"Alasdair."

"See, they fell into the MacDougalls' trap, too."

"It wasna their fault, though. Given my reputation, it wasna surprising. I was a troublemaker. Unpredictable. The outcast."

"Yes, but couldn't your father see you were incapable of stealing no matter how unpredictable you were?"

Anger rang in her voice, and her beautiful eyes threw daggers. His own clan hadn't believed him, and yet this lass, a stranger from another time, did. Elation spread through his whole body. He couldn't be more thankful to the faeries or destiny or whoever had sent Amber here to him.

"Nae. My da couldna. But it doesna matter anymore. My brother Craig and my cousin Ian came to believe me—although, Domhnall and Da still dinna completely trust me. Rightly so. I've done other shite I'm nae proud of."

He meant Inverlochy, of course. Getting Lachlan killed. Losing the siege to the English. Getting caught. Getting Amber tortured. That was all on him.

"But now that I ken where the MacDougalls and the English are going to attack, I can help the clan. I just hope they take my words seriously this time."

He hoped that when they saw a beautiful woman at his side, they wouldn't assume he'd been duped again. He had to keep his mind and hands off Amber long enough to do the responsible thing and warn his king.

CHAPTER 17

Two days later...

"What now, lass?" Owen asked.

They sat on their horses on top of a small hill. Amber stared at Glenkeld, the castle on the shore of the loch. The loch was still, and the castle, hills, and mountains were reflected on its smooth surface. Tiny compared to Stirling, it had one large, square tower and four curtain walls, more or less like Inverlochy. Smoke rose from somewhere behind those walls. Sheep and cows grazed around the castle walls, and the air smelled like manure, grass, and flowers.

This was Owen's home.

Not hers.

Amber bit her lip. Where was her home, anyway? Ever since her mom and dad had died, and Jonathan had sold the house to divide the profits between them, she'd had no place to come home to. She'd let go of her apartment before she went to serve in Afghanistan. In a way, the army was her home and her family.

Until that family had betrayed her.

So what now?

What she really wanted was to go back to her time, get the murdering, drug-smuggling bastard behind bars, and clear her name. A life in hiding, of looking over her shoulder, of anger at the injustice, would eat at her soul. If she were brave enough, she would make her way back to Inverlochy and go through the stone to the twenty-first century. She'd go to Jonathan. She'd hire an attorney, and she'd work relentlessly on gathering evidence against Jackson.

But those were only dreams. The reality was Jackson would crush her. She wasn't strong enough to take on a giant like him. She'd never confronted her brothers in the past, and she hated that she was a helpless coward.

"I don't know," she said. "I definitely can't go back to my time. They'll catch me there."

Owen presented a magnificent view—a medieval warrior sitting proudly on a horse. A strand of his blond hair fell across his forehead. The bruises on his face added roughness to his handsome features, and his bristle was turning into a short beard the color of wheat, white gold, and a little bit of amber. She could sink into his green eyes and be lost there forever. That would be a wonderful home for her.

"So if ye canna go back"—he swallowed—"what will ye do?"

He was perfectly still, waiting for her to reply, and yet she could see his chest rising and falling faster, and the vein in his neck pulsing quicker.

What would she do? She could stay here in this time.

Was she actually crazy enough to consider that? The brawny Highlander in front of her had nothing to do with it, she told herself. It was safer here...for the most part. When she wasn't being chased and tortured by the English.

"I suppose I could stay here. Your family won't want to put me in a dungeon, will they?"

He laughed. "Nae. Ye're safe with us. And I promise de

Bourgh wilna touch a hair on yer head if I have any say in that. So will ye be a guest of our clan?"

"A guest? Sure. And thank you for the kind invitation. But what could I do here? How could I earn money? I don't think I can do anything that's useful here."

"Usually, women get marrit, and their husbands provide for them. I could ask the clan chief, my uncle Neil, or my da to find ye a husband." His jaw tightened as he said that.

Amber laughed. "I'm not going to get married in medieval Scotland!"

"If ye plan to stay here, ye'll need someone to protect ye. Even a strong lass like ye needs either a father, or a brother, or a husband."

"I'm sure I'll be fine on my own. Maybe you can teach me some of that sword fighting so that I can protect myself."

"Aye. I can. But first, let's go home."

For the last two days, on their way from Stirling, they'd been careful to avoid the roads as much as possible. Dressed as English, danger lay from both the Highlanders, who could kill them on sight, and from the English, who might find out they weren't English at all. Not to mention de Bourgh's men were no doubt still looking for them.

Owen fascinated her. Not only was he ridiculously handsome, but ever since he'd shared the story about the gold, she couldn't help but feel a connection to him, like a miracle had happened and she'd scored a winning lottery ticket.

She loved riding next to him, and he told her more stories about his clan, explained about the war, and told her about Craig and Ian. She'd slept by his side, but he hadn't tried to kiss her or made any other move. He'd lain next to her as stiff as a statue.

She was puzzled by the sudden physical distance he kept after how close they'd been earlier, and she was also a little hurt by it. Why was she so unappealing to him all of a sudden? He'd wanted her before. She'd seen his very impressive erection at the inn. She'd felt it in his kisses and in the simple touch of his hand.

In his hug. Was he so appalled after her confession that he couldn't stand to touch her now?

Not that it should bother her at all. Caring for him would complicate everything. It was something she couldn't afford.

They rode towards the castle and stopped in front of the gates. Archers stood on the wall, arrows pointing at them.

"Who goes there?" a male voice rumbled.

"I thank ye for nae shooting us, Malcolm," Owen said. "Do ye nae recognize me?"

A man with white hair down to his shoulders and a white beard appeared from behind the rampart.

"Owen?" he said.

"Aye."

The man sighed and shook his head. "Only ye would come in bright daylight dressed like a Sassenach bastart. Let them in!"

Owen threw an amused glance at Amber. The gates opened, and they rode in.

Malcolm descended the stairs from the top of the wall.

"I was this close to giving the command to shoot ye," he said, pinching his thumb and index finger together. "Come here, ye rascal."

He took Owen in a bear hug, and the men clapped each other on the back.

"What's going on?" someone said.

∽

Dougal Cambel's angry voice made Owen's gut tighten. He released Malcolm and turned to face his father. Da marched towards them together with Craig, Domhnall, and several other men. Behind them, the northern wall with the crumbled part had short, sharp spikes installed into it. Owen's stomach churned as he imagined Marjorie having to fight off the MacDougalls. Craig had told Owen in confidence that the spikes had been suggested by a warrior from the future who'd helped Marjorie protect her son, Colin, and the castle. The gates were made of new wood—were they part of the defenses? His brave, strong sister... He wished he could've been here to protect their home. He'd missed her. With a bittersweet ache in his heart, Owen wondered how Marjorie's and Colin's lives were in the twenty-first century, and he hoped that man made his half sister very happy.

"Owen, son," Dougal said, "ye're alive."

Owen's father gripped his shoulder and squeezed it. The affection was unexpected, and Owen hugged him back but was ready for the questions he knew would come.

"What happened?" Craig asked. "Why are ye in Sassenach clothing? And who's the"—he frowned, eyeing Amber—"lass?"

"Yes, I'm a *lass*," Amber said, and Craig cocked his eyebrow. "Thank you very much."

Craig exchanged a look with Owen. No doubt, his half brother had recognized the accent. Everyone turned to study Amber.

Owen cleared his throat. "'Tis Amber. We were kidnapped together by Sir de Bourgh during the siege of Inverlochy. He took us to Stirling. We managed to escape but had to disguise ourselves as the English."

"We feared ye were dead," Craig said. "When we took back the castle, ye were unaccounted for. No one saw ye fall, and there was nae body. 'Twas like ye'd disappeared..."

It occurred to Owen that his brother might have suspected he'd gone through time. The thought seemed funny at first, but he realized it was a real possibility.

"I kenned ye were nae dead," Da said. "Ye're too cunning to let death take ye so soon."

"Didna feel that way at times," Owen said.

His father paled, and Owen's Adam's apple jumped as he struggled to swallow. This situation was too similar to what had happened to Ian. Many years ago, in a battle with the MacDougalls, everyone had thought Ian was killed and the

MacDougalls had taken his body. The Cambels had assumed he was dead, but he'd been sold into slavery and had only returned home from the caliphate this year.

Owen knew very well that his family didn't want to relive that horror.

"And who are ye, lass?" Craig asked.

Amber exchanged a glance with Owen, and he nodded, encouraging her to share the story they'd agreed on.

"I'm from the caliphate. I was hired by Kenneth Mackenzie."

Craig frowned as he studied Amber. His da and the rest eyed her dubiously.

"And how exactly did ye end up being kidnapped together?" the older Cambel asked as he looked between them.

"Owen helped me," Amber said, her voice ringing with gratitude. "He saved my life from the English."

Owen clenched his teeth. He'd rather they didn't know that.

"Ye helped a woman," his father said. "And ye lost the castle to de Bourgh. And got yerself kidnapped."

His upper lip rose in the same kind of disgust Owen had seen countless times. It had only resulted in a younger Owen wanting to rebel even more against him, to show his father that he didn't need his approval, that he couldn't care less.

But he couldn't afford to indulge in such behavior now. He had an important mission, a message he needed to deliver.

"No, you don't understand," Amber said. "He saved us. He was tortured and didn't say a word about the Bruce. He—"

Owen cared about the lass and was grateful she was defending him, but she was only making matters worse. The appalled expression on his father's face deepened. No doubt he thought Owen was hiding behind a woman, letting her fight his battles.

"Amber," Owen interrupted her. "Let me explain, aye?"

She closed her mouth, nodded, and stepped back.

Owen fixed his gaze on his father. "Aye. I did get myself kidnapped. And I didna succeed in keeping Inverlochy when

Kenneth Mackenzie fell. But I saw John MacDougall in Stirling."

Dougal crossed his arms over his chest. "Aye? And what did the man say?"

"They plan to ambush the Bruce when he moves to Lorne to attack them."

Dougal sighed. "Did he say that?"

"Aye."

Dougal threw a heavy gaze at Amber. "Did ye hear that, too, lass?"

"No. I wasn't there. But—"

Dougal shook his head once, cutting her off. "Do ye have any other proof, son?"

Helplessness weighed at Owen's shoulders as well as the sinking feeling of loneliness, of being a stranger in his own clan. Craig wore a deep frown, and doubt was written all over his face. Owen had let him down at Inverlochy last year, so he couldn't blame Craig for doubting him. Domhnall eyed him like every word out of his mouth was made of shite.

"I dinna have any proof other than my word, Da," Owen said.

"Aye. Well, yer word isna the most reliable source. And knowing how ye like to impress lasses... Ye having this information now seems too convenient."

"Ye think I'm lying?"

"Nae. I dinna ken if ye're lying. But I ken that where John MacDougall is concerned, one needs to be verra careful of trickery. Ye and John have that in common."

"Dinna put me in the same category as that bastart."

Dougal sighed. "Aye. That was too much. Let us forget the matter. Come, let us eat and drink to yer return and hear stories from the caliphate and from Stirling. Now that ye're back, there'll be entertainment enough."

He hugged Owen's shoulder and led him towards the great hall. Owen gave Amber an I-told-you-so glance, and she studied him with a worried look on her face.

No matter how much he tried to help his clan, they all had this image of him in their minds. He knew they wouldn't trust him. But even if they didn't believe him, he needed to get word to the Bruce. That was his mission, and he wouldn't fail this time.

CHAPTER 18

They settled at the table, the tension weighing on Owen's shoulders. Even knowing he needed to explain himself and try to convince his family what he'd said about de Bourgh was true, he didn't let Amber leave his side for a moment.

He felt protective of her. Not that anyone would harm her here. Still. She was part of him. She made him feel better about himself. She'd defended him back in the courtyard like an angry mother lynx. No one had ever defended him like that.

Not that he needed someone to defend him. But knowing that a woman had his back was new and fresh.

And he loved it. Too much.

He studied Amber's golden-brown profile for a moment as she chewed a piece of bread, her full lips moving seductively. They had tasted so sweet. So sweet he never wanted to stop kissing her.

People noticed her, he saw. The color of her skin was unusual, but they also stared at her beauty. How could they not? How could anyone not be mesmerized by those eyes and lips, that femininity wrapped in strength and power. She possessed the grace and confidence of a predator, and yet she could be as sweet as a domestic cat.

"Owen." His father interrupted his thoughts, and Owen turned to face him. "Drooling over another female, I see."

Heat rushed to Owen's face. He supposed he deserved that, but he wished his father would see the warrior in him for once, and not a jester.

Da cocked his brow and poured uisge into their cups. "I dinna blame ye, though, son. She is a bonnie lass. Never seen anyone quite like her. A dark beauty, eh?"

Owen glanced at Amber to make sure she couldn't hear this conversation.

"She's much more than that," Owen said, feeling protectiveness rising in him. "She's a good warrior with skills that ye havna dreamed of. And she's brave and strong." His fist clenched around the cup of uisge. "De Bourgh tortured her—a dozen lashes—and she didna say anything."

Dougal cocked one eyebrow. "Havna heard ye talk about anyone like ye talk about her. This one got ye right in the heart."

Did he hear sympathy in his father's voice?

"Nae." The lie scraped Owen's throat as he said it. She was not only in his heart, but she was also in his blood. "'Tis only that I admire bravery and strength—especially in a woman. Dinna see that often."

"Hmm." Dougal looked deeply into his cup of uisge and then threw back the liquid. "So tell me about John MacDougall. How exactly did he tell ye about their plan to ambush the Bruce?"

Owen's pulse galloped. This was his chance to convince his father he wasn't wrong. That he wasn't trying to impress Amber and really had information that could lead to a victory over the MacDougalls and the English.

"They thought I was unconscious," Owen said. "MacDougall and de Bourgh discussed their plans and didna ken I was listening."

"And how exactly do ye ken he wasna tricking ye? He's sly enough to set that up."

Owen's gut tightened till it hurt. "I just ken, Da. He had knocked me out. I lay there senseless—"

Dougal shook his head. "Son, I ken ye're nae lying, but it doesna mean he didna see ye were awake."

Acid rose in Owen's stomach. He remembered the terrible night he'd stood before his da, Craig, Domhnall, Uncle Neil, and his cousins, ashamed and helpless, repeating that he was innocent, that it was all MacDougall's ploy, that the gold had been stolen by a woman and someone had planted it in his room. Nothing had helped.

"He tricked me with the gold," Owen said. "But nae this time. They ken the Bruce is coming for them, and they'll set up an ambush at the Pass of Brander. They want to repeat the Battle of Dalrigh."

"The gold—"

"Right," Owen spat. The taste of the word was bitter on his tongue. "Yer son stole the king's gold. 'Tis what ye think, aye?"

"The old king thought that, aye," Dougal said through gritted teeth. "And it doesna matter what I think. It matters that we dinna let *this* king down. Because the freedom of our country lies with the Bruce. Everything we've been fighting for since William Wallace. We've never been so close. If the MacDougall let ye hear this information to set a trap, and the king walks right into it, he's finished. We're all finished. I canna take that risk, Owen. I just canna."

Owen shook his head, bitterness spreading painfully through his chest. All these years of trying to prove his worth to his clan, and he finally had information in his hands that could help, that could finally bring an end to the war.

"And what if I'm right?" Owen said. "And what if the Bruce walks right into a trap and they kill him?"

"Nae, I dinna believe that will happen."

"Ye dinna believe that because I brought ye this information.

If Craig had said the same, ye would be on yer way to the Bruce right now."

Dougal paled. "I ken what ye're thinking. Dinna dare go to the king with this. Promise me."

"Da—"

"Do ye ken what happens once the Bruce wins?"

"Peace."

"Aye. Peace. And we finally get our vengeance for everything *they* did to us. To Marjorie. Ian. Yer grandfather. We get our proper clan seat in Innis Chonnel back. Neil said the Bruce has promised him all of the MacDougall lands. The Bruce is considering marrying his sister Mary to Neil. We'd be related to the king himself. It means we'll be rewarded with wealth and power. Something we should've had long ago, but the MacDougalls took it from us."

"Da, I want all that for our clan, too, and 'tis why the king should be warned—"

"Nae, if ye tell him yer story and ye're wrong, we'll lose everything. He'll never trust us again."

Owen's throat vibrated with a silent growl. How could his father be so stubborn? Despite all of Owen's mistakes, his father should have faith in his son.

But he didn't. Trying to convince Dougal Cambel of anything after he'd made up his mind was useless.

Owen didn't know what to do now. Should he do as his da wanted and keep the information to himself? Or should he send a messenger to the Bruce and risk losing the king's favor again?

If he chose the latter, there could be no distractions.

There could be no Amber in his life. No matter how hard it would be, he'd need to distance himself from her. His family would not take him seriously if they thought she was distracting him. He couldn't afford his judgment being clouded. If he let a woman distract him again, he could lose everything. Worse. His clan could.

Scotland could.

He sipped his uisge and considered his options. He knew as surely as the sun would rise tomorrow that he *wanted* responsibility. He *wanted* to be a leader like his brothers and his father.

He *wanted* to see the respect and the admiration in his da's hard malachite eyes. Even if the price for that was letting Amber go.

"Aye, Da." Owen raised his cup of uisge. "Ye're right. Let's drink to that."

CHAPTER 19

Owen had kept Amber at his side since they'd entered Glenkeld Castle. After embracing his father, he'd turned to her and held her hand. The touch had sent a lightning bolt right into her core and set her blood ablaze. It was as though their connected hands sent sunshine through her.

They sat at a long table with the rest of the Cambels. Owen had let go of her hand, but their hips still touched, making Amber's head spin like she'd had a glass of wine on an empty stomach.

The ceiling inside the great hall was high, and the windows were small and let very little light in. Long tables and benches stood in two rows. At the other end of the hall was a great chair with a slightly smaller one by its side. The room reminded Amber of a church hall, but it smelled like beer and food.

Owen was talking to his father quietly when something changed in him. He shifted away from her. His thigh became as hard as a rock. He avoided looking at her, and something icy coiled in the pit of her stomach.

No, it was just her imagination, surely. She just needed to talk to him.

Amber glanced at the empty great chair. "Is your dad like the chief or something?"

Owen followed her gaze. "Nae. The chief of our clan is Uncle Neil, my da's older brother. My uncle and his sons are with the Bruce. He's the king's right hand, so my da needs to run things here."

Amber watched Dougal as he pulled a piece of meat off the leg of a fowl. He was talking to Owen's brother Domhnall, who sat across the table from him. His white beard moved as he chewed, his white hair was cropped short. She saw where Owen got his green eyes, straight jawline, and perfect nose. Strangely, Dougal reminded her of her own father. They both had a military strictness about them. His face showed little emotion, and his back was as straight as a pole. He had the wary look of someone who was used to dealing with enemies.

Would her own father have believed in her innocence if he'd been alive? Would she have gone to him for help? Probably not. He'd been part of the military system that had let her down. Would he have set that aside and trusted his daughter? Her whole life, all she'd wanted was for him to be proud of her. For her brothers to love and respect her.

She should've stood up for herself. Maybe then they'd have respected her more. But she dismissed the thought. Standing up to them would've only made the conflict worse.

Her body was already buzzing from sitting so close to Owen, so she ignored the cup in front of her and focused on Owen's tanned hand lying on the table. She could see fine blond hair on his wrist. She craved the touch of his hand, to have that jolt of electricity run through her again.

Owen's gaze trapped her, and suddenly, there was not enough air in the huge room. God, she hoped he couldn't see how he affected her. His thigh muscles stiffened and hardened. She shifted away from him, breaking the warm contact. But Craig sat on her right side, and she had to shift back to Owen so she didn't press herself tightly against his brother.

"So, the caliphate..." Craig said.

His green eyes were similar to Owen's. Both brothers were equally tall and strong, but Craig had dark hair. Where Owen was light and carefree, Craig's piercing gaze held her like a vise. He had the face of a detective.

She was overcome by the feeling he'd already caught her in a lie. She flashed a nervous smile.

"Yep." She cleared her throat. "The caliphate."

Craig scanned the people at the table around them and leaned closer to Amber. "Do ye by any chance mean the United States of America?"

What did he just say? "How the hell do you know?"

Craig chuckled and looked towards the entrance. A beautiful red-haired woman came in, her hand on her swollen belly. She wore the typical clothing of a medieval woman. Her long dress had long sleeves and was embroidered with Celtic patterns along the neckline. Her hair was done up in two ear-coiled buns tied with white ribbons. She spotted Craig, beamed, and made her way to their table.

"My wife, Amy, will tell ye how," Craig said.

His expression transformed as the red-haired woman approached them. The detective in him was gone, and his face was suddenly lit up with love, pride, and a hint of possessiveness. He stretched his arms out to her, and she came to him and laid her hand on his shoulder, then she took a place across the table from him. She glanced for a moment at Craig, and then her eyes moved to Amber.

"Hello," she said.

Was Amber hallucinating, or did she have an American accent?

"H-hi," Amber said.

Owen had mentioned there were more time travelers...

Amber and Amy kept staring at each other, neither daring to say a word. There were too many people around who could overhear.

Craig leaned closer with a mischievous glance. "United States of America. Discuss."

Amber blinked. "Are you from..."

Amy exchanged a careful glance with Craig, and he nodded. "Yeah," Amy said quietly. "North Carolina. You?"

Amber exhaled and looked heavenward. She was a time traveler, too! "Chicago."

A slow smile spread on Amy's lips. "Oh my gosh!"

She reached across the table, and Amber grasped her hands.

"It's so good to see you," Amy said. "Not that I'm lonely here"—she winked at Craig—"but no one understands what it's like to live in the past, you know, for people like you and me. But how did you? Why?"

Amber tensed and removed her hands. No matter how glad she was to see a woman from her time, she couldn't tell a complete stranger that the government wanted her for murder.

"Long story," Amber said. "And you're married to Craig and have a baby on the way? You decided to stay?"

Amy chuckled. "It's a long story, too. I went back at first, but I realized I couldn't live without this man."

"And you don't regret it?"

"No. Best decision of my life."

Amber looked around again, just to make sure no one was eavesdropping.

"I might want to stay, too."

"Oh." Amy smiled and raised her eyebrows. "For Owen?"

Owen's jaw worked, and a hot flush hit Amber's face. Craig guffawed, and many heads turned in his direction.

"No," Amber said. "Not for Owen. For me. It's better for me here."

Amy frowned, puzzled. "What do you mean, for you? Who in their right mind would voluntarily stay in the Middle Ages when there's medicine and toilets and showers and microwaves in the twenty-first century?"

Amber clenched her teeth. "Then I guess I'm not in my right mind."

Amy shook her head and smiled apologetically. "Sorry. I didn't mean to offend you. But what will you do here?"

"I don't know yet. But I can't go back."

Amy frowned, grimaced, and sucked in a breath.

Craig straightened up. "What is it?"

Amy shook her head. "Nothing. Just some Braxton-Hicks contractions... I think."

"What?" Craig said.

"Practice contractions. It's nothing. It doesn't even hurt, just feels weird."

Craig stood up. "Ye need to go and lie down. I'll come with ye."

"No, I'm fine. Seriously."

"Woman, dinna argue with me. Either ye go, or I pick ye up and carry ye. Yer choice."

Amy rolled her eyes and met Amber's. "Do you know that he kept me captive for weeks when we met? I suppose some habits never change."

"Amy Cambel!" Craig said, a warning in his voice.

"All right, all right. I'm going." She stood up. "Amber, please come and talk to me later? Please? I won't ask any questions you don't want to answer. I just want to talk to you."

Amber smiled. "Of course I will."

Amy made a small movement as though to kiss Craig but stopped herself and threw a quick glance around.

"We're not supposed to show physical affection in public," she explained. "I know, what's the big deal, right? You get used to it."

After she left, Amber looked at Owen. "No one else knows about her?" she asked quietly.

"Only Craig, our cousin Ian, and me—and a few other trusted men who'd rather die than betray her secret."

Rather die than betray her secret...

And they weren't even Amy's family. Were clan ties so strong even when people weren't directly related? If that was true, she really liked medieval times. Loyalty and belonging to a community above all. She could sign up for that. That was one of the things she'd been looking for when she joined the army.

But what about Owen? How could his family not believe him? They should. How was it possible they would protect Amy no matter what but wouldn't give Owen the benefit of the doubt? Surely, if he explained it better, they would see it differently.

Amber turned to Owen. Even if he was currently as warm as an ice sculpture and clearly not eager to talk to her, she had to make him see.

"You should talk to them again," she said quietly. "If you just trust them to believe you, they will."

Owen's face was a cold mask. He stared at the table and the corners of his mouth turned downward. "Ye have nae business talking about it. Ye dinna ken."

"I do, actually. I see so much more trust in your family than in mine."

"Lass, dinna make me—"

"Owen, please, if you'd just get over yourself—"

"Get over myself?" he shouted, and faces turned. His father glared at him.

"Owen, lower yer voice," Craig said.

Owen looked around, his chest rising and falling quickly, his hands shaking. He got up from the bench. "Stay out of this, Amber. Ye've done enough harm already." He marched through the great hall and outside, and Amber felt Dougal's eyes on her.

Maybe she'd kick herself for this later, maybe Owen would never speak to her again, but she raised her chin and met his father's gaze.

"You should trust him, you know," she said. "You're his family. Open your eyes. Your son is so much more than you give him credit for."

Dougal's jaw opened, and he stared at her in disbelief, but before he could answer, she stood and walked out.

CHAPTER 20

Owen shoved a piece of parchment rolled in leather into Malcolm's hand.

"Be careful," Owen said. "I dinna trust no one with this but ye."

Malcolm gave a solemn nod and hid the parchment in the inner folds of his coat. One of the most loyal and dependable men of the clan, Malcolm had always seen through Owen's shite. Had seen him for who he was—a lad with bad luck and big brothers to live up to.

Malcolm placed his gloved fist against his heart. "I'd rather die than let anyone get this."

Owen looked at Malcolm's claymore with the Cambel clan coat of arms on the hilt. "'Tis better ye take this sword." He handed him the English sword he'd taken from the guard in Stirling. "Ye better have nae other sign ye belong to our clan on ye. If anyone stops ye, ye're just a traveler."

Malcolm took the sword. "Look after my claymore."

"Aye." Owen took the man's sword, and Malcolm nodded and mounted his horse.

"Godspeed," Owen said and clapped the horse's side. He exhaled a long breath as Malcolm galloped out of the castle. It was done. Now he could only pray to God that Malcolm would get to Inverlochy safely. Owen would go himself, but he knew his father would never allow him to leave the castle. He might even disown Owen and ban him from the clan if he caught him trying to get to the Bruce.

Owen looked around the courtyard. Most of the clan was still eating inside the great hall. Malcolm had no idea Dougal didn't want the Bruce to get the message. If he did, would he still believe in Owen and deliver it?

There was one person who stood by the great hall and watched him, her dark eyes piercing. Owen's breath caught at the sight of Amber.

He was still furious with her. Mostly because she might be right. He did need to talk to his father again. Sending a message behind his father's back was not only wrong, but it was also treachery to go against his chief. Well, his father wasn't chief, but he was in charge while Uncle Neil was away.

Amber marched towards him.

"What did you do?" She propped her hands on her hips and glared at him like an angry cat. She stood close enough for him to reach down and kiss her.

But he couldn't.

"Ye should go and rest after the long journey," Owen said.

"Did you just send that man with a message to the Bruce?"

He put Malcom's claymore in its scabbard and walked towards the big tower. "Dinna fash about that, Amber."

She followed him. "You did, didn't you? What about talking to your father again? I heard him forbid you from sending the message. He'll be furious."

"Aye. But he wilna find out until the Bruce arrives."

"You *invited* him here?"

Owen entered the tower and climbed the stairs. His bedchamber was on the top floor. "Aye. We must come up with a plan for the ambush at the Pass of Brander."

Her face darkened with worry. "Owen, you might have created a big mess for yourself."

He shook his head. "It doesna matter. I ken I'm right. I also ken the Pass of Brander well, and what John MacDougall described in his plan, it matches perfectly."

"I believe you. I just wish your stubborn father would, too."

"Ye're from the future. Dinna ye ken what happens?"

"Unfortunately, I didn't study history in much detail. But I remember Robert the Bruce is supposed to be a great warrior and a great military leader. I think he's successful."

Owen sighed with relief. "Good." They'd reached the door to his room, and he pushed it open and went inside. Amber followed.

"But I also have no idea if you can change the future with your actions," she said. "Amy and I being here could change the course of history."

That thought chilled Owen's bones. "Aye, I wilna treat this as a certain future. I need to make sure it happens, nae matter what."

Amber looked around his room, her eyes lingering on the swords, shields, and bows hanging on the walls.

"If I stay longer with your clan, I want to earn my keep."

"Nae need, lass. Ye're my guest, under my protection."

She didn't respond, just gave him a frown. "Look. You don't need to feel responsible for me, okay? You got us out of that mess in Stirling. You saved my life, and I'll forever be grateful. But that doesn't mean you owe me your protection or whatever."

She was right, of course. But she didn't know he'd lose his ability to breathe if anything happened to her. Knowing she was alive and well was more important than food and water.

"Aye. It does. In fact, I want ye to stay in this room. The way here was hard on yer back. Ye still need to heal."

"What? Take your room?"

"Aye."

"And"—she swallowed—"will you sleep here, too?"

"Nae. I'll sleep in the great hall with the clan warriors. 'Tisna a bother, dinna fash. I'm used to sleeping wherever."

"Where would I have slept if not here?"

"Probably with the maids, somewhere on a mattress on the floor. Let me take a fresh tunic, and I'll leave ye."

He took off the English tunic and walked shirtless to one of the chests in the room. He picked up a tunic and froze as he noticed her watching him. Without looking away, she walked over to him. Her sweet scent brushed against him, and all his senses heightened. Her lashes trembled as their eyes locked.

Take me into your arms, her eyes begged. *Kiss me...*

Oh, he really wanted to. His body reacted before his mind could stop him. He dropped the tunic and took her into his arms. Her breasts pressed against him with each heavy breath she took.

Her lips were right there. *Just reach down and taste their lush sweetness again, lose yerself in her scent. Cup her face and feel her smooth skin.*

His bed was right there, too. The room had shrunk to the size of a box. How easy it would be to pick her up, take two big steps, and set her on the mattress. To lie down next to her and undress her and worship her body.

His father's words came to mind. *If ye're wrong, we'll lose everything.*

Giving in to his desires now would cloud his head. He'd be more likely to make a mistake and therefore endanger his mission.

He tensed his arms to stop from running his hands up her shoulders and neck and burying his fingers in her hair. He wanted to take her face between his palms and kiss her so hard she would forget her own name.

She put her hand on his chest, her palm burning his bare skin. He held his breath, unable to move. If he lifted a finger, his restraint would burst. The perfect seductress, she ran her hand up his chest, causing blood to flow to his cock. He cursed inwardly—such a simple gesture, and he was ready to go.

She reached his neck, where his wound pained him. Without touching it, she reached up and cupped his face. Her lips were so close, and she stretched up to kiss him.

He wanted to, so much. But if her lips touched his, he'd be lost. He gently removed her hand from his face, hating everything about rejecting her. He released her and stepped back.

"Ye should stay away from me, lass. I am nae right for ye."

Amber's eyes clouded with hurt. His heart clenching at seeing her like this, he picked up the fresh tunic from the floor and pulled it over his head.

"You're unbelievable," she hissed.

Like a coward, without looking at her, he left his bedchamber. He wouldn't let his clan or his king down by giving in to the distraction of a beautiful woman. He'd stay focused and redeem himself, even if it meant losing Amber forever.

CHAPTER 21

"May I come in?" Amber asked.

Amy lay on her bed, and an old woman touched her belly. The bedroom was round and rather spacious. There was a narrow window with open shutters that let light in, and flames played in the fireplace. Chests stood around the room, as well as several chairs.

Amy looked up and beamed. "Hey! Yes, of course."

Amber came inside and stood by the bed. A lavender canopy was suspended from the ceiling above it, and four posts stood at each corner of the bed.

The old woman straightened and looked at Amber, her bright eyes sparkling with curiosity. She was small and dressed in a simple brown dress and wore a white kerchief on her head. Her face was leathery and wrinkled.

Amy sat up. "Amber, this is Isbeil. She's Glenkeld Castle's healer."

Isbeil leaned over the bed and picked up her basket. "Another one from yer time?" she asked casually.

Amber was rooted to the spot, not sure she'd heard the woman correctly. Amy chuckled. "Yeah. She knows. Nothing can get past Isbeil."

Isbeil gave out a small, humorless chuckle. "I can practically smell the faerie magic around ye two."

"You know about faeries?" Amber said. "You know who Sìneag is?"

"Oh, aye. 'Tis the faerie that plays with destinies." She looked at Amy, and her eyes softened. "Yer babe is fine, and ye are, too. 'Tis a little early for the womb to tighten so, but ye're still closed. Dinna fash yerself."

"Thanks."

Without saying another word, Isbeil left the room. Amber watched her in fascination. The woman looked ancient and yet appeared full of energy and moved swiftly.

"How does she know?" Amber said when the door closed behind Isbeil.

"Your accent. But she'll keep her mouth shut. I trust her. One thing about the Middle Ages is that people live so close, everyone's in everyone's business. They think I'm a weirdo, but they're good people and have accepted me."

Amber smiled and shook her head. "Yes, these times are so different from what I'm used to. Makes you appreciate more what we had—the freedom, the conveniences—doesn't it?"

"Well, yes. But no conveniences in the world would make me abandon Craig. What we have, the happiness—no modern conveniences could ever trump that."

Amber chuckled politely. Lucky Amy. Deliriously happy with Craig, having a family with him. Jealousy stung Amber. She was falling for Owen, but unlike Amy, she'd never be with the man she loved—not with anyone. She just couldn't depend on a man. Or trust him. Especially one like Owen.

Besides, he'd said she should stay away from him. Her cheeks warmed in embarrassment as she remembered her pathetic attempt to kiss him. She shook her head to get rid of the thought. "Speaking of conveniences, do you happen to have any spare clothing? I'm still in this stinky English uniform, and we were on the road for days."

"Yeah, sure. I'll give you a few of my dresses." She stood up and threw an estimating glance at Amber. "Though I think they might be a bit too short for you. But I can ask my maid to make a dress in your size, no worries. You want to try something on?"

Amy leaned over one of the chests, and Amber pulled the tunic over her head.

"You have a maid?" she said.

Amy sighed. "I know. I have a maid. Sounds so posh. But you get used to this stuff. I refused in the beginning, but with time, I realized I couldn't weave cloth, make dresses, do the laundry—and make no mistake, you have to wash everything by hand in cold water. There's also running the kitchen, doing the cleaning... It's a lot of work. Besides, it's nice to know I'm giving a good girl the opportunity for honest labor. Here." She handed Amber a blue dress, a pale red dress, and a couple of undertunics.

"Thanks."

Amber turned around to put the dresses on a chair so she could try one on, and she heard a gasp.

"Amber, what happened to your back?"

She froze. "I was flogged in Stirling."

"Flogged? Hold on, let me have a look." Amy came closer, and Amber felt a light touch on one of her sutures. "The wounds look good, though someone did a very rough job. But these stitches need to come out, so you don't get an infection. Do you want me to do that? I brought some medical supplies with me the second time around."

"Can you take them out?"

"Of course. Here, lie down," she said. Amber lay on the bed, and Amy went to one of the chests and began rummaging in it.

"You still have your modern shoes, I see. Hold on to them. They're so much warmer than these." She showed Amber a leather shoe with a flat sole. "I'll ask my maid to order some in the village for you. You'll need them sooner than you think when yours wear out."

"Thanks so much."

She found a metal flask, no doubt from the twenty-first century, and something that looked like a first aid kit. "I wish there'd been someone for me in the beginning to help with all this stuff."

She came back to the bed and placed her tools on the covers. She took out sharp scissors, tweezers, cotton swabs, and adhesive bandages. Wow, the woman was a miracle.

"So this is what you do as a wife?" Amber said. "Run the house?"

Some liquid gurgled briefly—alcohol, as far as Amber could smell. Amy rubbed a wet cotton swab against Amber's wounds, and they stung. "Yes. Craig and I have our own estate, but we came here because it's safer. He has to go with the Bruce a lot, and he'd rather keep me and the baby in the castle. We don't have as many men as Neil and Dougal have."

"What did you do before—back in the States?"

Amy took the scissors and the tweezers, and Amber felt a small tug against her back, then a pulling, stinging sensation. "I was a search and rescue officer."

"I was in the military, an officer. Served in Afghanistan."

Amy put a small part of the catgut thread in a wooden bowl. "Oh, wow. A warrior woman..."

"Not anymore."

There was another pull and the snap of the scissors. "If I ask why, you won't tell me, will you?"

Amber sighed heavily. "I don't think you want to know."

She was pretty sure Amy wouldn't want a suspected murderer anywhere near her family.

"So if I'm not a soldier anymore—or a warrior, or whatever it's called here—what can I do to earn a living?"

Amy chuckled. "Good question. Most women get married and run households. But I gather that's not what you want to do."

"Definitely not."

"Some women brew beer and sell it to taverns. They're called alewives, and they do really well for themselves. Some own and run taverns and inns. Farming is essential, though you probably can't do it alone. You can also work in the castle. There's plenty to do here. Women work for the lady of the house as maids, wet nurses, and so on. Do you have any medical skills?"

"Only basic stuff. Stopping bleeding, stabilizing broken bones, and so on. Just what combat lifesaver training entails."

"Right, so you can't be a healer?"

"What, administering herbs and leeches?" Amber chuckled. "No. Nor do I want to."

"And I assume you don't want to be a nun?"

Amber chuckled again. "I'd rather brew beer."

Amy's fingers moved faster now. *Click, click, click*, went the scissors. "Stay with me then, until you get used to this life. Until you know what you want to do."

Amber released a long breath, her chest aching dully. Here she was, thousands of miles and hundreds of years away from home, and yet she'd met warm, kind people who cared about her.

Still, she'd be a fool to completely trust strangers. And she didn't want to be an imposition. Her first instinct was to leave and make her own fortune. But Owen was right. There seemed to be more danger to a woman alone these days, especially since she looked so different from everyone else, and the English were still out there hunting for her. She could always leave later, once she knew how she could earn her living and lead a safe life.

"Thank you, Amy," she said. "I really appreciate your kindness. Owen also insisted I stay until it's safe, as his guest."

Amy pulled on one knot too hard, and Amber bit her lip.

"Okay, then it's settled," Amy said. "You're staying with us. I'm so glad to meet another time traveler."

"I'll stay, but only if I can repay your kindness one day."

"Oh, please, don't worry." Tug. *Click*. Tug. *Click*. "So what's going on between Owen and you, by the way?"

Amber felt heat rush to her face. "Nothing. We were unfortunate enough to get kidnapped together, and he saved my life when I was flogged. Now he insists I'm his guest and under his protection."

"Under his protection? Really..."

"I don't want it. It's overprotection. He even gave me his bedroom. The gesture means a lot to me, but honestly, I just want to be left alone."

Correction. What she wanted was him. But having him was out of the question, no matter how out of breath he made her, how alive he made her feel—like she could finally relax and be herself. Like she didn't need to justify her very existence.

Amy cocked one eyebrow. "I don't think being so protective is very typical of him."

"And what's typical of him?"

"I'm not sure I've ever seen him with the same woman twice. And yet he's giving you his bedroom and taking you under his wing."

Amber shook her head, but her pulse accelerated. "He just feels responsible for me."

"Owen can be a joker, and he makes mistakes, but he means well. And I know if it comes down to it, he'll defend his clan until his dying breath. He might be a playboy, but once he falls in love, I don't think he'll fall out of it. Mark my words, it'll be forever."

Amber chewed on the inside of her cheek. *Falls in love...* She remembered his lips on hers, the way he called her "lass." From his lips, the word sounded charged with pure sunshine. But he wasn't in love with her. Of course not. Maybe a little infatuated, but nothing more.

And yet a tiny part of her heart wished he was in love with her. He was a wonderful man, the best man she'd ever met in her life. He wasn't perfect—and that was exactly why she loved him.

Loved him?

No, she didn't love him. How could she after such a short

time together? Maybe *she* was infatuated with *him*. She was definitely very attracted to him. How could she not be? He was absolutely gorgeous. Simply being in the same room with him brought her a deep sense of peace, as though she'd found a part of her soul she'd lost a long time ago. As though finally, the hard journey was over and she'd arrived home.

The only thing was, how could she trust that feeling?

CHAPTER 22

Three days later...

Owen slammed the door to the stables shut behind him. The warm scent of horses, hay, and manure enveloped him, taking him away from the heated discussion he'd just had with his father. It seemed everything Owen did aggravated Dougal.

Owen had suggested he could train the young warriors, and surprisingly his father had allowed that. Craig and Domhnall had watched as he'd taught two dozen men in the courtyard, showing them movements he'd learned to use when fighting in close proximity. Some of the men were surprised; they'd never seen him take any kind of initiative.

While the men were taking a brief rest, Owen had asked his father if he could teach the men on a regular basis. Dougal had answered that was Craig and Domhnall's task. He didn't trust that Owen would stick to it. His refusal and distrust were like a hard slap across Owen's face.

His first instinct was to rebel and to flee, just like he had so many times before, but his new, responsible self protested. He would stay and prove everyone wrong. Show that he'd changed. That he could take responsibility and be trusted.

His second instinct was to find Amber and kiss her. Talk to her. Make love to her. Let her distract him.

But that would be a mistake. He'd been so good during the past three days, avoiding her even though it felt like he were pulling his own teeth.

He marched towards a stall to take a horse and ride north to a little cove on the loch where he always escaped when he felt like he did now—like an outsider in his own clan.

When his eyes had adjusted to the semidarkness of the stables, he realized he wasn't alone. Amber stood by a horse one of the grooms was saddling for her.

"Hi," she said.

Owen's stomach clenched at the beautiful sight of her. He'd seen her walking here and there, with Amy for the most part. Everything brightened and gained color when he saw her. He longed to go over to her and just stand near her, to bathe in her presence as if in sunlight.

There was nowhere to run now.

"Lass," he said and nodded. He walked to another horse and began saddling it.

Stop thinking of her.

She came to stand by his horse. "Going somewhere?" she asked.

His jaw clenched. "Aye," he said without looking at her. He put the saddle on the horse's back and began fastening it. "Ye?"

"Yeah. I'm tired of sitting inside and doing nothing. I just want to go for a ride."

He stopped. "Alone?"

"Yeah."

His nostrils flared. "Lass, we talked about this. Ye shouldna go out alone. 'Tis too dangerous."

"I'll be fine. Not that you'd want to go with me." She turned to walk away and then threw a glare over her shoulder. "You've been behaving like a dick ever since we got here."

The groom snorted, and Owen suppressed a growl. He knew his distance was hurting her, but he didn't want to argue in front of others.

She wasn't leaving him a choice now. "Ye're nae going anywhere, lass."

She snorted. "You have no right to command me, pal."

What was happening to him? He was never this bossy with women. That was because he'd never cared about anyone like he did about her. "I do when 'tis in yer best interest."

"My interests are none of your concern."

He walked out of the stall and stared at her. "If ye insist on going alone, I'll take ye over my shoulder and lock ye up. Ye can either come with me or stay here. Yer choice."

She crossed her arms over her chest. "Go with you? I thought you were avoiding me like the plague."

Owen pressed his lips together tightly. "I was busy."

She raised one eyebrow. "Right. Busy running in the other direction when you see me."

"Are ye coming or nae?"

"Only if you promise not to behave like a jerk."

"A what?"

"I believe the lass means an arse," the groom said. "Yer horse is ready, my lady."

"Thanks."

"Please wait with the horse outside while the lady and I talk," Owen said as he glared at her. Once the groom left, he sighed. "Fine, I wilna behave like a *jerk*."

"All right then."

A moment later, they'd mounted and were heading out of the castle. With Amber riding by his side, he needed a distraction from *this* distraction. He urged his horse into a gallop, enjoying the whistle of the wind in his ears and the hard rhythm of the horse under him. The loch was to their left, stormy and gray under a sky the color of woodsmoke. There were woods and rocks to their right, where trees and bushes swayed in the wind.

The place wasn't far, and they soon arrived. There was a small inlet that created an oval pool. The shore rose steeply towards a cave half hidden by bushes and undergrowth.

The view from here took his breath away. The loch spread in front of them to the left and to the right. On the shore across from the cove, there were green hills and mountains covered partly by purple fields of heather.

"Why did you want to come here?" Amber said.

Owen tied his horse to a tree and stood by the shore, allowing himself a deep, cleansing breath and feeling the tension and anger in the pit of his stomach melt away.

"'Tis where I used to come as a lad when everyone seemed to have forgotten about me. And when even my pranks didna attract my da's attention." He chuckled softly to himself.

Amber walked to him and stood by his side, facing the loch. "This is a beautiful place to run away to."

"I'd sometimes sleep in that cave." He pointed up towards the cliff. "There's a bit of magic there. I discovered it when my mother died. I was a lad of twelve years old. She became sick very quickly and died."

"I'm so sorry, Owen. I remember when my mother passed away. Nothing comes close to that kind of loss."

He sighed. Sadness crippled his heart, but knowing Amber had gone through the same thing somehow made him feel better.

"My ma was Craig and Marjorie's stepmother, but she treated us all the same. As though they were hers."

Amber smiled softly. "She sounds like an amazing woman."

"Aye. I think she's watching over me. I realized it first when I came here. 'Tis why I keep coming back."

"Really? Why here?"

He studied her, contemplating if he should open up to her about it. This was the first woman he'd ever loved. With her, his soul wanted to share everything that was dear to him. Gray clouds spread across the sky, but the sun shone brightly between them. Yes, she was watching over him. That was a sign.

"Come, then. I'll show ye."

He took her by the hand and went up the slope with her. They passed the bushes and the undergrowth and entered the cave. It smelled like rotting leaves and something earthy, animallike even. The cave was rather small and deep, and although the sun was high, it was hard to see what was in the black depths.

The opening of the cave shone with brilliant crystals that sparkled like a night full of stars. There was the same wonder in Amber's big eyes that he felt in his heart. God almighty, even this divine creation of nature didn't come close to the beauty of this woman.

Their eyes locked, and he forgot to guard his fascination. It was just like that night in the inn where they'd been naked in front of each other, sheltered from the world like nothing existed but them.

He saw the decision in her eyes. She crossed the distance between them, took him by the collar of his tunic, and brought his face to hers.

The kiss was like plunging into the waters of the loch—fresh and delicious. He sank into her with the inevitability of a rock heading towards the bottom.

Her scent filled every bit of his body. Her lips caressed and her tongue teased, hungry for him, and she pressed herself against his chest.

Let her go. Tell her no. Release her. Stop.

All in vain. She was water, and he'd been thirsty his whole life. Nothing could stop him from drinking his fill. Here, in the cave that gave him strength in the moments when he needed it, he'd have her. He'd make her his.

He deepened the kiss, devouring her mouth. Claiming her. Possessing her.

He was instantly hard and throbbing for her, his blood like fire. She rubbed herself against him, as impatient as he was. He took her face in his palms, then traced his fingers down her body. He cupped one breast through her tunic, and it was warm and lush against his skin. He circled her nipple with his thumb, and she sucked in a quick breath and arched into him. He reached under her tunic and cupped both her breasts with his hands. They were so soft and warm. He massaged them, rolled her hardened nipples between his thumbs and index fingers.

She let out the tiniest whimper of pleasure from the back of her throat. He imagined her making the same sound as he drove into her for the first time. He broke the kiss and slid her body to the ground. He looked down at her breeches and realized they were his. Why did seeing a woman in his breeches bring his blood to boil even more?

He pulled them down her hips and stared at the black triangle of hair he'd craved ever since he'd seen her naked in the inn.

"So beautiful," he whispered.

He spread her folds and put his mouth on her, blood pulsing hard in his ears.

A growl sounded from somewhere nearby.

Owen was so drunk from the succulent, wanton taste of her that he didn't make the connection at first, but Amber tensed and shifted.

The growl came again, closer, louder, more urgent.

Everything seemed to happen slowly. Owen went cold all over, as though a bucket of ice water had been thrown over him.

A bear.

His mind knew he needed to react, but his body still refused to move. Distantly, he remembered bears liked to nap during summer days and hunt at night.

Like in a nightmare, his body felt as slow and heavy as a boulder. He rose to his feet and shoved Amber behind his back while removing his sword from its sheath. The beast emerged out of the darkness, roaring like a monster from an old tale. He was big, fat, and brown, and he stood before Owen in the sunlight, his jaws open, yellowish fangs bared.

All Owen could think about was Amber. *Don't let any harm come to her. Do anything to protect her.*

His sword flashed in the sunlight as he swung it in warning before the beast. It roared again—a heart-stopping sound—and launched itself at Owen.

Owen roared at the bear, too. It hugged him in a deadly embrace, claws tearing the flesh of Owen's back, but before it could sink its teeth into Owen's shoulder, he thrust his sword upward through the animal's jaw and into its skull. The bear fell into an impossibly heavy heap of stinking fur.

"Owen!" Amber cried.

He kicked a heavy paw off himself, and she helped him stand up and dragged him away. They both stood at the mouth of the cave staring at the dead animal, a pool of blood forming around its head.

"Are you okay?" she said. "Let me see."

She touched his shoulder in an attempt to turn him and see his wounds, but he jerked away.

This was his fault. She'd tempted him. And after all the promises he'd made to stay away from her and not get distracted, he'd done it again. He'd gotten distracted and they both could have died.

She frowned at him, surprise and hurt in her eyes.

"We almost died because of me," he said.

Her face went blank. "What?"

"Aye. If ye had nae kissed me, if I had nae given in to yer charms…"

Now it wasn't just a matter of failing his king and his family, it was a matter of failing *her*. She'd almost been hurt because of his inability to be responsible and focus.

This was a good slap in the face, a reminder that he couldn't give in to temptation.

Next time, it might not be a bear. It could be an English sword that put an end to everything he was fighting for.

CHAPTER 23

One week later...

THE WATCHMEN ON THE WALLS SHOUTED AND RAN, AND OWEN stopped in the middle of the courtyard on his way to the great hall.

Someone was coming.

His heart drummed against his rib cage. He saw Amber in the courtyard and longed to talk to her. She was the only one who knew he'd sent a messenger to the Bruce.

In a dark-blue dress, her hair split into two braids and joined at the back of her head, she looked like a noble lady from his time. Ever since Amy had given her some clothes and helped her look less like a woman from the future, he'd imagined her here with him like that every day, and something ached sweetly in his chest.

Something that would never be.

"'Tis the Bruce!" one of the sentinels cried. "And his army." The man ran towards the great hall to tell the rest of the clan.

Owen's gut churned. His father was about to find out he'd disobeyed him. "By God's bones..." he muttered.

He was in trouble whether the Bruce listened to him or not. Rather than confront his father, he rushed to see the Bruce's arrival for himself.

He flew up the stone stairs attached to the wall and stood there watching the crowd of men move over the green hills towards the castle from the north. A standard-bearer rode ahead displaying the Bruce's colors, two red lines crossing like a letter X on a yellow background.

"Owen!" a furious cry came from the courtyard.

Owen gritted his teeth and went down the steps under the lethal gaze of his father.

"By God's blood, what did ye do?" Dougal growled. "Did ye send word to him?"

Owen stood before his da, a part of him trembling like a little boy, but he raised his chin high. He had nothing to prove and nothing to apologize for. He hadn't made a mistake this time.

"Aye," he said. "I did."

"Ye stupid, stupid lad. What if ye bring shame on this family again?"

"I wilna. If 'tis shame that comes, it will be mine and mine alone. I swear if I'm wrong about this—and I'm nae wrong—I'll leave forever, and ye'll never see me again."

"This canna be undone. And there's more at stake than shame. The lives of so many people, the destiny of our country—"

Craig came over to them, obviously just as angry as their father. "'Tis too late to argue about this. We must decide together what to say to the king. Do we stick to Owen's suggestion about attacking at the Pass of Brander? Or do we talk the Bruce out of this?"

Their father glared at Owen, then spat on the ground.

"I dinna want to stand ashamed of my son in front of a king again."

The rumble of horses' hooves thundered in the air and vibrated the ground. The king rode through the gates and into the courtyard surrounded by men. Uncle Neil was at his side, as well as Owen's cousins, Goiridh and Anndra. He recognized James "Black" Douglas, one of the Bruce's favorite officers. Malcolm rode in as well and dismounted at the far side of the procession.

The king dismounted, and so did Neil and the rest. Owen took a deep breath. He locked his eyes with Uncle Neil, but the older man's expression was unreadable. What did he think of the whole matter?

"Welcome, Yer Grace," Dougal said. "Hope yer journey was good. We didna ken of yer arrival."

"Aye," the Bruce said. "But the message yer son sent was very important. We must act. Where's Owen?"

Owen stepped forward. "Aye, Yer Grace, I'm here."

A tall, mighty man with the neck of a tempered warrior, huge shoulders and arms, the king wore a look of grave intensity. Owen had never spoken to the king directly, and being under his penetrating gaze made his skin itch. What if he was wrong? What if he was putting the destiny of his king and Scotland in jeopardy?

"Come," the Bruce said. "We must talk somewhere quietly and decide what to do."

"The great hall?" Neil asked Dougal.

"Aye, of course. Owen, make sure no one enters but those who're supposed to be there. Craig, Domhnall, come with."

Owen's teeth clenched. He wasn't even invited?

"Father," Craig said quietly while Uncle Neil showed the king to the great hall. "Owen should be there. 'Tis he who heard the news."

Dougal eyed Owen heavily and shook his head. "Aye. No way of turning this around, anyway."

Owen was about to walk with them to the great hall when

Amber caught his arm and stopped him. Her delicious scent reached his nostrils, her full lips close to him.

"Owen, don't falter," she said. "Don't let them intimidate you. You got this."

Even though he'd kept his distance from her all these days, she didn't hold a grudge and still supported him. Gratitude spread through Owen's limbs with tingling warmth. And then he had a thought. "Come with me. Ye're from the future. Ye might have some good ideas."

"Me?"

"Aye. Please. Amy's helped Craig with her skills from the future. She knows how to track missing people. She boils milk and water and cloth, claiming it kills some invisible sickness. It sounds like witchcraft to me, but it works. Ye are a warrior from the future. Ye might ken something we dinna."

Amber glared at him. "Didn't you say I was distracting you?"

Guilt pinched him. "I will try to contain myself," he said through his teeth. "If ye can help, 'tis more important."

She tapped her foot nervously and held his gaze for a few moments. "Okay. Let's go."

"Aye."

They walked to the great hall. It was being emptied for the discussion. The Bruce had appointed his own men to watch the entrance, and they blocked the way when Owen and Amber approached.

"The king wants me there, lads," Owen said.

"'Tis nae about ye," one of them said. "She canna enter."

Amber took a step back. "Seriously, Owen, I don't think I should be in there."

"Nae, ye should. She's with me, lads. She's a known military strategist from the caliphate."

The guards exchanged a look, but one of them shook his head.

"The Bruce will be cross," Owen said.

"I didna hear nothing about anyone from the caliphate," the guard said.

Craig appeared from the doors. "What's taking so long, Owen? The king is asking for ye."

"These good men dinna want to let Amber in."

Craig frowned, clearly confused. "Amber? Why would she—"

"Aye, she's a renowned military strategist from the caliphate. And the king would verra much appreciate her advice."

Craig's forehead flattened. "Oh, aye. Lads, let her in. The king wants her in here."

The guard sighed and stepped aside, letting Owen and Amber pass.

Men stood around one of the tables, the benches set aside. The king himself, Uncle Neil, Dougal, Craig, James Douglas, the Bruce's brother Edward, and several others stood around the table. Their presence suffused the great hall with a palpable pulse of power.

"Owen Cambel"—the Bruce raised his head—"finally." He frowned at Amber. "Why is this woman here?"

"Lady Amber's a traveling mercenary from the caliphate," Owen said. "She was hired by Kenneth Mackenzie."

"The caliphate?" The Bruce's look sharpened. "Dinna women there sit inside harems and produce children? 'Tis what I heard."

Amber raised her chin. "Not all of them. The strongest ones build their own lives. At least, that's what I wish for them."

His strong lass. But would the Bruce believe her?

"Why are ye here?" the king asked. "A woman doesna belong on my military council."

If the wrath of the king fell on Amber, it would be Owen's fault. He needed to protect her. "I believe her unique knowledge from the caliphate might be beneficial. I have seen her fight and she possesses military skills I havena seen before. She is an asset to ye, Yer Grace."

The Bruce held him in his long gaze, then Amber. "'Tis most unusual, but these are unusual times. I'll allow it. But rest assured, if I suspect foul play, ye will be held prisoner, Lady Amber."

Owen suppressed an urge to shield Amber from the king's words. Another threat of prison... That must be hard for her.

The Bruce gestured for them to come closer. "Tell me what happened, Owen. How did ye come to hear the information about MacDougalls and the ambush?"

Owen walked towards the table, feeling the eyes of every man on him. His da's gaze was especially heavy. Owen could physically feel it on his skin. But his father was not his concern now. He went to stand at the table and met the king's eyes. They were dark and piercing, the eyes of a man who knew what he wanted and expected much from himself and the people around him.

A man who'd made himself king.

He wouldn't forgive a weakness, or a mistake.

"As de Bourgh took Inverlochy, he took me prisoner." He looked back at Amber, who stood behind him. The Bruce studied them both. "As well as Amber. De Bourgh tortured her, trying to find out anything that would compromise ye or the campaign. And when it was my turn to be interrogated, John MacDougall showed up."

The Bruce's sharp gaze pierced Owen. "Aye, and?"

Owen's fists clenched as he remembered the rage that had thundered in his body. "We talked. As ye ken, our clans have a history."

The Bruce shook his head briefly. "As does mine with his."

"Aye. He beat the shite out of me and knocked me unconscious. When I woke up, de Bourgh and MacDougall didna ken that I was listening, and they discussed their plan. Yer peace treaty with the MacDougall ends in a sennight. He kens ye're coming for him since he's the last strong clan in Scotland that stands against ye. And he kens the only way to his lands is through the Pass of Brander."

"Aye."

"He wants a repetition of the Battle of Dalrigh. He will ambush ye there."

The Bruce stared at him for a long time, and Owen felt rooted to the spot. The anticipation of awaiting his king's response was like cold iron solidifying the marrow of his bones. What would it be, shame or victory? Would he lose everything over this? Would he dishonor the reputation of his family in front of yet another king?

"And ye're certain of this?"

Owen found the ability to speak again. "Aye, Yer Grace. I heard it with my own ears. Ye ken I have nae reason to lie or deceive ye, and I swear 'tis the truth."

The Bruce looked at Dougal. "Ye look dubious. Speak yer mind."

Owen's eyes locked with his father's. His features hardened, his mouth curved into a bitter grimace. If his father said one word against him, Owen was done. His chest tightened so hard, he stopped breathing. A drop of sweat snaked down his spine.

Dougal sighed and looked at the Bruce. "If my son says 'tis the truth"—he tapped his thumb against the table—"'tis the truth. Clan Cambel has always been loyal to ye. And we always will be."

Relief flooded Owen, and an enormous weight on his chest lifted. His father nodded to him ever so slightly. Whether he believed Owen or not, he was on his son's side before the king, and that was what mattered. Warmth spread through Owen, and it became easier to breathe.

Uncle Neil added, "I stand by my brother and my nephew's words, Yer Grace."

Owen's throat tightened. Now it was ironclad—if the chief of a clan gave his word, the whole clan stood behind him.

The Bruce gave a curt nod. "Aye. Now what about the Pass of Brander? Does anyone ken it?"

"Aye, I do," Owen said. "I used it several times on my way to and from the MacDougalls' when I was fostered there."

The Bruce nodded. "Good. Now tell me how exactly ye think they're going to try to ambush us and what we can do to counter them."

CHAPTER 24

Amber felt Owen's relief in her own bones. His shoulders and face relaxed, and she knew how grateful he must feel that his family was standing by him. She wished the same for herself, that her own brothers would support her in difficult times, but she doubted that would ever happen.

Aunt Christel was the only one she'd been able to turn to for help. And unfortunately, she'd probably gotten her innocent relatives in trouble for harboring a criminal. Had the police questioned her aunt and cousin? Had they pressed charges? God, she hoped not.

She was proud of Owen for stepping up and holding his ground. The Bruce was intimidating, and she could imagine he was scary for those not on his side. But Owen hadn't faltered. He'd defended himself and stuck to his word.

Something she hadn't done. Something she'd never have the courage to do in her own time. She imagined standing up for herself. Hiring a lawyer, fighting the good fight against Jackson.

But it would be useless. She'd lose. There was nothing that she could do to defend herself. All the evidence was against her. So many witnesses had seen her and Bryan fight at the bar. Bryan hadn't given her anything to prove that Jackson was smuggling drugs, only that name: Aman Safar. So even if she could accuse him of Bryan's murder, without any evidence, she couldn't prove he had a motive.

And she'd run from the authorities, which only made her look guiltier.

Owen took a pile of soot from the dead fireplace and poured it onto the table.

"The Pass of Brander is a narrow and dangerous track." He drew a line in the soot with his finger. "'Tis only a few yards wide. On the right, it borders the precipitous side of the Ben Cruachan Mountain." He ran his hand over the small pile of soot and made a broad, cone-like shape next to the line he'd drawn. "And on the left side, it drops into the waters of Loch Awe." Owen drew waves on the other side of the line.

The Bruce scratched his bearded chin. "There's nae better place for an ambush."

"Aye." Owen drew a line crossing the path. "MacDougall will block the way and put some of his men right on the Pass." Then he poked the sooty surface several times on the pile indicating Ben Cruachan. "Here, on the mountainside above, he'll place men who'll hurl rocks and boulders down on yer warriors below."

Neil Cambel put his hands on the table and leaned over the drawing. "'Tis just like at Dalrigh."

"I wasna at Dalrigh," Domhnall said. "What happened?"

The Bruce's eyes darkened, as did those of most of the men around the table. Owen rubbed his shoulder.

"'Twas two years ago," the king said. "After the Battle of Methven, when the English destroyed us. We fled westward, only five hundred of us. The MacDougalls blocked the path before us, and we didna have a choice but to fight. There were a thousand of them, all trained warriors. We had the remnants of my exhausted army, women, the elderly, and children."

Amber swallowed hard as images of blood, pierced flesh, and dying people invaded her mind. She'd seen her fair share of torn body parts and blood soaking the ground. War was war.

She studied the Bruce's mournful face, his dark eyes full of regret and pain. Would he let his people down, these Highlanders who had put everything on the line for their king?

"As ye can see," the Bruce continued, "we escaped. Yer uncle, and yer father, yer clan brothers, too. James Douglas and Gilbert de la Haye were wounded, among others, and we put them on boats to escape. Then we had the worst winter of my life, hiding in the Isles and thinking the war was over."

"'Tis nae over," Owen said and slammed his fist against the table. "'Tis far from over. We ken what they have in mind. We can strike back."

"Aye," the men echoed.

"And we can finish the MacDougalls forever," Craig said. He locked his eyes with Owen. "I ken who else would like to be at that battle."

"Ian," they both said.

"Aye, Ian," Dougal said.

"'Tis my nephew the MacDougalls sold into slavery," Neil explained to the Bruce.

"Aye," the Bruce said. "Any Cambel is welcome to fight against our common enemy."

"So what do ye want to do, Yer Grace?" Owen said.

The Bruce sighed and studied the drawing thoughtfully. "How steep is the slope?"

"'Tis quite steep," Owen said. "There are few places where one can climb it. I ken them."

"Aye. Good. Then we need to take advantage of the knowledge. The biggest threat, of course, are the forces hidden up the mountainside. Owen, ye ken the terrain well. What do ye suggest?"

Amber bit her lip, nervous for Owen. This was his moment to shine or to fail.

"I suggest ye take the Pass as if ye dinna ken of the ambush. That'll blind the MacDougalls and make them feel as though their plan is working. In the meanwhile, have some of yer men attack the enemy waiting to ambush ye in the mountainside, mayhap from their flank."

"Aye," the Bruce said. "'Tis what we'll do."

Amber remembered a similar situation in Afghanistan. They'd arrived at a city in six Humvees. They'd driven around a corner and found a street barricaded with old cars and rubble. Bullets and grenades had rained down on them from behind and above.

If it wasn't for another unit that had come from the east and air support, Amber didn't think they'd have made it out alive.

They'd been able to take out the snipers from the air. Obviously, the Bruce couldn't use choppers, but his men could climb even higher and ambush the ambushers from above.

"There's something more you can do," Amber said.

Everyone looked at her, and she bit her tongue, instantly regretting her interference.

"Woman, ken yer place," Dougal barked, and men chuckled.

"Da, let her speak," Owen said. "With yer permission, Yer Grace."

The Bruce pierced her with his eyes, and she cowered. What the hell did she know about medieval tactics and Scottish terrain?

The Bruce shook his head. "We dinna have time for a woman's opinion. Ye're here as a courtesy to Owen Cambel. Nothing more." He turned to the men. "Now, I think our knights should attack the blockade. And the Highlanders—"

"Forgive me, Yer Grace," Owen said. "But ye should listen to what Amber has to say."

The Bruce shot him a murderous look.

"Owen, ye ken I respect yer opinion, but why should I trust a woman?"

"If ye trust my information, ye need to trust her."

"Owen—" Dougal said.

But Owen insisted, "I beg of ye, listen and then decide. She has significant military experience. Ye *want* to give her the opportunity to talk."

The Bruce held Owen in his heavy gaze. New worlds must have been born, lived, and died before the Bruce spoke again.

"All right." He looked at Amber, who was still rooted to the spot. "Speak. Fast."

Every man in the room glared at her, their attention heavy and estimating. Damn it. She could be wrong about this, and what then? Would she condemn the battle and the whole war to failure?

She walked towards the table on weak legs but with a straight back. She'd give her best advice and let them decide if it was a good plan.

"You should ambush them with your own ambush." She leaned over Owen's drawing and drew a line an inch from the dots he'd marked on the mountainside. "Put a line of archers here. As many as you can, and let them attack these guys from behind and above. At the same time, have your Highlanders launch at them from the side, as Owen suggested."

Owen nodded, pride shining in his expression. The Bruce propped his hands on the table and studied the diagram closer. "The main threat will be too busy fighting both sides. And the knights will finish those who block the Pass."

He looked at Amber again, surprise and a hint of respect shining in his eyes. "Aye. This will work." He turned his attention to a handsome man with long, dark hair and the longest beard in the room. "Douglas, yer men will be up on the mountainside. Ye and they ken how to move quieter than a cat."

He looked at Owen. "Since ye ken the land, I want ye to lead the Highlanders and attack from the side." He pointed at the dots.

Owen's chest puffed up. Amber thought he'd stopped breathing. A smile threatened to spread across his lips, but he tensed his mouth, and his eyes flashed.

The Bruce met Neil Cambel's gaze. "I will lead the knights."

Owen squeezed Amber's hand under the table. She returned the gesture and intertwined her fingers with his. The connection of their hands sent electricity through her, a bizarre combination of desire and trust. Her whole body relaxed at the touch, filling with warmth and a soft, barely noticeable buzz. It was as though every cell in her body had come alive.

The Bruce looked straight at her. "I want ye to fight with us."

Could she serve another leader who could use her so easily in his manipulations? A man who had all the power? She couldn't do it again.

"No."

The air became thick and charged. Every single man stared at her in disbelief. The Bruce's eyes turned as sharp and as dangerous as a snake's.

But the worst response was Owen's. He gaped at her with the pained expression of someone who'd just been betrayed.

CHAPTER 25

Owen felt his nostrils flare. Amber held her chin high, her back straight, her face not faltering under the heaviness of the gazes of a dozen battle-clad warriors. How could she say no when his people so clearly needed her, when the king himself had asked her to join them? If Owen wanted to be a successful leader, he needed to have all the best people on his side.

"Nae?" the king asked, his voice low and calm, but apprehension crackled around him like the air before a storm.

As angry with her as he was, Owen realized she might be in danger now, and he shifted to stand between the Bruce and Amber.

The Bruce was a good leader, a strong warrior, and the king Owen was ready to lay down his life for. But Amber should make no mistake. He was ruthless. He was powerful. He could also be cruel.

After all, he'd murdered his opponent, Red John Comyn, in a church and proclaimed himself king. He'd raided and burned all of the Comyn lands in the east. He was a man who showed no mercy to his enemies.

Owen hoped Amber wouldn't become one. And that he

wouldn't need to choose between the woman he loved and his king.

"No," she repeated.

Hell...

Out of the corner of his eye, Owen saw his father's face tighten and harden like a rock. Uncle Neil's eyes bulged, darting between Amber and the king. The rest of the men stood immobile like statues. Only Craig moved, shaking his head.

"Ye can fight, canna ye?" the Bruce said, his voice still low. "Ye're a mercenary and fought for Mackenzie, aye? And if ye fought for Mackenzie at Inverlochy, ye fought for me."

Amber nodded, swallowing.

"So am I to assume ye dinna stand by yer own battle plan? How do I ken ye're nae a spy hired by my enemies?"

"Amber isna a spy," Owen said.

The Bruce looked at him as if he were a noisy fly.

"Answer me, lass," the king said, his nostrils flaring.

"Had you asked me a month ago," Amber's voice rang out loudly in the silent hall, "I'd have said yes. But not because I wanted to. Because I'd be afraid of you, of your authority, of your power. I've made myself small and obeyed the orders of my commanders my whole life. My father. My brothers. My superiors in the army. But the same superiors I trusted and fought for betrayed me."

She inhaled sharply.

"So I won't give anyone else power over my destiny. You fight for Scotland's independence, King. I will fight for only mine. This is not my war. And you're not my king. I have no king."

The Bruce held her in his hard gaze for a long time. It was so quiet, Owen imagined he could hear mice scratching in the corners.

The Bruce crossed his arms on his chest. "Why did ye agree to serve Mackenzie in Inverlochy?"

Amber's shoulder twitched. "I needed protection from those who chased me."

"Who chased ye?" The Bruce frowned.

Owen might regret it later, but he couldn't leave Amber in peril, fighting her fight alone. Even if it might cost him his king's favor.

"The English," Owen said.

The Bruce raised one eyebrow, the weight of his gaze like a boulder on Owen. "Are the English yer enemy?" the Bruce asked Amber.

"Aye," Owen answered for her.

Amber nodded. It was at least partially true, after what de Bourgh had done to her.

"So if the English are yer enemy, will ye at least join me against them?" He chuckled, his mouth askew. "Even if I am nae yer king?"

She shook her head. "Forgive me, Yer Grace, but no. I have fought against enough enemies. I'm done fighting."

The Bruce nodded once, his lips pinched in his beard.

"I'm nae used to being rejected three times, my lady. Still, 'tis yer right, and I appreciate words said honestly. It takes courage to say nae to a king, and ye dinna lack any. I'll take yer valuable advice and let ye go. But if ye wilna show yer loyalty to me by fighting by my side, ye need to leave this council now."

Amber untangled her fingers from Owen's. "Of course."

She locked her eyes with Owen's, and his stomach squeezed in awe at her. It was only a brief moment, but it felt like it lasted for a lifetime. It was as though Amber and he were the only two people left in the world, and there was no yesterday and no tomorrow. No enemies, no one to judge them, and no one to respond to. She wasn't a distraction. She was the only thing that made sense.

When she walked out, she left him with his chest hollow and scraped out.

"Owen! Owen!" He heard a voice calling him and turned his attention to the men around the table, his head still full of Amber.

The Bruce, Neil, Douglas, and everyone else stared at him, waiting. He only now noticed his father had come to stand right next to him.

"What is it?" Owen asked.

The Bruce raised his eyebrows, his eyes hard in annoyance. "Is there a route up the mountainside?"

Owen cleared his throat. He needed to shake off his feelings for Amber and concentrate on the task at hand. If only it were so easy.

"Son," Dougal murmured next to his ear, "ye need to focus. Ye lead one third of the Bruce's army in this battle. Ye canna let a lass distract ye this time."

Owen nodded. For the first time in his life, he completely agreed with his father.

"Aye," he said to Dougal, then leaned over the drawing on the table and drew a thin, circuitous path on the right side of the mountain flank up the hill. "Here."

And as the line got closer to the dots representing the MacDougalls, he realized with the clarity of the waters of Loch Awe that everything he'd ever wanted had finally happened. He'd been given great responsibility. He was a leader. He could finally make his clan proud.

He couldn't let his love for Amber interfere with that.

CHAPTER 26

Owen sat in the courtyard staring at the flames of the campfire, deep in thought. He enjoyed the murmuring voices around him. The whole courtyard was full of campfires and warriors eating and drinking.

Craig was there, and several others, including two Mackenzie brothers, cousins of Kenneth. A worm of guilt turned in Owen's gut—he was at fault for Kenneth's death.

"I am sorry for yer cousin's death," he said.

"'Tis nae yer fault, Cambel," said Angus, clearly the older one, with black hair and black eyes. "'Tis war. People die."

Raghnall, the younger brother, who had the same raven hair but was even taller and leaner, sighed. He had a crooked nose and one eyebrow with a scar. He looked like someone who'd been in his fair share of fights. "Aye. We're all going to die." He raised his cup of uisge. "So better savor the joys of life while it lasts." He downed it and grunted.

"I'm nae surprised to hear ye say that, brother," Angus said. "Nae wife, nae children, and nae land."

Raghnall threw a dark glance at him. "Nae land? I'm nae Mackenzie nae more, am I?"

Craig frowned. "Aren't ye two brothers?"

Angus and Raghnall exchanged a heavy look. "Our father disinherited me," Raghnall said. "He said I shouldna bother coming back to Mackenzie lands or consider myself part of the clan."

Something cold and heavy settled over Owen's chest. Would that be his destiny if he failed this mission? What if they made their way to the Pass of Brander tomorrow, but no enemy arrived? What if there was a different trap waiting for them?

"Father died," Raghnall said. "Our brother is chief of the clan now. And I'll be on my way home after this battle. He may reconsider and take me back."

"What did ye do that yer da disinherited ye, man?" Owen asked.

Angus looked pointedly at the fire. The two didn't even sit next to each other, and Owen wondered if the Mackenzies were as close as the Cambel brothers.

"Many things I regret," Raghnall said.

Angus raised his eyebrows. "Ye do?" His voice had the quality of thunder.

Raghnall shrugged. "I've lived as a homeless rogue for years. A warm bed and a steaming bowl of stew every night is what I want. 'Tis time to live like a man again."

Angus's face darkened. He leaned forward and placed his elbows on his knees, the muscles of his huge shoulders bulging under his tunic. Owen wouldn't want to get on the bad side of this man. His eyes were like the black clouds of a gathering storm. For a moment, Owen saw bottomless pain there, the pain that the saddest songs are sung about.

"The warm bed is cold when ye lie there alone, and the steaming stew dinna taste good if 'tis nae the woman ye love who cooked it." His voice cracked at the word "woman."

Raghnall chuckled. "I ken ye dinna want to marry, but trust me, brother, any bed and any stew is better than none."

Silence hung around the fire. Angus picked up a stick and

stabbed at the burning logs, sending a frenzy of sparks into the air.

"Ye dinna want to marry?" Craig asked.

"Only if I must to protect my clan," Angus said.

Raghnall rummaged in his sack and retrieved a lute. He brushed his fingers against the strings once, producing a beautiful, sad sound.

"Ye've been doing that yer whole life," he said. "Ye're clearly lonely. Dinna ye wish to find someone ye love?"

Angus glared at him. "Never mind about me. Why dinna ye marry if ye want a warm bed?"

Raghnall laughed and played a cheerful tune. "A man dinna need a wife to keep his bed warm. Aye, Owen?" He winked.

Owen looked away. He actually couldn't think of anyone in his bed but a certain beautiful woman from the future.

Craig arched one eyebrow. "I reckon he'd have agreed with ye before. Now, I dinna think he will."

"Shut yer mouth," Owen growled.

Raghnall's occasional chords grew into a melody, and he began to sing.

Oh, road before me, bring me favorable wind,
  Oh, deep blue sea, be gentle with me.
  Pick me up, tired, sick, and lonely,
  And take me to the lass who waits for me...

He had a pleasant, melodic voice, and Owen was thankful for the distraction. Owen didn't know if Craig suspected he had feelings for Amber, but he didn't need an additional reminder of her when he was doing everything in his power to keep his mind on the mission.

"Have a cup of uisge?" a familiar voice sounded.

Owen turned. Ian stood behind him, as tall and as big as he

remembered, and whole. Both Craig and Owen stood and took Ian in a heartfelt embrace.

"My messenger was fast," Owen said. He'd sent a boy earlier to Dundail to ask Ian to join the fight. "I didna expect ye till the morn."

Ian looked at the sky. "'Tis nae long till the morn. I hurried, dinna want to miss my chance."

"How are yer wounds?" Craig asked.

"I'll live. If the MacDougall is going to be there, 'tis my chance to get revenge for what he did to me."

The three Cambels exchanged a look. This battle meant everything to the clan. Owen could pull it off. If only he could keep his heart and cock under control and stay away from the first woman to make him feel alive.

CHAPTER 27

The next day...

Amber watched the courtyard where Owen barked instructions at the men who were training. His affable expression and easy half smile were gone, replaced by the determined frown of a man who knew what he wanted and was going for it. He walked straighter, and he seemed bigger, as though he'd gained muscle since she'd seen him yesterday at the Bruce's council.

The gracefulness of his body was the same—the way he swung the sword, the way he ducked and lurched and evaded blows like a predator on the hunt. Collected. Controlled. Deadly.

She was relieved that the Bruce had let her go after yesterday. The fact that she'd stood up for herself and defended her position in front of the most powerful man in Scotland showed she'd changed, too. Owen still had her back and was ready to vouch for her and potentially lose everything he'd been fighting for, and that was life changing for her.

It was magical.

And it had hit her right in the heart.

The world had stopped. The universe had consisted of him alone. That handsome, strong, and brave Highlander with the kindest heart and the most beautiful body she'd ever seen. The man who'd stood by her side more times than anyone back in the twenty-first century.

Electricity crackled over her skin just from looking at him. This man had more courage in one drop of his blood than she did in her whole body, despite fighting in a war for years.

The man she loved.

Yes, she did love him. The understanding was like a small, personal sun had been born in her chest and radiated warmth and light into every cell of her body. Like she'd lived in darkness her whole life, and had finally come out into the light. Had finally found what was missing in her life.

Him.

Everything she was screamed that she loved him.

She wanted to tell him. He should know. She wanted him to know.

For the first time in her life, she wanted to be vulnerable and open. She wanted to tell him, even if he might not want to hear it. Amber marched towards him, determined. She wouldn't be stopped.

She'd make him listen to her.

"Owen!" she said as she walked through the muddy courtyard. Men glanced at her. Servants stared. Only Owen didn't react. "Owen!"

She came to stand by him and took him by the biceps, turning him to her. His mouth tight, he glared at her, making her stomach drop. Was she completely wrong about him? Wrong to believe he might have feelings for her, too?

No, she reminded herself. *Don't be discouraged. Just tell him how you feel.*

"What is it, lass?" he said with annoyance in his tone. The man he was training threw a curious glance at her.

Mind your own goddamn business, she thought.

"Can I talk to you, please?" she said.

Owen looked back at his student, clearly irritated. "Can it wait, Amber?"

She was digging her own grave. But she couldn't stop. "No."

Her hand was still on his arm, the touch so pleasant, like licking a spoonful of warm chocolate.

Thunder rumbled somewhere in the distance. The sky darkened. A cold gust of wind played with Owen's hair. It was wet from exercise, but not in a yucky way. In a sexy, masculine, please-take-a-shower-with-me way. She itched to tuck the strand behind his ear and reveal his handsome eyes the color of spring moss.

"Aye." He turned to the training men. "Lads, continue till the rain starts."

He reached out and gently removed Amber's hand from his biceps, making her gut churn.

Not good. Oh man. She was doomed, wasn't she?

He gestured towards the donjon. He was so cold, so distant, as though they hadn't lived through life-and-death situations together, hadn't kissed and told each other about the worst things that had ever happened to them.

She had a really bad feeling about this.

They walked through the courtyard into the tower. There was a storage room on the ground floor, with crates and sacks and barrels. The only light came from three torches on the walls. They stood facing each other.

Two strangers.

A maid came down the stairs. Oh God. Was Amber really going to pour her heart out to him while people were walking around?

"Can we talk somewhere private, please? In your room?"

"'Tis nae proper, Amber. We're nae marrit. Ye canna be with me alone in a bedchamber."

Amber snickered. "First of all, you and I have been in much more compromising situations alone. There's not much you haven't seen, or that I haven't."

Owen's eyes burned, and his jaw muscle flexed. Finally, some sort of reaction.

"Second of all, I don't care about my reputation. I'm no virgin, and I have no intention of getting married or whatever it is you guys save your women's reputations for."

Owen's face gained an intensity she hadn't seen before.

"I just can't talk to you while people are walking around like this. Please."

"Aye."

They climbed up the stairs to Owen's room, where Amber had been sleeping since they'd arrived at the castle. When they entered, the wind howled, sending a cold rush of air through the single window. It slammed the shutters closed. Another roll of thunder sounded, and lightning flashed through the slits in the shutters.

Owen looked around. "'Tis dark. I'll build up the fire."

He went to the fireplace and put wood in it, blowing on the dying embers. Amber's hands shook. How could she tell him? Did it even matter? God, was there a way to tell him that wouldn't result in him rejecting her?

"Owen?" she said.

"Hmm?" He took a poker and stirred the wood. Sparkles flew from the embers. The fire kindled and began burning brightly.

Be brave. Be strong.

"Please, look at me," Amber said.

Owen sighed and stood to face her, but he didn't come closer. Could she say it? *Just blurt it out.*

Her heart beat against her ribs like a fist, and she rubbed her damp, shaking palms against her dress. She was drenched in sweat.

"I..." She took a step towards him and locked eyes with him. His were so indifferent, as if he were looking at a tree instead of her.

"I'm thinking I'd like to build clocks. I repaired one with my mom when I was a teenager, and I enjoy engineering. And it drives me nuts that I don't know what time it is. So as soon as I know you're safe after the battle, I'll leave. Get hired somewhere as apprentice. Go from there."

He nodded, his face still a stone mask. Only the shadows of sadness appeared in his eyes. "Good. 'Tis a useful craft, Amber. I understand for a woman from the future it might seem normal, but I dinna ken if a man will agree to hire a woman as an apprentice. Besides, ye'll need to go to a big city for that, or a monastery. Clocks are a rare treasure."

It would be a profession, something to do in the Middle Ages, and yet she was still running away from the shadows in her past. She'd confronted the Bruce yesterday, and she'd started going through different options for potentially confronting the monster in the twenty-first century. But it still seemed hopeless.

"When is the battle?" she said.

"We leave on the morrow."

"Tomorrow." Her throat clenched. Lightning flashed again, wind rattled the shutters, and thunder exploded somewhere above their heads.

He might die tomorrow...

She took another step towards him and noticed with a painful realization that he tensed. He might have stepped back, too, if the fireplace wasn't right behind him.

"Owen, I—"

She felt as if she were in a ship out in the open ocean, lost in a storm. She looked into the abyss, wind flapping her skirt, death everywhere in the waters rocking against black cliffs sharp as razors. There was only one place in that sea where she could land and be safe.

Her stomach flipped, her breath caught and disappeared, and she jumped.

"I love you," she said.

His eyes widened, and his face distorted in a grimace of longing combined with physical pain, as though she'd just stabbed him in the gut.

"Ye—" he said.

"I love you. I've fallen in love with you."

He inhaled sharply, shakily, closed his eyes for a long moment, then swallowed, his Adam's apple working.

"Jesu, Mary, and Joseph..." he muttered and looked at her. "Amber, I dinna ken what to say."

"You go to battle tomorrow, and I just couldn't let you go without you knowing. I suppose I want to know how you feel about me."

Oh God, this confession was like pulling teeth out of a healthy mouth. Was a love confession supposed to feel this way? Wasn't it supposed to be all passion, tears of happiness, and hot kisses that promised a lifetime together?

He kept silent, only breathed heavily and eyed her as though he were a lion and she an antelope.

"Because if you feel the same about me, I won't leave. I'd like to stay." She paused. Was he really not going to say anything? His chest rose and fell quickly, his mouth pressed tightly in a thin line, and the sinews on his neck bulged. He looked as if he were having a stroke.

"Stay with you, that is. If you want me to." She inhaled and exhaled audibly. "Say something. I'm dying here."

"Lass..." His voice rasped like sandpaper. He shook his head. "I canna. I need to focus on the battle. I lead those men on the morrow. Their lives are my responsibility. I canna fail."

Amber frowned, confused. "What does that have to do with anything? I'm just asking how you feel—"

He crossed the distance between them in three broad strides and loomed over her. Lightning lit up the room and half his face. His eyes burned, devouring her, dark with a mixture of desire and pain and longing.

He took her face in his hands, the touch charging her skin like lightning had struck her.

"If ye want to leave and make clocks, ye should pack yer things and go."

The words lashed her worse than Jerold Baker's whip.

"There's nae future for us," he said.

Thunder rolled again, deafening her. Or did her ears refuse to work so that they wouldn't hear him?

"I canna be with ye."

She stopped breathing, heartache suffocating her. But why was he still holding her face in his hands, why was he looking at her like he wanted to kiss her? Why was he torturing her?

A battle was fought behind his eyes, desire and restraint. And then, surprising her, he leaned down and kissed her. It wasn't a passionate kiss. It was one full of despair and softness. There was no tongue, but their lips melded together. Then he stopped, fell to his knees and hugged her waist. He pressed his forehead to her stomach and stayed there, frozen. She couldn't move, was afraid to spook him, afraid to lose this strange, unexplainable moment of tenderness.

Rain hit the shutters hard. Lightning blinded Amber, and thunder shook the world.

Owen stood up and looked at her. "The kiss was a goodbye." He gave her a curt nod. "Godspeed, Amber."

And then he left, taking her broken heart with him.

CHAPTER 28

She loved him?
She loved him...
She loved him!

The words drummed in Owen's ears, louder than the storm thundering outside the great hall. The room was packed with warriors; Owen didn't remember it ever being so full. The king, his knights, and some of his Highlanders who could fit, were seeking refuge from the downpour. The rest of the army were camped in the tents by the castle walls, provided with as much food as the castle cooks could serve.

Owen stared at the bowl of stew in front of him. He stirred it mindlessly with his spoon. He had no appetite whatsoever. The room around him was loud with dozens of voices talking, laughing, singing.

He'd be leading these men tomorrow. But all he could think about was Amber.

Amber who loved him.

Owen had hurried out of his chamber as fast as his feet could carry him.

He'd run away. Run away from happiness. From the woman

he loved—the strongest, most beautiful and perfect woman in the world.

Head hung between his shoulders, Owen reached for the cup of uisge.

He'd run away so that he could stay focused and win the battle tomorrow.

Because he'd been an idiot in the past. Infatuated by beautiful women. Led by his horny cock. He'd always taken the easy way.

He'd not taken anything seriously.

Finally, he'd gotten what he wanted. He was leading the men into battle against his clan's archenemies, the MacDougalls, in a battle that might decide the destiny of Scotland.

A battle where he might die.

He didn't mind dying for his family and for what he believed in. But could he die without telling Amber how he really felt?

Could he die peacefully after he'd hurt her so much? He'd seen the pain he'd inflicted on her by saying nae. He'd hurt her so much he wanted to punch himself in the face.

But it was better this way, wasn't it? He'd promised he wouldn't get distracted, and this was him keeping his promise.

What he wanted most was to take her in his arms, lay her on his bed, and show her exactly how much he loved her. He wanted to scream, "Stay with me. Marry me. Be with me. Be mine. Forever."

Instead, he sat in the great hall, holding himself back with all the restraint he had. He hated himself for hurting her. She didn't deserve the pain he'd inflicted on her.

He needed to tell her. He needed to explain. If she was leaving soon, and he would never see her again, he needed to tell her he couldn't be with anyone.

Not just her.

Owen climbed off the bench and rushed out of the great hall into the stormy, flashing darkness outside. The wind hit him hard with a freezing wave of heavy rain. Thunder rolled over his head as he ran through the muddy courtyard into the donjon. He climbed up the stairs, jumping over two at a time. He opened the door without bothering to knock and stood still, rooted to the spot.

Amber was naked from the waist up. She leaned over a basin, frozen with an ewer in one hand, water still pouring over her arm. Her skin glowed in the light of the fireplace, golden brown against the white cloth.

So smooth, so inviting, so beautiful.

He was hard in an instant, pulled towards her as if she'd put a charm on him. Their eyes met. Her sweet, full lips parted. Fire played in her dark eyes.

She loved him. He was going to battle. He needed to explain to her why he couldn't be with her.

Only he couldn't think of a single reason.

Lightning flashed outside and brought him out of his stupor. He crossed the space between them and stood in front of her in a moment. She dropped the ewer and it splashed water on them both.

He didn't care. He took in every detail of her pretty face. Her long eyelashes, the thin scar above her eyebrow, lips so full and so desirable, he didn't think he'd seen anything more beautiful.

"God, help me," he whispered.

Forgetting everything, he plunged his hands into her hair and kissed her. The moment their lips touched, thunder cracked the sky above them in a deafening roll. Owen's blood turned to fire. She gave out a small, feminine whimper—a mixture of surprise and pleasure—and wrapped her arms around his back, pressing herself to him.

He kissed her with more vigor, only now realizing how starved he was for her. How much his soul, his body, and his heart had been deprived of her this whole time.

She melted against him, arching her back into him, one hand burying into his hair at the back of his head, pulling him closer to her.

He wanted her so badly, he was ready to go fight the whole world to have her. Her mouth was delicious and wanton, responding to his kisses with the same passion as his. His hands shook, and he could barely breathe.

He wanted to take her like an animal. Make her his. He picked her up and carried her to his bed. He laid her down and stretched beside her.

Watching him from under her eyelashes, she asked, "What about you not being the man for me? That you can never be—"

"All lies. All I can think of is ye. I burn for ye. I live for ye. I havena really lived before ye. I'm only starting to live now."

He moved his mouth to her neck and started kissing her there, inhaling the clean, feminine scent of her skin. He gently nibbled his way down her neck, and she rewarded him with a throaty moan that made him all but burst into flames.

Down he went, brushing his lips over her silky, perfect skin. When he reached her breasts, he had to stop himself to admire the dark nipples, the round, full, beautiful hemispheres. He reached down and bit her nipple.

"Ohhhh..." she cried.

"Sorry, lass, was that too much?"

"No. Oh, no. Do it again."

He obliged, taking the whole nipple into his mouth and sucking. She arched, her eyes rolling back. He covered her other breast his palm and began gently twisting the nub between his fingers.

"Owen..." she whimpered breathlessly.

"Aye, my sweet lass."

"Ah..."

The sound that was born from her throat sent a jolt of pleasure right into his groin. He'd never heard anything so beautiful and alluring. He wanted to bury himself deep inside her. Touch her everywhere. Dissolve with her.

Lose himself in her.

AMBER WAS IN HEAVEN. SOMETHING LIKE BLISS WAS BUILDING inside her. She felt like a wild creature, with no thoughts of yesterday, and no worry about tomorrow. Her body was free, living to follow its instinct.

Because she trusted him.

There was no fear. No worry that if she moved the wrong way, he'd get too excited and hurt her.

She wanted him. Everywhere. His mouth on her breasts, his skin on her skin, him buried deep inside her. She rolled from the bed and stood before him. Owen's eyes filled with awe, and her chest tightened with a sweet ache. She pushed the night shift down her hips.

"God almighty, there's nae a woman more beautiful than ye," he whispered, his eyes dark and intense and burning.

The words were like a caress over her skin.

"You're not so bad yourself." She let his gaze run up and down her body—for the first time in her life, she wanted to be this open. Wanted him to see her.

She went back to bed, climbing over him and straddling him. He sat up and took her into his arms. She winced as his hand touched her tender scars.

"Forgive me, lass," he murmured, kissing her chest above her breasts.

"It's nothing." She cupped his face. "Your touch is healing."

His eyes gained the dark intensity of malachite. "No one has ever said that to me before. I've been nothing but trouble."

"To me, you've been nothing but a blessing."

He kissed her tenderly, taking his time, as though kissing her was his only purpose in the world. When she was breathless, he pulled away and went back to her breasts. He sucked on the hard bud of her nipple, sending a jolt of pleasure through her. Hungrily, he sucked harder and took more of her breast into his mouth, his tongue working wonders around the nipple.

He moved to the other nipple and bit it ever so slightly, and a throaty moan escaped Amber. He slid his hand between her legs and brushed his fingers up and down her cleft. A tremor of pleasure ran through her.

"Does that please ye, lass?" he murmured.

"Yes..."

He released a masculine sound of satisfaction and slipped his fingers between her folds. He found her swollen, sensitive knot and began rubbing it gently up and down and in circles. Amber gasped as a small convulsion went through her.

He laid her gently on her back, then settled himself between her thighs and put his mouth on her. Sweat misted Amber's skin. A trembling moan escaped her throat. Her breath gusted as he spread her folds and licked between them. The flutters of his tongue teased her, driving her crazy. She dug her fingers into his hair, her pelvis bucking with the rhythm of his mouth.

He drove her to a delirious peak of blinding pleasure, making noises as though he was the one about to fall apart, not her. He inserted a finger inside her and began circling it, bringing her to the next level.

An intense, magnificent pleasure was building in her, and with a loud moan, she exploded and fell apart like stardust. She tightened in a ferocious convulsion, a blazing eruption, the orgasm cascading through her in a searing wave.

Owen climbed up and stretched out next to her, taking her into his arms.

"Ye're so bonnie when ye find yer release. I havena seen anything so beautiful as ye," he said, his voice a husky rasp.

Amber opened her eyes and met his gaze, breathless. Love for him spread through her, and she thought she'd never seen anyone so handsome. He eyed her with male pride and a hint of possessiveness. He traced a finger down her cheek, down her neck and towards her breast, circling her nipple gently with his knuckle. It hardened from sweet pleasure in response. The sensation shot straight through her core.

Amber bit her lower lip, surprised at her reaction. She'd just come, and yet she was ready to go again.

Yes, she thought in surprise, yes. She wanted him. She wanted him inside her, driving into her, owning her, making her his.

She reached out and kissed him, trailing her fingers down his hard body, over the crisp hair on his chest, his solid six-pack, and down to his erection. She circled the base of his cock, and he sucked in air with a hiss.

"Lass..." he groaned, his voice a hot warning.

"Hmm," she mused and began stroking his hardness up and down.

A low, animallike growl escaped his throat. "Christ, these sweet, sweet hands..." He looked at her with an insatiable hunger.

"I canna hold much longer, lass..." His voice was thick and husky. "I want ye... Will ye be mine?"

Be his...

"Yes."

He rose to his knees and with a lightning-fast movement, he yanked her up towards him. It was too fast. Too hard. For a brief moment, it reminded her of being with Bryan.

"No!" Amber straightened as a ribbon of fear twisted in her gut. "Not too rough."

"Lass, ye can trust me. I'll never do anything to hurt ye."

That was something she knew without a shadow of a doubt. Owen had protected her ferociously and saved her life several times.

"But you'll see my scars... They're ugly, and they'll never go away..."

He kissed her and pressed his forehead against her. "There's nothing ugly about ye. Ye're the most perfect woman that has ever walked the earth."

"But—"

"I want ye. Scars and all."

He turned her around so that she was on all fours and started kissing her scars so gently it felt like cool feathers stroking her heated flesh. The onslaught of emotion brought tears to her eyes. He turned her face to him and kissed her mouth. She reached out between her legs and took his cock. She directed it to her entrance and arched her back to let him inside her.

He pushed in and entered her, filling her.

"So soft and warm, lass," he groaned.

Every rock-hard inch of him stretched her. She expanded in all directions, warm and pliable, like modeling clay in his hands. He cupped both her breasts and played with her nipples, rolling them between his thumbs and index fingers, sending waves of sheer elation through her.

He glided in and out of her, his lips on her mouth, his hands on her breasts, naked lust in every stroke of his tongue. He made chest-deep grunts, like he couldn't get enough of her. And when she didn't think she could take any more, his hand went between her legs and pinched her clit. She shuddered and cried out as glorious waves of pleasure assaulted her from all sides.

She tilted her head back as he dove inside of her in long, unyielding strokes, continuing to fondle her swollen clit. She bucked back with his every thrust, her breath ragged.

Owen kept murmuring how perfect she was in his arms, how beautiful she was, how much he wanted her, and how he couldn't ever get enough of her. Time slowed, and Amber had the wildest sensation of falling into the center of the world.

Her body shook on the edge of a climax. Intense, out-of-control spasms began to build within her. A wave of pleasure slammed into her, and her muscles tightened, the spasms racking her body as she convulsed in white-hot, blinding bliss.

Owen stiffened, growled like an animal, and thrust into her, hissing her name. They collapsed on the mattress, warm and lax and hugging each other.

As Amber looked into Owen's eyes, the fog of naked lust

faded away, and her heart started to hurt again. Was he just hungry for her, or had this meant more?

She needed to know.

But as she opened her mouth to ask, he turned away, an expression of regret clouding his face.

CHAPTER 29

What the hell did I just do?

As the warmth and heaviness started leaving his sated body, cold realization crept into his mind.

He'd just done exactly what he'd promised himself he wouldn't do. Lose his head. Give in to distraction. He sat up, leaving the gorgeous, warm body of the woman he loved. His heart missed a beat at the loss of her touch, and his skin chilled.

"I shouldna have..." Owen said.

She sat up, too, gathering the blanket and clutching it to her chest. He couldn't bear to look into her eyes. Fear gripped his heart. This distraction might ruin any chance of a successful battle tomorrow. Now that he'd tasted this woman, knew what it was like to lie with her, to have her trembling and shaking around him, he never wanted to stop.

He knew he couldn't afford to let his feeling guide any of his decisions. He couldn't trust himself. His heart and his head always led him in two different directions.

"Why?" she said, hurt tight in her voice. "Was it bad?"

He turned to her. "Bad? That was the closest I've ever felt to God."

Her expression was part surprise, part understanding, part wonder.

"Then why?" she said on an exhale.

"Because I ken now, just like I ken that the sun will rise in the morn, that one time with ye will never be enough."

Amber inhaled a shaky breath. "Then what's the problem? I don't want us to stop at one time, either."

Owen slouched and ran his fingers through his hair. "My whole life, every mistake I've ever made was because I've let my cock lead me. I canna allow it now, not when the king himself has appointed me to lead his troops."

"That's all I am to you?" she said, her voice breaking. "A distraction? Something your cock can't resist?"

She may as well have just stabbed him with a knife right in his heart.

"Nae, *mo chridhe.*" *No, my heart.* "Ye're so much more. Ye're everything."

Her eyes widened. She inhaled shakily again and moved closer to him, just an inch.

"But 'tis precisely the problem. My heart is full with ye. And when my heart is full, and my cock throbs, my head stops working. I need my head to be clear on the morrow."

She groaned. "But it doesn't need to be like this. People love. They can be happy with someone and still focus."

"Lass..."

She covered his forearm with her hand. "I can help you focus. We can be each other's support systems."

Owen's heart ached. How he wished he believed this could be true. How he wished he could have everything—to have Amber and be the man he wanted to be. He reached for her and cupped her face, her bonnie, perfect skin like flower petals against his fingers.

But that was simply impossible for him. A life where he was a responsible leader and had the woman he loved in his arms was only a dream.

"'Tis good that ye leave on the morrow, lass. And I'm sorry if I hurt ye. But we canna be together. If I want to be a leader worthy of my king's trust, the leader my clan deserves, I canna let my feelings for ye cloud my judgment." He shook his head. "Based on my previous mistakes, I ken that can be lethal."

He thought of Kenneth, of Lachlan, of his grandfather. Of so many more lives lost in the feud with the MacDougalls.

"Owen..."

But before she could say something to change his mind, he stood, pulling his breeches up, then putting on his tunic and his shoes.

"Too much is at stake, Amber. The king's life, the lives of my clansmen. Yer life."

Amber stood and wrapped the blanket around herself, her shoulders and her arms still bare. God, she had the most beautiful, sculpted shoulders, the muscles on her biceps clearly defined in a feminine way. He itched to brush his tongue along them.

That was exactly why he couldn't stay.

Amber's eyes filled with hurt. "You know what, Owen. Go. Whatever. I never should have said anything about loving you. Now you feel like you've won, don't you?"

Owen frowned. "Won?"

"Yeah. Won. Got the girl. Because all you have are bullshit excuses. You've always been a player, haven't you? All you wanted was a piece of ass from another time, am I right?"

All wrong. All lies. But it was better this way, anyway. Better she believed that and left and never returned. He walked to the door, opened it, but turned to look at her for the last time.

"If I never see ye again"—his throat fought the onslaught of emotion—"I want ye to ken ye're the best part of my whole life."

He left, aching as though he'd just torn his heart from his chest and left it with her.

CHAPTER 30

They marched early the next day. As the castle got smaller and smaller in the distance, Owen finally allowed himself to look back at the tower where his bedchamber was, hoping he'd get a final glance at Amber. The window was heartbreakingly empty.

Leaving without saying goodbye to her was one of the hardest things he'd ever done.

The back of his horse swayed as he rode. The trees to the right rustled in the wind. Loch Awe to his left was stormy and gray with angry waves crashing against each other. The army was headed northeast, to bend around the loch's most northern point.

The Bruce was worried that MacDougall had planted scouts that would spot the army moving, so James Douglas had gone ahead with his archers to position them above where the ambush would take place.

Owen rode next to his father, Craig, Ian, and Domhnall. Their whole clan rode behind them, along with the Mackenzies, Camerons, Macleans, Mackintoshes, MacKinnons, and others. The king, Uncle Neil, and the rest of the knights rode in front of them.

The way was windy and cold after the storm of last night. The small army of men following him wasn't enough to make Owen focus on the task ahead. Even with the wind blowing in his face and the breathtaking beauty of Loch Awe that opened up in front of him, all he saw in his mind was the beauty of the woman he loved.

Time passed quickly, even though they made one brief stop to rest. The closer they got to the Pass of Brander, the tenser the men became, and the warier their faces grew.

They arrived in the early afternoon of the same day. Through the gaps between branches and leaves, Owen saw three birlinns, West Highland ships, on the river.

"MacDougalls," he muttered and pointed for his father and his brothers to see. He exchanged a glance with Ian and Craig.

The tension in Owen's shoulders released. The enemy was here, just like he'd known they would be. He hadn't let his king and his clan down.

"Ye were right, son," Dougal said, narrowing his eyes at the river.

"Aye," Craig said. "Well done, brother."

They reached the mouth of the Pass. To their right, the steep flank of Ben Cruachan started. Owen saw a small mountain path starting between sparse bushes and trees up the slope. He'd take that path with his men as soon as the king gave him the signal.

To their left, behind the bushes and undergrowth, there was an almost vertical drop into the river. The path before them grew more and more narrow. No one from the birlinns could see them through the bushes.

The Bruce stopped the procession, and they waited until a figure climbed down the steep slope of Ben Cruachan—the messenger from Douglas to say that he and his men were in position.

Owen rode forward to the king.

"'Tis all true," the Bruce said when he saw him. "There's an ambush. The road is blocked. Douglas has taken up his position. Are ye and yer men ready?"

Owen's heart beat hard against his rib cage. Was he ready? Was he focused? Would he lead his men to victory?

He inhaled deeply, his chest rising, his shoulders straight, his head high. Amber's face was in his mind, and her sweet voice rang in his head. But surprisingly, that didn't feel like a distraction. She gave him strength and power.

She gave him love.

Now he knew who he wanted to fight for. He wanted to fight to return to her. To tell her he loved her.

He only hoped he wasn't too late.

"Aye, Yer Grace," Owen said. "I'm ready. So are the Highlanders."

The Bruce's eyes shone with dark determination and a fierce, unapologetic drive for victory. "Then let's finish the bastart MacDougalls."

"Aye," Owen said. He would have roared, but they still needed to be quiet.

"Go. As planned."

"I'll see ye on the battlefield, Yer Grace."

They nodded to each other, and Owen rode back to his men. He halted and faced his troops. Some of them were on horses, too, but most were on foot.

"'Tis time," he said, trying to keep his voice as low as he could. "Those of ye on horses, leave them here. We go up on foot."

They dismounted and tied the horses' reins to the bushes and trees. The Bruce's troops moved forward, and Owen, his father, Craig, Ian, Domhnall, and the rest of the Highlanders took the barely visible, winding route up the slope.

Owen crouched as he went. Bits of gravel crumbled from under his feet. Bushes and undergrowth grew increasingly sparse the higher they went. He could see the Bruce and his troops down below as they moved. He could also see that the road in front of the Bruce was blocked by at least five hundred men.

Five hundred Englishmen. He saw the red flags with golden lions. Oh, he hoped de Bourgh was somewhere down there. He hoped today the man would pay for what he'd done to Amber. He wished he could be the sword that would pierce his heart.

If the Bruce got any closer, the MacDougalls hiding above would rain down arrows and boulders on him and his knights. Why was Douglas not taking action?

Then arrows flew from somewhere high in front of them, and pained cries and yelps came from the bushes. When the last arrows from Black Douglas landed and the war cry of his men came from above, Owen knew they were charging the MacDougalls.

It was his time to shine. His time to show to everyone he wasn't just a jester and a rebel. He wasn't just a sword. He was a leader.

"*Cruachan!*" Owen straightened to his full height and pumped the fist with his sword into the air.

"*Cruachan!*" the Cambel men echoed.

Somewhere behind them, other clans called their war cries, and they all mixed together in one Highland roar as they surged forward.

The time had come for the MacDougalls to pay. He'd fight for Amber. For Marjorie. For Ian.

He'd fight like the leader he should have always been.

There they were, the MacDougalls, at least a thousand of them. They were disoriented and already dealing with Douglas's force, which had crashed into them from above.

A man ran at Owen. He swung his claymore and it clashed with the man's ax. More men collided, and the ring of metal against metal pierced the air. Shouts and cries of pain came from below. Owen's opponent deflected his sword and slammed a shield into his face. Owen ducked, but the shield caught him and cut the skin on his cheekbone. He slashed his sword across the man's head, and the enemy fell, blood spraying everywhere.

Owen moved to another man, then another, fighting his way through the forces. Battle rage roared in his blood, searing his veins.

Two men came at Owen, one from either side. One swung an ax, the other a sword. Owen deflected the sword with a grunt and barely ducked the ax as it swooshed by his head. The swordsman raised his weapon to slash Owen's side, but before the man could lower his blade, a spear cut through his chest. He froze and fell, lifeless. A few feet away, Angus Mackenzie nodded to Owen.

The man with the ax stared at the corpse for a moment, his eyes wide. Raghnall Mackenzie appeared behind the man and tapped him on the shoulder. The man turned, and Raghnall punched him in the face, sending his head jerking backward.

He roared and launched at Raghnall, hammering at him with the ax as though he were a log. Raghnall deflected the ax, but the man turned his weapon slightly and hooked Raghnall's claymore between the ax's crescent blade and handle. He jerked Raghnall's claymore from his hands and lifted the ax for a lethal blow. Owen surged forward and thrust his claymore into the man's side. He grunted and fell, clenching the gaping wound.

Owen leaned down, picked up Raghnall's sword, and threw it to him.

Raghnall caught it and grinned. "My thanks."

More enemies came at them, and the battle continued. At some point, Owen was aware that Ian, Craig, and his father all fought by his side, too. He didn't know how much time passed—it all flashed in a blur of metal, blood, and distorted faces.

The fighting slowly descended down the mountainside as the MacDougalls were losing, caught in the Bruce's vise from two sides. And then there he was. With dark, cold eyes, and wearing English armor.

De Bourgh.

A low growl escaped Owen's throat. Oh, the man was his.

Owen half slid and half walked down the slope, his lungs burning, his muscles ringing with exhaustion.

It didn't matter. The man would pay for everything he'd done to Amber. Not to mention what he'd no doubt done to Muireach.

De Bourgh had just pierced the neck of one of the Bruce's knights when he saw Owen coming towards him. When Owen reached even ground, the man's eyes widened in recognition. He wore good, expensive armor. Owen had but his *leine croich*—a long, quilted coat—chain mail coif, and his helmet. But de Bourgh wouldn't leave this battlefield alive.

They lunged at each other, each with a roar, their swords clashing. De Bourgh was smaller but quicker than Owen. He struck at Owen from above and the side. Owen deflected his blade, but the impact resonated in his bone marrow. Another blow came from the other side, and Owen barely had time to meet the blade.

He needed to go on the offensive. He slashed his sword at de Bourgh's face, but the man deflected and crashed the hilt of his sword into Owen's face in a bone-crushing thrust. Owen heard the crack of bone and his head burst in white, blinding pain, sparkles flashing in his eyes. He staggered back for a moment, his arms searching for support.

De Bourgh grabbed Owen's coif and hauled him forward. He rammed his helmet into Owen's face, but Owen ducked and thrust his sword into the man's stomach. De Bourgh jumped to the side. The chain mail prevented the blade from running de Bourgh through, but he was wounded, and he yelled and staggered.

Roaring with rage, de Bourgh slashed low and opened Owen's thigh. Red-hot pain burned through Owen's leg, and he sank to one knee. De Bourgh raised his sword to serve the final blow, and Owen's life flashed before his eyes as he stared at the unyielding blade. He realized how useless his romantic conquests had been. How silly he'd been to rebel against his father to prove a point and draw attention. How much time he'd wasted arguing and joking around when he could have been enjoying precious moments with his brothers and his father.

Most of all, he realized how last night with Amber had been the best night of his life. How just that night was worth every mistake, every doubt, every quarrel, because they'd led him to her.

The love of his life.

And as the sword was about to reach his head, he closed his eyes.

I love ye, Amber...

CHAPTER 31

Amber ran, the sword in her hand a useless, heavy toy she had no idea how to use. As she evaded men fighting with swords and axes, she looked for Owen and wished she had a gun. Owen had never shown her any sword-fighting techniques, and she was out of place here.

The battle was in full swing. The iron tang of blood was rich in the air, and the sound of metal clashing rang in her ears. Men fought, wounded one another, and died. All around her were spilled guts, open gashes, and cries of pain.

War was war, even in a different century.

Her gaze bounced off the faces, looking for Owen's handsome features, his blond hair, his chiseled cheekbones, and short beard.

At least she hadn't seen him among the fallen.

Good. Good.

Earlier this morning, she'd watched the army march off north, and everything inside her had gone nuts. Her gut had burned, her breath ragged and erratic.

She'd known then that she had to join the battle. Not to fight for the Bruce, but to protect Owen. She just had this feeling, this dark, cold premonition. She had to go.

She'd run to Amy and asked for a sword and a horse. And then she'd galloped after the army. It hadn't been difficult to follow their trail. She was just afraid she was too late.

Suddenly, someone grabbed her braid from behind and yanked her back. Pain shot through her scalp. Someone wrapped a strong arm around her shoulders, blocking her arms.

"Why do you have a sword, woman?" the man said.

He turned her to face him, and she saw he was a young man about twenty years old, blond, and square-jawed. Surprise and lust spread on his face as he eyed her up and down.

"Do Scots have dark-skinned women now?" With another hand, he pressed the blade of a bloody ax against her throat, and the cold metal chilled her skin. "You're not going to fight me, are you?"

Fear gripping her limbs in its cold claws, Amber wriggled and thrashed.

And then she saw Owen.

And de Bourgh.

They were fighting, their swords flashing.

Oh, thank God he was alive. Now she just needed to get to him. To help.

"Go to hell, you jerk!" she cried, raised her leg, and stomped on the man's foot with all the strength she had. He yelled and let her go, but he grabbed her by the arm again. Fighting this guy would delay her getting to Owen.

Then a familiar figure appeared next to the man. He was tall and had black hair and battle scars on his face.

"Hamish..." she whispered.

Ragged sprays of blood stained his face and his coif, and cold battle rage flashed in his eyes, as though death looked at her. Last time she'd seen him, he'd helped them and saved Owen's life. Whose side was he on now?

"Here, Hamish, help me deal with her," the blond man said.

Hamish's eye twitched, his nostrils flared. He shoved Amber

away from the blond man and slashed his sword at him. The man deflected the blow, astonishment on his face.

"Go, Amber!" Hamish barked. "Now!"

Amber turned and ran towards Owen. De Bourgh had just raised his sword over his head and was about to kill Owen.

"No!" she yelled, her screech enough to distract the man.

With all her might, she stabbed her sword at de Bourgh, but the blade only jumped off the iron armor without penetrating it. At least she'd stopped the blow aimed for Owen's head. De Bourgh staggered forward and looked at her, surprise and annoyance distorting his face.

Owen stared at her with wide eyes.

Damn, that gash on his thigh didn't look good at all. "You won't take him from me," she growled at de Bourgh and threw the sword aside. The thing was useless in her hands.

Amber launched herself at him. When she'd almost reached him, she rotated and kicked him in the chest. The kick was powerful enough that he fell on his back.

The heavy armor made standing up a struggle, and she stood over him, her foot on his neck.

"I can crush your throat with one good stomp," she said. "Your airway will swell, and you won't be able to breathe. It's a bad death."

"You won't do it," he mused, seemingly unaffected by her threats. "You're way too noble to kill a man without giving him a chance to fight back."

"She is," Owen said as he came to stand on the other side of de Bourgh. "But I'm nae." He put the tip of his claymore next to Amber's foot on the man's neck.

He briefly met Amber's eyes, and for the first time, she was a little afraid of him. It was a lethal stare.

"This is for Amber," he grumbled and pressed his sword down.

De Bourgh made a gurgling sound, and his eyes bulged with fear as he died.

Amber closed her own eyes briefly, until she felt Owen collapse by de Bourgh's side.

"Owen!" she cried and rushed to him.

He was ashen. How had she not noticed that at first? He was losing too much blood.

"Ye came..." he whispered. "Why did ye come, lass? Ye should be far away from here."

"Shut up." She took a dagger from his belt and cut several long pieces of cloth from her cloak. The material was far from sterile, but it would have to do. "I need to stop the bleeding or you'll—"

She didn't finish. She couldn't allow herself to even think about it. He hadn't said he loved her. But she loved him. That was why she'd come. She loved him, and she couldn't stand the idea that he could die. She had to protect him.

It looked like she'd come exactly at the right time.

She pressed the cloth firmly against the wound, but it soaked through quickly. To elevate the gash, she bent his knee and propped his leg against the ground. She pushed more of the pieces of her cloak against the cut, but he was still bleeding. Oh no! The only way to stop it was to find the femoral artery pressure point. She tied a long piece of cloth around his thigh to keep pressure on the wound as much as possible, then she pushed her fingers against the artery in his groin and watched the cloth under her fingers like a hawk.

Owen chuckled. "Lass, I want ye, too, but shall we wait until we're alone?" His voice was weak and slow, as though he were drunk. She would've appreciated the joke if she wasn't rigid and cold from fear for him.

She kept watching the compress. "Don't you dare die, do you hear me?"

"Why would I die? I'd hate to go when I've only just found the woman I love."

"What?"

"I'd hate to go—"

"Not that." Her heart stopped beating and then launched into a gallop. "You love me?"

He smiled weakly and lifted his hand to touch her face. Around them, the chaos continued, but everything slowed down and blurred, as though an invisible, protective dome had landed over them.

"Aye." His eyes were ablaze, a deep green, the color of the ocean. "I love ye."

Amber's vision blurred, her eyes burning. "You idiot. Couldn't you tell me earlier?"

"Ye didna ken?"

"Of course not. I was afraid you were just using me for sex. That I was a conquest. That you were pretending to care about me."

"Can ye please kiss me? I'm having a little trouble moving."

"I can't move, or you'll start bleeding again."

She stared into his eyes, so handsome and so dear. The dearest set of eyes in the whole world.

"I love ye more than life itself," Owen rasped. "I need ye, lass, more than my next breath. Staying away from ye all this time was like pulling teeth. I hated it. But I needed to keep my head cool for this to work." He gestured to the battle.

Amber shook her head, tears of happiness springing free. "And it did work. Look. The MacDougalls are running in all directions."

Owen looked around and frowned when his eyes fixed on something. "Is that Ian and John MacDougall?"

∼

OWEN HELD HIS BREATH, WATCHING AS HIS GIANT RED-HAIRED cousin grappled with the treacherous MacDougall fifty feet or so away from them. Ian was huge, the tallest of all Cambels, but MacDougall was no small man, either.

The MacDougall was in iron armor, while Ian, like many

Highlanders, wore only a *leine croich*, and a chain mail coif around his head, neck, and shoulders.

The two exchanged blows, the MacDougall coming at Ian with heavy downward strikes like a blacksmith. Backing up, Ian took shelter from the storm of iron under his shield. His bone marrow must have been reverberating from the impact of those strikes.

"Come on, brother," Owen muttered.

Ian wasn't Owen's brother, of course not, but it felt like he was. And this was the chance for Ian to get his revenge for what the MacDougalls had done to him. Owen had sworn he'd avenge Amber, and it felt right having just done so. He wished that for Ian, too.

One of MacDougall's arms was still obviously weaker than the other, and clearly wasn't healing properly. The wound Marjorie had given him might just kill him yet by limiting his fighting ability. This would be her vengeance, too. MacDougall lowered his sword for a moment, and Ian used that pause to thrust his claymore towards the man's shoulder. MacDougall managed to bring his sword back up and deflect the blow. Ian struck again from the side, but MacDougall deflected that, too.

Ian was getting angry now. Owen had seen his cousin fight in the battle at the MacFilib farm, and knew he could be an animal. A lethal predator. He roared like a bear that had been poked too many times. He grabbed MacDougall by his breastplate and yanked him forward.

MacDougall's helm fell from the motion, and Ian slammed his fist into the man's jaw, and John fell. Ian grabbed an ax that lay nearby, and with a giant swing, he brought the ax down on the MacDougall's arm at the elbow, between two mail plates.

MacDougall's resounding scream made many men turn their heads in horror, and the remaining MacDougalls quickly scattered. Only a few ran towards Ian, ready to fight for their laird, who clutched the stump of his arm.

Ian raised the ax for the final blow when one of the MacDougalls threw a hand in the air in surrender.

"Please! Please. Mercy."

Ian stilled and watched the man in confusion. Then his expression flattened, and he let the ax fall. He looked at the MacDougall again. "Take him. Flee like the shite flies ye are."

The men grabbed John MacDougall under his arms just as Robert the Bruce came to stand next to Ian. The men tried to hurry, but it was impossible carrying an almost limp MacDougall.

"Wait," the king said.

They turned, and MacDougall opened his eyes.

"'Tis over for ye, John, ye ken?" the Bruce said. "I am the King of Scots."

MacDougall managed an expression of disgust. "Yer reign will never be just, the blood of thousands of yer countrymen is on yer hands." He spat bloody saliva at the Bruce's feet. "Ye murdered my kin."

"Yer whole family are treacherous bastarts. John Comyn was, and ye are, too. Now leave. Either ye die from blood loss, or ye live the rest of yer life a powerless cripple, always licking English arse and begging for protection. Both outcomes will be punishment enough for ye. Either way, I will give yer lands to yer worst enemies, the Cambels. Ye and yer clan are done."

John's lips pressed in a thin line, and his beard trembled in silent rage. The Bruce gestured with his head for them to leave and the men who supported the MacDougall hurried off with him.

Owen was sure they'd head towards the birlinns he'd seen earlier on the river.

The Bruce looked around at the last few enemies making their escape. "Get them!" he roared. "And let's take Dunstaffnage!"

That was where the old MacDougall, John MacDougall's sick father, resided. The men around the king pumped their fists in the air. Those who had horses mounted them, and those on foot gathered weapons and shields. Soon they all charged forward with victorious roars and cries. The Bruce noticed Owen on the ground and rushed over to him.

"Owen." He sank to his knees, worry in his eyes. "Oh Christ, man, ye're wounded badly."

"Is there a medic here? A healer?" Amber said.

"Aye. We have several. They'll stay and help ye, aye?"

"Thank ye, Yer Grace," Owen said.

The Bruce took Owen's hand between his palms. "Nae, Owen Cambel. Thank *ye*. If it wasna for ye, I'd likely be dead or defeated. Ye've done everything right, man. Ye've done everything right." He looked at Amber. "And ye, too, lass."

"Thank you," Amber said.

He looked at Owen again. "I must go and deliver the last blow, but once ye get better, I promise ye an estate in the Lorne for yer service. Ye'll be the lord of yer own house."

Gratitude and pride overflowed in Owen's chest. He'd done everything right. The MacDougalls had been crushed. He hadn't brought shame or embarrassment on his clan. On the contrary, the king was going to grant all MacDougall land to the Cambels.

And Owen had played a part in that.

"Godspeed, Yer Grace," Owen said, and the king smiled back at him through his beard. "Make them pay."

The Bruce nodded and walked away. He mounted his horse and spurred it on, heading west with his knights to the heart of Lorne.

Owen looked at Amber. He had everything now. Tiredness was pulling him into its dark, warm embrace. He was slipping away, and he didn't know if it was into death or an exhausted sleep. But wherever he went, he wanted to know Amber would not leave him.

"Stay..." It was all he managed to say before he sank into complete darkness.

CHAPTER 32

The next day...

Amber stroked Owen's pale cheekbone. He was as handsome as ever in the semidarkness of his bedroom. The fire crackled softly. The shutters were open and the sunlight coming through the window fell on his chest.

Amber sat on his bed. She hadn't left him for a minute since yesterday on the battlefield. A healer had treated the wound as best he could, and Amber had taken Owen back to Glenkeld together with several other wounded on a cart.

When they arrived, Amy had treated his wound again with fresh cloth she boiled. She'd also disinfected the wound with alcohol, an even stronger version of moonshine that was poisonous to drink. She had stitched the gash in his thigh, and now, thankfully, the bleeding had stopped completely. Owen had received the best medical care available given the medieval circumstances.

His lids fluttered, and he opened his eyes. Amber's heart

burst with joy when she saw him awake. He'd slept most of the night after Amy had stitched him up—a procedure during which he'd been awake and wheezing loudly through the pain.

"Amber," he whispered.

His eyes were still clouded from the pain potion Amy had given him.

Amber cupped his jaw, tears of joy prickling at the corners of her eyes. "Hey. How are you feeling? Do you want some water?"

He smacked his lips tiredly. "Aye. My damn arms feel like they weigh ten stone each."

"Yeah, it's the blood loss, buddy." She helped him drink. "Are you in pain?" she asked when he finished.

"Aye. My leg feels like 'tis on fire."

"You'll be okay. We got the bleeding to stop, which is the most important thing. He got you good."

"He paid for it."

"Yeah. He did."

"Any news of my father and my brothers? Ian?"

"They all went to Lorne with the Bruce. No news from there yet, but I saw all of them alive before they left."

Owen sighed, relieved. "Thank God. And thank God ye're alive. But how stupid of ye to show up on the battlefield." He paused. "Ye shouldna have come."

Amber swallowed. "Do you want me to leave now?"

He inhaled sharply and held her gaze.

Say no. Please, say no.

"Nae," he said, and she was suddenly light as a feather, like she could fly up into the air.

"I want ye to never leave. I want ye to be mine. Forever."

Her heart burst with love and gratitude. Every cell of her body lighting up like Times Square.

"Do ye want to stay with me?"

Her mouth opened to say, yes of course, there was nothing she wanted more than that.

And yet…

There was this nagging feeling in the pit of her stomach that she couldn't. That she still had a job to do in her time. That she'd never be happy and complete if she didn't take care of that last thing.

She'd stood up for herself in front of a king. She'd endured torture and imprisonment in the fourteenth century. She damn well could clear her name and stand up to a bully back in her time. She needed to stop the drug smuggler from hurting others, or she'd always be running away.

"I can't." Her voice dropped.

Owen stilled, and it seemed as if he'd stopped breathing. His eyebrows furrowed. And if it was at all possible, he seemed to pale even further.

"Why?" His voice was so low, it sounded like a raspy whisper.

Amber licked her lips. How she hated to hurt him like this. She could only hope he'd understand.

"I've been a coward, Owen. Back in my time, I ran away. I've learned so much about bravery and strength from you and because of what I've been through, but I'm still running."

Amber's throat clenched, and she swallowed a hard, painful knot. "I was terrified to stay and fight to clear my name. To fight a drug smuggler and murderer. To get justice for those he harmed."

Owen's mouth curved downward in a pained grimace. "Ye dinna have to worry about that, lass. Yer life can be here, with me. Can ye nae forget all that?"

She shook her head.

"I thought that was exactly what I could do. But seeing how bravely you fought, risking everything to save your king and your country... I should be like that. I'm a soldier, too. It's my job to risk my life for my people. And yet I cowered instead of rising to the challenge."

"Lass, no one would blame ye—"

"No, Owen. I love you, and I want to be with you. But if we want a chance of a happily ever after, I cannot let myself be a coward. You don't deserve that." She let out a quick breath and looked straight into his eyes. "I need to be my own goddamn hero."

"Aye. Be yer own hero, lass. Ye're verra much mine," he said with pride in his voice. Then he sighed, and his eyes clouded with sadness. "'Tis goodbye, isna it?"

"I hope you understand."

He gave several small nods, thoughtful. "I do. Course I do." He covered her hand with his. "I'm proud of ye, lass. Though I wouldna think any less of ye if ye just let all that go."

"Thank you."

He pushed himself up and sat straighter. He looked at one of the chests by the wall.

"Can ye do something for me?"

"Sure."

"In that chest, can ye find a small brown leather pouch and bring it here?"

"Okay."

She stood and went to look in the chest he'd pointed at. Sure enough, she found the leather pouch and brought it to him. He opened it and took out a ring.

Amber's stomach dropped, and her head spun like she was falling into the center of the earth. A ring...

"My mother gave it to me before she died, and I never thought I'd need it. Mayhap in yer time people are happy to be *dating* their whole lives, or however ye call it. But we're in my time. And in my time, I'd need to marry ye to make ye mine. I'll never want a wife who is nae ye."

He held out the ring to her.

"I want to marry ye."

Amber took the ring, and it burned her fingertips. It was a simple silver band with two curls coming together in front with a beautiful Celtic finishing.

Her eyes blurred, tears stinging them. "I want nothing more than to put it on my finger and say yes."

He swallowed hard. "But ye dinna plan to return." There was a finality in his voice.

"I want to return." Amber climbed onto the bed and shifted closer to him, trying not to touch his thigh. "But I have no idea if I can. No matter how hard I try, they still may put me in prison or..."

Or sentence her to death.

Owen's face fell.

Amber took his hand in hers. "Bottom line, I may not be able to come back." She put the ring in his palm and closed his fingers over it. "So I can't promise to marry you. I'm not selfish enough to make you wait your whole life if I can't."

"But ye want to marry me?"

"Of course I do."

He put the ring back in her palm. "Then I'll wait for ye forever."

"Owen—"

"Nae. Shush. If I can't marry ye, I'll never marry. And I'd rather spend the rest of my life hoping every day that ye come back than spend it with a woman I dinna love."

She let the joy of hearing those words seep into every cell of her being and shake up the swarm of butterflies in her stomach. She cupped his bristled jaw. "Then whatever happens, I won't stop until I can find a way to get back to you. I'll turn the world upside down if I have to."

She leaned down and kissed him, setting the butterflies into an erratic dance.

And as his arms wrapped around her, she begged time to stop so she could drink in these precious moments with Owen since they might very well be his last.

CHAPTER 33

Two weeks later, 2020

JONATHAN'S HOUSE LOOKED JUST LIKE AMBER REMEMBERED from when she'd visited five years ago. It was a light-green, two-story building with a big porch. Trees with Spanish moss grew around the house, its long silver streams hanging from the branches, creating an idyllic picture of a Southern family home.

Her heart squeezed in a dull ache. She'd missed her family. Her mother, father, and her three brothers. The house reminded her of where she'd grown up, and she wondered if Jonathan had chosen it for that reason.

She couldn't win this battle alone. She needed Jonathan. He had connections in the military and in the police. He could help her.

She had traveled back to the twenty-first century eleven days ago after a three-day journey on horseback from Glenkeld. She'd had no money, no passport, no phone, nothing but her clothes. Owen had given her his dagger, and Amy had suggested she take some pieces of jewelry to sell to an antiques dealer. That way, she'd have money to travel to the States.

Amber didn't want to ask for more help from Aunt Christel. She didn't want to put her in more danger than she already had.

She'd gone through the stone and walked to Fort William, where she'd sold the jewelry and the dagger. With his eyes shining, the pawnbroker had paid her 25,000 pounds. He'd agreed on the price too quickly, which made her think she could have done better.

Still, the money was enough to buy a fake driver's license and passport off the dark web that were good enough to pass through border control. It took a week for the ID to arrive, and then she was suddenly Susan Francis, born in New Hampshire and residing in Inverness.

She'd considered contacting Jonathan to let him know she was coming, but in the end, she'd decided not to in case his phone was bugged. One heart-stopping flight and two security checks later, and she was in New Orleans.

From there, she'd used a rental car to get to Nicholson, and now she sat in the driver's seat wearing a wig of short black hair in a bob cut. She'd gone for a suburban-mom look of checkered shirt, mom jeans, and comfortable but stylish sneakers. Just in case, she put on a baseball hat to hide a bit of her face.

When she saw Jonathan leave the house, her heart thumped. Her brother was older, and gray hair touched his temples. With age, he looked more and more like their dad. He was the same height, had the same build. His broad shoulders even slouched in a similar way, and her heart squeezed at the thought.

He got into his car and drove away, and as if in a thriller movie, she followed him. As far as she could tell, they had no tail. He arrived at the parking lot of a Costco, and when he got out of the car, so did she. With her pulse racing a hundred miles per hour, she jogged to him before he reached the entrance.

"Jonathan," she said, and he turned to her. His eyes widened in surprise, and he glanced around.

"What the hell, Amber? What are you doing here?"

Her back tensed and her gut tightened. Was this a mistake? Would he betray her like he had when they were young?

"Can we please talk?" she said. "Somewhere private?"

He muttered something, took her by the elbow, and led her across the road into a small park. The air was humid and rich with the scent of flowers. They sat on a bench looking out over a small pond. Strands of Spanish moss hung from the trees surrounding the water. Mothers pushed strollers, elderly women power walked, and teenagers rode bikes and skateboards along the path.

"Talk," Jonathan said. "You were all over the news a month ago. We went out of our minds searching for you."

The accusation in his voice surprised her. Had he been worried about her?

"So? Did you murder him?" he said.

Amber's nails bit into her palm. Did he even have to ask? Of course he wouldn't believe her. How had she ever thought he would?

"What do you think?"

"I didn't think you could, but you running and hiding didn't look very good."

A slow smile bloomed on her face. Her brother was on her side. "I was set up. That's why I'm here. I need your help to prove I'm innocent."

He sighed. "Why didn't you come sooner?"

"Because..." She fingered the nail of her thumb. "I didn't think you'd believe me."

"What? Why?"

"You know why. We haven't exactly been close. We never really were. I didn't think you'd want to risk anything to help me."

Jonathan sighed and massaged his face with his hands. "Yeah. Well, you're wrong. I have your back."

Her brother had always been intimidating. Their father had

treated him as his heir, the perfect son. The image Amber had helped him maintain when she'd taken on various little sins that he'd committed.

But now, looking him in the eye, she didn't see annoyance and arrogance like before. She saw guilt.

And love.

He covered her hand with his.

"I'm sorry for what we did when we were kids. I know it was wrong, but I was young and stupid. And cowardly. Dad loved you so much, I didn't think anything could change that."

She snorted. "What? Me?"

"You never stood up for yourself. You never said anything."

"I didn't say anything because I thought you'd despise me even more if I did. All I was trying to do was get on your good side. For you to see we were on the same team."

He sighed. "But we never were, were we?" He shook his head. "You know, after Dad died, I realized how many mistakes I'd made. How precious the time we had together was. I'd give anything to have him and Mom back."

"Yeah. Dad was the rock. Without him, the family fell apart. There was no one to protect us."

"Yes. There is." He squeezed her hand. "Me. I'll help you."

Hope and love filled her chest. She understood now how Owen must have felt when his father had supported him in front of the king. Her brother had her back now.

"Thank you." She squeezed his hand back, and tears welled in her eyes. "You have no idea what it means to me."

He smiled warmly, his eyes watery. He pinched the bridge of his nose and wiped the tears in the corners of his eyes.

"So tell me everything, and start from the beginning," he said, businesslike.

"Okay."

Amber told him about Bryan. How he'd gotten into debt with Jackson and become irritable and angry.

"I thought it was his pride," she said. "That he hated owing anyone anything. But now I think he hated being involved in a crime like that. Bryan was hotheaded, but he was a good man. I think he felt guilty that he was helping Jackson smuggle drugs into America."

"Can you remember any information? Anything he said that might help us find proof?"

"He mentioned Aman Safar, the owner of a teahouse in Kabul. But he didn't like to talk about anything he did with Jackson. He got so angry and agitated when I asked questions. Anyway, it got worse and worse, and one day he said something about making a deal with the devil."

Jonathan nodded thoughtfully. "Jackson."

"Yeah. I realize that now. Back then, I had no idea what he meant, and he wouldn't say. Soon after, we split up, but I saw him getting more and more irritable." She looked down at her hands. "Now I think he was trying to figure out how to get out of the business with Jackson. I should've been more understanding. But I thought he just wanted to get back together."

"Stop the guilt, Amber. If you'd known and tried to do something, who knows what Jackson would've done to you. Or if you'd even be alive now."

"Still. Maybe Bryan would be alive now."

"All right. Tell me what happened the night of the murder."

She told him, her hands shaking as she revisited the evening, every little detail. How she'd pushed him in front of everyone. How she'd discovered him later in a pool of blood. How he'd told her about Jackson. And how Jackson had found her there.

"And then what?"

"I pointed the gun at Jackson, tied him up, and ran away. There were a lot of witnesses that saw me being aggressive towards Bryan. It looked like I had killed my ex-boyfriend. Best case, I'd be charged for manslaughter. Worst case, Jackson could pin a murder rap on me and make sure I got the death penalty. Knowing him, I just didn't think there was any way for me to fight it. I felt so helpless. He's a freaking major, Jonathan."

"Yes. I know. It was stupid, Amber. By running, you signed your own guilty plea."

She sighed. "I'm here now. And I want to fight. First, I need to find Aman Safar. He might come forward and talk. If not, maybe we can find other evidence through him. Maybe even record Jackson in action."

Jonathan propped his elbows against his knees and leaned forward.

"No," he said. "Not you. I'll go."

"Jonathan, no. It's my mess."

"It is. But every time you go through airports and security, you're pushing your luck."

She opened her mouth to contradict him, but he waved his hand and continued.

"I know someone in the military police. They might give me an idea of what they have on you and what the charges are."

No. That was too dangerous. She didn't want to involve her brother that much. "Jonathan—"

He didn't let her continue. "Also, once we have any evidence, I think it might be wise for you to come forward. They'll arrest you, of course, but I'll bail you out. And if we get something on Jackson, we might be able to strike a deal. Kyle knows a stellar military defense lawyer."

Amber shook her head. This was too much. She thought Jonathan might give her advice or call someone for her. This was so much more. This was risking his own freedom.

"They might come after you for helping me…"

He looked at her with sadness in his eyes. "How many times did you take the blame for me and our brothers? It's time for me to pay you back."

CHAPTER 34

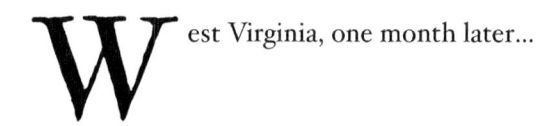

West Virginia, one month later...

Jackson's house looked just like him: large and imposing.

So this is where the drug money goes.

Her stomach in knots, her palms sweaty, she fought a battle inside her head. Despite her earlier bravado and her decision to come back and clear her name, her confidence and her bravery were gone. She wasn't sure this was the right decision. In fact, she'd started to think this was the biggest mistake she'd ever made. This pathetic attempt of hers might just ruin her life forever.

And she might never see Owen again.

She got out of the car. Her heart thumping, she shifted her shirt. The wire attached to her skin was scratching her.

"Jonathan, please don't let me down," she whispered.

Of course, she had no way of knowing if her brother could

hear her. She had to assume he could. They'd checked the connection, after all.

Deep breath in, long breath out. She marched towards the house. Jackson was currently on leave, which was a stroke of luck. She would've found a way to get to Afghanistan if he hadn't been, but that would've made this so much harder.

She had no doubt that news of Bryan's murder and her involvement had rushed through the base like a swarm of hungry rats. There had been newspaper articles and even TV coverage. A crazed woman killing her boyfriend on a military base was a newsworthy event.

Well, to hell with everyone. To hell with Jackson. That was what Owen would have told her. To hell with them all.

Her anger gave her strength. Yes, good. She needed that.

She also needed to talk to Jackson. She knew he was divorced and lived alone. After some surveillance, she and Jonathan also knew he didn't usually go anywhere or have any visitors during lunchtime.

She stood before Jackson's door and could hear his voice booming through it. Bastard. He was always loud, his presence palpable. Amber knocked vigorously.

He opened the door after a few moments, his phone pressed between his ear and his shoulder. The foyer behind him was large, with a big staircase leading upstairs. He filled the whole space, and Amber felt as if she were back in de Bourgh's torture room. There were likely no instruments of torture in the clearly expensive, modern house. But the man was more dangerous to her than all of Jerold Baker's tools combined.

"Just get your ass down here and show me your game," he said in his thundering voice. Then he erupted into laughter so loud Jonathan's eardrums must have popped from where he sat listening through the wire.

"I'll call you back," Jackson barked into the phone and then shoved it into the pocket of his jeans.

He looked like a lion sighting the weakest antelope in the herd, and an icy trickle of sweat snaked down her spine.

"Well, well, look what the cat dragged in," he said slowly and stood to the side.

"Major," she said by way of greeting and walked inside.

He shut the door with finality.

"What are you doing here?" he said. "Aren't you hiding?"

"I came to save you from the capital punishment that you deserve."

He raised his eyebrows, clearly amused, and came closer to her. Then he took his cell phone out.

"You have thirty seconds to tell me why you're here, and then I'm calling the military police."

"I have evidence against you, Ronald," she said. "Evidence of your drug smuggling, proof of your motive for killing Bryan. I've come to give you the courtesy of turning yourself in and getting a better deal. If you don't, I'll give them the evidence."

His amused expression fell for a moment, but it returned quickly. He looked her up and down, in an assessing way. Did he suspect she was wearing a wire?

"I don't know what drugs you're talking about. And me killing Bryan—that's just bullshit."

But he wasn't calling the police. He wanted to know what she had on him.

"Is it?" she said and walked farther into the foyer. That might be a mistake. He could try to cut off her exit. "Then why aren't you dialing?"

"What *evidence* do you have, Amber?" he said.

"You ship the drugs on C-17s. And you have a man on the inside who oversees the deliveries and doesn't let the dogs get close. I know all about Aman Safar, and I know all that because Bryan was helping you. He wanted out, and he threatened to report you. That's why you killed him."

He shook his head, his eyes turning dark and threatening.

"Princess, wake up. I want to know what the fuck you're smoking to get these ideas."

He wasn't budging. She had to up her game, which meant taking bigger risks.

"Okay," she said and took a few steps towards the exit. "I gave you a chance."

He moved so fast she didn't see him. He slammed his palm against the door, his mouth turning into a snarl.

"No. You haven't given me anything. What exactly do you have on me?"

Amber was rooted to the spot. Not exactly a confession, but she was getting closer. Sweat dampened her skin. She looked straight at him. Man, she had much less courage than she was trying to show.

"Aman is ready to come forward and give a statement against you."

His expression went blank. "What?"

"He made a deal with the US government. His family is going to be moved to the US while he serves time in prison. He's terrified of you."

"You're bluffing."

She cocked her eyebrow. "Do you want to try and find out?"

He shook his head. "I wasn't born yesterday, sweetheart. You can't prove shit."

"Then remove your hand and let me go."

His palm gathered into a fist on the door, his knuckles white.

Instinctively, her body tensed. He was going to snap. But he might snap physically at her and not confess, and she needed him to say the words. Those words would set her free.

This wasn't working. She needed to up her game even more.

"Everyone in your drug organization is terrified of you," she pressed. "Bryan was ready to rat you out. Now Aman. You're done, Ronald. Because you can't shut Aman up. You can't kill him like you did Bryan. The only chance you have is to come forward."

He narrowed his eyes. "How did you get here?"

She blinked. "What?"

"You're in hiding. No one knows where you are. You were last seen in Scotland. How did you cross international borders? Fake passport?"

"Yeah. Fake passport. Why?"

"Did anyone help you get this information?"

Wires connected in her brain. He wanted to know if anyone knew she was here. In case he wanted to make her disappear.

"No," she said, hoping it would ease his suspicion. "No one knows."

Something changed in his eyes. In one slick motion she almost missed, he grabbed her by the throat and slammed her against the door, choking her. Her throat clenched, pain tearing it apart. She desperately gasped for air, but only gagging sounds came out. In an onslaught of panic, she clawed at his hand around her throat, but it was useless.

"You should have stayed away, princess. You should have hidden like a bug under a rock."

Her lungs were burning. Her vision was going black. Jonathan was probably going crazy listening to her choking. No one except him knew she was here. Everything was a bluff, orchestrated to get and record a confession out of Jackson.

And she was losing. She was about to die. For nothing.

"Ah," he said, pressing his fingers tighter around her neck. "Look at you. You have the same look of helplessness Bryan did just before I pulled the trigger."

Her mind was going blank. She was oxygen-deprived, and judging by the pain, he might have crushed her airway completely.

She'd gone too far. She was dying.

She'd never see Owen again. Her fiancé. The man who had brought happiness to her life, even in her darkest moments.

And then, as though on a distant whisper of wind, she heard his voice.

Be yer own hero, lass. Ye're verra much mine.

She had to live. She had to choose to live. She almost had Jackson.

For Owen.

Gaining strength from the earth, something she'd learned from kung fu, she reached deep inside herself, because in every cell of her body was love for Owen.

She kicked Jackson right between his legs.

He released her and doubled over, stepping back.

She coughed, desperately sucking in the air. She held on to the door, her legs barely keeping her up. Breathing was painful, but she needed to get oxygen back into her system. Her work wasn't yet done.

He was still clutching his groin but was already standing straighter. He lurched to a console by the wall, opened a drawer, and took out a gun.

Amber didn't have time to waste. Her body was recovering, and she took a step to give herself room, rotated, and kicked him in the face. He fell back, and she took his gun and pointed it at him.

He threw his arms up in surrender.

"You're done now, Jackson," she choked out. "Jonathan, did you get all that?"

Her phone vibrated in the pocket of her jeans. She answered it with one hand.

"Hey, sis. You all right?"

"I'm fine," she rasped. Her throat was killing her. "Did you get all that?"

"Yes. The military police are on the way. Erickson, my contact, says it's enough for a confession. You're free."

Amber exhaled, relief flooding her system like sunlight. She'd cleared her name. She was free. And this guy would be behind bars, getting what he deserved.

When the military police arrived and arrested Jackson, Amber went out of the house and breathed in clean air. She watched as they loaded him into a car, and she took lungfuls of air, letting the freedom seep into every cell.

The police car drove away, and someone walked towards her —a female figure in a green cloak... Sìneag? A chill and a thrill ran through Amber. What did she want? Where had she even come from? It looked like she'd emerged from thin air.

She beamed as she approached Amber, dimples forming in her rosy cheeks. Could anyone else see her? There was no one around. Her brother had gone with the police to hand over the evidence and the taped confession. The suburban street looked calm and ordinary. Seeing Sìneag here made Amber's head spin.

"I see ye did well, lass!" Sìneag said when she came to stand by Amber.

"Um. Thanks." Amber frowned. "Why are you here?"

Sìneag looked around in wonder. "I love the United States of America. 'Tis so much more interesting than wee ol' Scotland. There's so much delicious food, things I havena even heard of in two thousand years."

Amber's skin chilled. Two thousand years?

"Speaking of..." Sìneag looked Amber over. "I have something important to say to ye. A warning." Her eyes flashed mischievously. "But in the best Highland tradition, I'll only give it to ye if ye bribe me first with something delicious and unusual." She swallowed. "Well. Anything, really."

Amber's eyebrows rose to her hairline. "You want some food in exchange for information?"

"Aye."

Amber shook her head with a smile. "The fact that you're a faerie may not be the weirdest thing about you, Sìneag." She walked to her car and opened the passenger door. She found a bag of peanuts in the glove compartment and gave it to Sìneag. "There you go. Food. Now what did you want to tell me?"

Sìneag's eyes practically sparkled. She opened the bag and stared at the contents in wonder.

"Those are nuts," Amber said. "Salted peanuts."

Sìneag took a peanut out and studied it in her hand. Then she put it in her mouth and chewed slowly, crunching with her eyes closed.

"'Tis delicious." She looked at Amber, and there was sunshine in her eyes. "Thank ye." She put another nut in her mouth and chewed.

"So? What did you want to say?"

"Oh. Aye. Now that ye conquered yer enemy, what do ye plan to do?"

"Go back to Owen, of course."

She smiled. "Good. But I must warn ye. 'Tis the last time that ye can cross the tunnel of time. A couple only gets three times."

Amber bit her lip and nodded. Three times... This would be her last time through. Goodbye to the twenty-first century, goodbye to her brothers, to her friends. She'd never eat peanuts, she'd never be able to go to a doctor, have her teeth cleaned, have a cup of coffee. If she and Owen had any children, they wouldn't get vaccinated or go to school.

"Does it change anything?" Sìneag asked.

Did it? She could still stay. Live her life here in the relative safety and stability of the modern world.

And howl every day inside, missing Owen. This life, full of conveniences, of being warm and sated, would be empty without him. She'd never respect herself if she chose comfort and material possessions over love.

"No," Amber said, and she knew in her gut this was the right decision. "I belong with Owen. You were right. He's the love of my life, and the man I'm destined to be with."

A smile bloomed on Sìneag's lips, so wide it threatened to cut her face in half. She sighed happily and popped another peanut in her mouth.

"Another couple found happiness thanks to me," she said. "Yer world is so much more fun than the land of faeries." She cupped Amber's jaw, and her touch was cool and sent a small vibration through Amber that reminded her of standing next to a giant speaker at a concert. "I'm a faerie, and love for me isna possible, so I live vicariously through ye and others. Now go to him. Be happy. And I'll look for another couple to torment."

Amber opened her mouth to ask why Sìneag would never be able to find love, but the faerie disappeared.

Amber sighed and shook her head. What a beautiful, wonderful, strange creature. Sìneag may be her favorite person in the world after Owen.

Because she'd brought them together. And now Amber could finally go to him.

CHAPTER 35

Inverlochy Castle, three months later...

OWEN PACED THE UNDERGROUND STOREROOM. HE THREW periodic glances at the rock.

"The damned rock," he mumbled.

He'd been visiting here every day since he'd arrived at Inverlochy a moon ago. And every day, it remained still and refused to bring Amber back.

A nerve on Owen's cheekbone kept twitching. Could he do something? What?

He'd asked that question hundreds of times every day since Amber left. And the answer was always the same. Nothing. He couldn't do a damn thing to help her or to find out if she'd been successful in her mission.

And even if she had been successful, what if she'd changed her mind? What if she'd decided he wasn't worth leaving her comfortable and safe life in the future for?

A hundred knives carved into his heart at the thought. Even

though he'd told Amber he was happy to wait, he hated feeling like this. Helpless. At the mercy of destiny.

His whole happiness depended on this rock. This silent, cold stone.

He stopped himself from kicking the damn thing and walked out of the storeroom. He climbed the stairs and went out into the courtyard.

It was winter now, and the ground was covered with a thick layer of snow. The atmosphere had changed in Inverlochy since the Bruce had won the Pass of Brander. There were no more enemies in Scotland.

The MacDougalls had run to England, so had the MacDowells of Galloway, and the Comyns. There was still no peace with England, but that was a distant threat now. The Bruce had relaxed his forces in Inverlochy, and there were fewer soldiers here now, though the castle was still fortified and prepared for whatever was to come.

The Bruce had delivered on his promise and bestowed all MacDougall lands to the Cambel clan, which had suddenly made his family one of the most powerful clans in Scotland. Like the Bruce had promised, Owen had received an estate in Lorne, which he still hadn't visited. As soon as he'd gotten better, he'd ridden to Inverlochy. There was no treasure or estate in the world that would make him miss the arrival of his bride.

After Kenneth's death, Alexander MacKinnon had become the constable of the castle, and allied clan members could come here for a rest during their travels.

Owen marched through the courtyard to the opposite wall. He'd suggested that while he was living here, he'd serve as part of the garrison. But he didn't tell anyone he was waiting for Amber.

The air was crisp, and the sky was blue and cloudless. The sun shone brightly, and the snow was such a brilliant white that Owen squinted as it hurt his eyes.

He entered the tower to climb the stairs and walk onto the wall to keep watch. Despite the more relaxed situation, they still needed to keep an eye out for any threats. Who knew if the English would decide to attack? There was no signed peace treaty yet.

Angus and Raghnall Mackenzie came to stand next to him. They watched the white vastness of the Highlands spreading before them and exchanged a few words. Then Raghnall glanced behind Owen, and a look of surprise and admiration appeared on his face. With a tightening in his heart, Owen turned.

His heart stopped. She stood there before him, alive and well and more beautiful than he remembered. She was dressed in a long, woolen cloak trimmed with fur. Under it, she had on men's clothes: leather breeches that hugged her legs and tall boots. She wore a white woolen hat, and a single braid came out from under it.

Her eyes were misted with tears. "Owen..." she whispered, and he felt like his body was filled with air instead of blood, and he was about to soar.

With the brightest smile, she crossed the space between them. But before she could hug him, she slipped. He caught her before she could fall.

"Thanks," she muttered. "Damn ice."

Without another word, and without paying attention to the Mackenzies and others staring from the courtyard, he brought her closer and hugged her.

His bride...

"Lass," he whispered, inhaling her delicious scent, that exotic, mysterious sweetness of spices and fruit he knew only from her.

She felt both strong and fragile in his arms. She wrapped hers around his neck, and he felt something warm and wet against his cheek.

He looked at her without letting her go. She was crying. "Amber?"

"I'm okay," she said. "I'm just so happy to see you... There were moments I thought I'd never— And I thought maybe you'd change your—"

He swallowed her words with his kiss, plunging into the delicious feast of her lips. The world stopped existing, everything disappeared except for him and his bonnie bride. She softened against him, setting his blood ablaze. He deepened the kiss, hungry for her, his heart beating painfully hard.

When he broke away, and she sagged against him, breathing harder, he said, "I was going mad waiting for ye. What took ye so long?"

She shook her head once and chuckled. "You know, trying not to get caught...or killed. Jackson almost choked me to death."

Owen felt blood leave his face. "What?"

She grinned. "It's okay. I won. You saved my life, again. I heard your voice in my head, and it gave me the strength to fight. I kicked him in the balls. He's in prison now. So whatever you did telepathically, thanks."

"Ye're welcome, lass. Didna ken I did anything except tear my hair off my head. Any longer, and ye may have come back to a bald man."

"I'll take you in any shape and form."

"I almost kicked the rock into dust in frustration. 'Tis probably a trench down there where I paced daily."

She laughed, and the sound reverberated in his chest, melting the last tensions, reservations, and fears. She was truly here, truly in his arms.

"Come, lass." He took her by the hand and led her down the stairs. "Ye must be freezing. I'll warm ye up. There are fewer warriors in the castle now, so more spare rooms."

They went down the stairs and reached the courtyard.

"I'm so glad you waited," she said.

He looked around to see if anyone was watching, then he slowly ran his hand down her cloak and took a handful of her arse, though it was mostly fabric. "Let me greet ye properly, like I've wanted to all this time without ye."

"And you think I'll just stay with you in the same room without being married?"

He stopped and stared at her in astonishment. "What?"

"Just kidding."

He shook his head, and in one swift movement, he picked her up and threw her over his shoulder. Amber squealed and beat against his back with her fists. Without a care about who saw them, he clapped her arse. "Jesting, huh? Dinna give me—what did ye call it—a heart attack?"

"Let me down!"

"In a moment, lass. When ye're in my bedchamber, and I've barred the door. I wilna let ye out even if the English come knocking again."

He reached the small tower and quickly climbed the stairs to the first floor with his bonnie, precious load on his shoulder. Inverlochy Castle was a royal castle, and Owen took her to the room designated for honorable guests. It was where the Bruce would sleep should he come to stay. A fire burned in the fireplace, and it was warm and dry in the room. He set her down on the bed and stretched on top of her.

"I missed ye, lass."

She ran her fingers through his hair. "I missed you, too."

He kissed her deeply, settling his weight between her legs. He was already hard and aching for her. He undid the fastening on her cloak.

"Was it hard to say goodbye? To leave everything behind?"

She bit her lip. It was swollen from the kiss, and he ached to take it between his own teeth.

"My brother Jonathan helped me clear my name. Without him, it would never have worked."

"Aye. Kin."

"While we worked together, we grew closer than we've ever been. In the end, it was hard."

"Did ye tell him ye were marrying a man born hundreds of years ago?"

Her smile was sad. "No. He'd put me in a hospital for the mentally ill or something."

"So what *did* ye say?"

"I said I was going to travel the world. Then I arranged for my aunt Christel, who lives near Inverlochy, to send him a letter a month from when I left that explains the truth. I wrote that he may think I'm insane, but he should know I'm happy, and that I found love. And that love is worth going crazy for."

He kissed her again, loving her, appreciating her like never before. He kissed her chin, then down her neck, inhaling her scent as though he wanted to make her a part of his bloodstream. He ran his hands down her body, undid the belt on her tunic, and went under it with his hands, brushing his fingers up her soft skin.

She threw her head back and arched into his touch. He pulled her tunic up and marveled at her beautiful body.

"How lucky I am." He kissed the undersides of her breasts. "Ye're a woman like nae other. Made of pure wonder and brought to me through time by magic."

She stilled, looking at him with something like reverence in her big eyes.

"Mine," he whispered through a hard knot in his throat. "Ye're my wonder."

She sniffled a little, and he came back to her breasts. "So beautiful," he said and took her nipple in his mouth.

He sucked and licked it, fondling the other one with his fingers.

"So soft," he whispered, tracing his lips down her stomach.

"So delicious." He undid the fastening of her breeches and pulled them down, then with some difficulty unlaced her boots and pulled them off, too. He stared in awe at her graceful hips, at her stomach, and at the triangle of dark hair in the apex of her thighs.

His cock twitched, hardening and aching. He pulled her breeches off, nested between her spread legs, and slowly kissed her thigh from knee to groin while kneading and massaging the other thigh. She rewarded him with a low, sweet moan and the curling of her toes. He reached her sex and inhaled her scent, so feminine and deliciously wanton.

Desire for her set his blood on fire. He spread her folds and put his mouth on her sex, licking and suckling her sensitive bud. She was already wet and tasted divine.

She started making small whimpers of need, like a kitten, and he felt a surge of a male satisfaction that he was the one giving her this pleasure. He wanted to give her more. He wanted to give her everything.

To be everything for her.

Everything she'd ever want and need.

He inserted a finger inside her warm wetness, and she clenched around him. He craved for her to clench like that around his erection, to plunge into her silky depths and feel that she was his. That she belonged to him.

He began moving his finger in and out of her, but she suddenly sat up. She was flushed, and her full lips were parted. She panted, her eyelids half closed, her eyes like a dark night.

"No," she said. "That won't do."

"Nae?"

"You. I want you. Not your finger. Inside. Now."

He shook his head with a soundless laugh. "Happy to oblige, lass."

He pulled the tunic over his head and unfastened his breeches. She eyed him with appreciation, her gaze moving slowly up and down his body. He loomed over her, his hands on either side of her head, and supported himself on straight arms. "Lass, stop looking at me like I'm food, or I'll blush," he purred.

"You're better than food." She slapped him on his arse and pressed on his hips, urging him to come closer. "You taste better, and nothing brings me as much pleasure as you." She dug her fingernails in his arse. "Now prove it."

"I'll need to talk to ye about yer manners." He palmed his erection, but she brushed his hand away and took his cock in her hand. She positioned his tip against her entrance, and he groaned from the hot, wet feel of her.

"Is yer back healed enough for this?" he said.

"Yes, it's fine." She wriggled against him, her sleek movements driving him wild. "Your leg?"

"I'll live."

"Good. Now take me."

He looked deeply into her eyes. It was amazing how much they'd survived together. How much they'd both changed. And how much happiness there was still to come.

He thrust into her, pleasure shooting from his toes to the very tips of his hair. She moaned and arched her back, closing her eyes. She clung to him, wrapping her arms around him, her fingers digging into his muscles.

He started driving into her, his desire wild and hot. He was as deep as he could go. She wrapped her legs around him, and he buried his face in her neck, inhaling her scent. He breathed heavily, unevenly, his heartbeat erratic.

She wriggled under him, meeting each thrust like a perfect wave. They climbed towards the climax together, sweat misting their skin. Her moans of pleasure spurred his own hunger. Her head was thrown back against the mattress.

And then he was there. He arrived at the peak with her, bucked, and lost himself into her body, wild and furious waves of pleasure crushing him. He dug his fingers into her hips, feeling her clenching and unclenching around him, her body shuddering and tensing under him. She cried out his name like a prayer, and he tried to hold on to the reality that this divine woman, a goddess from another time, was his.

This happiness, this expansion of his heart and whole body,

was going to be his future. His love for her opened him up and filled him.

She was his first love. She was the first woman to touch his heart. And as long as he lived, his heart would whisper her name with every beat.

EPILOGUE

Six months later...

The road was quickly disappearing under the horses' hooves. Amber thought that the Pass of Brander couldn't be more beautiful in this weather. Owen rode next to her and eyed everything with a relaxed alertness, ready for any threat.

The summer air was warm, and the sky was blue, the sun making the colors around them brighter and more vivid. River Awe, murmuring to their right, was brilliant, almost sapphire blue, and the mountains around them were lush with greenery. A breeze touched her skin and brought the scent of river water, grass, and flowers. The air was alive with birdsong and gently rustling leaves.

They were on their way from Owen's new estate, Kinleith, where they'd spent the winter and spring, to Glenkeld. After that, they would continue down south. They had no destination and no goal. Amber had suggested they might travel around

Europe, and Owen, who'd never been anywhere apart from Scotland, loved the idea.

The secret of Amber's true origin, as well as Amy's and Kate's, was kept safely within a close group of people. The past six months had been blindingly happy. She'd never thought she could be this joyful and content.

And now that she knew she could stand up for herself and those she loved, now that she knew how David must have felt when he'd confronted Goliath, she knew she and Owen could do anything as long as they were together.

And they'd decided what they wanted together was adventure.

They'd gotten married on his new estate a month after she'd returned. Although she didn't want to live the life of a housewife, she'd enjoyed a few months of her and Owen in their own little cocoon, settling into the new house, and starting things their own way.

She'd bought a few books on ancient clocks and clockmaking back in the twenty-first century. Mechanical clocks had just recently been invented and were expensive and only available in cities. Amber was curious to see if she could make one of her own. Making clocks meant reconnecting to her mom. She knew that every time she worked on one, her mother would be right there with her.

When they descended from the Pass of Brander and reached the flat, sandy shore of Loch Awe, Owen said, "Do ye feel like making a stop? I'll catch ye a nice fish and roast it over the fire."

She knew that tone. That little smirk in his voice meant he had something in mind. Something she'd love, and he didn't want to spoil the surprise. She knew that was the perfect moment to play along.

"A nice roasted fish sounds great."

They dismounted and settled on the small beach. Owen started a fire and began undressing, and Amber stilled, admiring his powerful body, his muscles playing as he moved. She'd been married to him for a while now, and he still stole her breath away.

He removed his pants, too, and glanced at her over his shoulder.

"I don't think you need to be that naked to fish." Amber chuckled. "Though I'm not complaining."

He walked to her, and she admired his long legs coiled with muscle. "Come swim with me."

Amber stood up. "Swim? I don't really feel like it. The water must be cold."

"I'll warm ye up, lass, dinna fash."

"No, thanks." She took a step back. "I'm good and warm here."

He stepped forward. "Lass..."

She squealed and darted. He reached her in two large steps and caught her by the waist. In a practiced move, he threw her over his shoulder and walked to the water.

"No, Owen! I don't want to change! Owen, no..."

He walked into the water until it reached his ankles and then stopped. "If ye dinna want to get yer clothes wet, ye better undress, lass. Either way, ye're going into the water with me. I have something in mind that ye'll love."

She grunted through a smile. "All right, all right. There's no changing your mind, you stubborn Scot."

"'Tis exactly right." He put her back on the shore, and she undressed under his watchful eye. She didn't need to worry about the cold. The sun was warm, but mostly, the heat in Owen's gaze was enough to make her feel as if she were on fire.

"Good lass." He smacked her on her behind possessively, and she hid her smile at the look of male pride on his face. "Come on." He picked her up and took her into his arms like she weighed nothing. With a satisfied grin, he walked into the loch.

Amber hissed as cold water touched her behind. Owen kissed her while still walking, and she melted, forgetting everything. Then they were deep in the water, and he moved her so that her arms were wrapped around his shoulders and her legs around his waist.

The water was not cold anymore, and swimming in it with Owen felt wonderful.

"Now see what a nice fish I caught," he said.

"Just don't roast me over the fire."

"Oh, nae. But I do have a spit I'd like to put ye on."

His erection brushed against her butt cheeks, hot and hard.

"Well," she murmured. "I don't mind being put on that spit."

She kissed him, and his lips were soft and giving but also demanding, and she was more than happy to grant him whatever he wanted from her. Their tongues met, gliding, sliding, playing, and teasing until they were both breathless. Amber was burning with need, and the strange sensation of being weightless in the water added an edge to her excitement, a new sense of relaxation and softness.

"Gentle and slow?" he asked.

"Oh no, baby. Hard and fast. This water thing is amazing."

She grinded her pelvis against his hips to show him she was ready, and he guided himself to her entrance. In one hard plunge, he was deep within her, and she shifted her hips to meet him.

She gasped as he stretched her to the limit, his heat invading her. He was diving into of her, his breath gusting hard against her throat. She welcomed him even deeper, taking him all the way to the root.

He began to move faster, gliding in and out, precisely and relentlessly. Every rock-hard inch of him brought her pleasure. He whispered how good she felt to him, how he never wanted to stop, how beautiful she was.

In no time at all, she was coming. A violent wave came over her, and she yelped at its intensity. She bucked and tilted her head back as convulsions slammed through her.

He stiffened and cried out her name as if he were unraveling and couldn't stop. They shared a moan, breathing as one. When they both finally stilled, Owen held her in his arms, and she enjoyed the scent of him, the feel of him around her. She took in the unprecedented beauty of the nature around them. No noise of cars, no white stripes from airplanes in the sky, no smell of gasoline. No pollution.

The loch and the hills and the trees were pristine and untamed. And she felt as if she were part of them, dissolving in their beauty.

"I'm so blessed," she said, looking at him. "You are the highlight of my life, the best thing that has ever happened to me."

He brought her closer to him. "I love ye, Amber."

"I love you, too," she whispered and kissed him.

They swam a little in the loch, then got out and ate some bread and cheese they had with them. It was already afternoon, and they wanted to reach Glenkeld before nightfall. The whole clan was gathered there to celebrate the official bestowment of Lorne to Neil Cambel, Owen's uncle.

They arrived before sunset. When they entered the great hall of Glenkeld, Amber saw that the majority of Cambels had already arrived, and the room swarmed with people. The aromatic scents of roasted meat and freshly baked bread spread through the air.

Dougal and Chief Neil sat at the high table, and Amber looked through the crowd for Amy and Kate. She spotted both women sitting next to Craig and Ian and made her way to them.

"There you are!" Kate exclaimed, standing up and extending her arms to Amber.

They hugged, Kate's scent enveloping Amber. She always smelled like home and something like vanilla, although Amber knew it was impossible because there was no vanilla in medieval Europe.

They'd met at Amber and Owen's wedding and, as with Amy, they'd immediately understood each other well. Kate was different from anyone Amber had connected with in the twenty-first century. She was soft and sweet, but there was a hard core within her, and a strength of character that Amber admired right away.

Amy joined the hug.

"That's right. Let's give everyone a reason to stare," Amber said.

"I don't care," Kate said. "I'm so happy to see you girls." They broke off the hug, and Amber went to sit on the opposite side of the table next to Owen. "I was waiting for you to join us, because I made something special."

There was a large plate on the table covered with a linen cloth. Amy leaned in a little and sniffed. "What did you make?"

Ian cocked his head and chuckled mysteriously. "She let me try it, just a little piece." He looked around, and when he saw no one was listening, he leaned forward and added in a low voice, "'Tis a little piece of heaven from yer time."

Amber said, "Oh my God, what is it? I'm dying to know now!"

Kate giggled and lifted the linen. The plate contained a significant pile of doughnuts.

"Doughnuts!" Amy and Amber cried in unison.

"Oh my, how I miss coffee..." Amy said through a mouthful of doughnut. "These are divine, Katie!"

Amber bit into a doughnut and closed her eyes in sheer bliss. It tasted as good as the ones she remembered. The men were also helping themselves, and everyone let out orgasmic sounds, moaning and humming in delight.

"How did you make these?" Amber said. "Can you even make them with the ingredients of medieval Scotland?"

"Yes! The ingredients are all the same, save sugar. But honey does the job perfectly. Also, wheat flour is a bit of a challenge, but Ian splurged a little for me. And here we are."

"Katie, for ye... For this"—Ian gestured appreciatively with a piece of doughnut in his hand—"anything."

Kate giggled. "You certainly inspire me to bake"—she winked to Amy and Amber—"some buns"—she waited—"in the oven."

Amy got it first. "Oh! Congratulations, you two!" She clapped her hands and hugged Kate. Owen and Craig exchanged a puzzled gaze.

Amber grinned. "They're expecting a baby," she explained to the two Highlanders, and smiles spread across their faces. She looked at Kate. "Congratulations!"

"Thank you." Kate and Ian exchanged a gaze full of tenderness and love.

"Honestly, the doughnuts were more for me than for you guys. I'm craving carbs!" Kate giggled again.

Amber thought she had a delightful, infectious laugh, and she laughed, too.

"'Tis a joy to see Ian so content," Owen said to Amber quietly, a grin on his face. "He came back from Baghdad broken and desperate. Now look at him. A husband. A future father. Happy. Whole."

Enjoying Ian and Kate's happiness, she pressed herself against Owen's side, and even the brush of his skin sent a charge of electricity through her. She'd gotten used to holding back on touching him in public, and she was actually enjoying the secret touches under the table, or the occasional brush of a hip, or a stolen kiss.

"Welcome to fatherhood," Craig toasted. "May yer family grow, strengthen, and prosper. I'm happy for ye, Ian."

All of them, save Kate, clunked their cups of ale together.

"What about you two?" Amy winked. "Any news of more little Cambels to come?"

Amber exchanged a glance with Owen. They'd talked about it and decided they weren't ready. Amber followed her cycle strictly for birth control. Although that method was not guaranteed, and they'd still be happy if she got pregnant, for now they both wanted adventure.

"Not yet," she said. "And there won't be for a while."

Amy threw her hands in the air in a gesture of surrender. "All right. All right. Got it. No more questions."

"Though I dinna mind practicing," Owen said.

Amy closed her ears with her fingers. "Don't even want to hear about practicing."

The six of them laughed warmheartedly.

Dougal appeared behind Owen. "Son, I wanted to greet ye. How was the journey?"

Breaking all conventions, Owen stood and hugged his father, both clapped each other's backs. "Good, Da, thank ye."

"Amber"—he nodded to her—"ye look well."

"Hello, Dougal."

Though Dougal liked her, there was a little awkwardness between them, but Amber was sure it was only because he didn't know her very well.

"How are ye both?" he asked.

"Well. We're heading south to visit the Bruce."

"Oh, aye. 'Tis good. He has the highest regard for ye. The war isna over yet, so be careful. King Edward still refuses to acknowledge Scotland as an independent kingdom, and the Bruce its king."

"Aye."

Dougal clapped Owen's shoulder amicably. "Ye did well, son. I couldna be more proud."

He walked away, and Amber saw Owen's gaze follow him, and that his eyes were wet.

He came back to sit next to her, and Amber tangled her fingers with his under the table. "I couldn't be more proud of you, either," she whispered. "Of us."

"Oh, lass, 'tis I who am proud to be the husband of such a wonderful woman as ye. Ye're my treasure."

And even though people would stare, she leaned over and kissed him. She couldn't wait another second to show him how much she loved him.

Because the biggest treasure in her life was her Highlander's love.

Thank you for reading HIGHLANDER'S LOVE. Find out what happens next Sineag sends Rogene to Owen's sword-brother Angus Mackenzie in HIGHLANDER'S DESIRE.

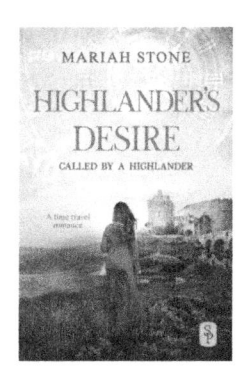

He's engaged. She refuses to alter history. Their love is forbidden. But destiny binds them. Will they risk their lives and Scotland's future by choosing desire over duty?

Read HIGHLANDER'S DESIRE now >
"This book is so outstanding. I was on the edge of my seat throughout this book. I even talked to the characters, even though they did not listen. lol!"

Sign-up for Mariah Stone's Newsletter:
http://mariahstone.com/signup

Feeling like a billion dollars?

Other mysterious matchmakers help people find their soulmates across the ages; also in modern times. If you haven't read Channing and Ella's story yet, be sure to pick up AGE OF WOLVES.

There's more to tattooed billionaire, Channing Hakonson,

MARIAH STONE

than detective Ella O'Conner could have ever imagined—something mystical and ancient.

Read AGE OF WOLVES now >
⭐⭐⭐⭐⭐ *"Great twists and turns. I just couldn't stop reading!"*

Or stay in the Highlands and keep reading for an excerpt from HIGHLANDER'S DESIRE.

~

Eilean Donan Castle, May 2021

Rogene Wakeley laid two long candles neatly next to each other on the polished antique sideboard. Taking a deep breath, she told herself she was 99.9 percent happy for her friend.

Karin was getting married in Eilean Donan, having her dream wedding to the love of her life in the most beautiful castle in Scotland.

Rogene glanced at the fine painting hanging above the table on a rough stone wall. The portraits of generations of clan MacRae looked at the guests from the walls of the Banqueting Hall, surrounded by rococo and neoclassical furniture. Rogene took the bottle of whisky out of the bag and placed it near the silver quaich, a traditional, shallow drinking cup the couple would use as part of the wedding ceremony.

She glanced over her shoulder to make sure the guests were fine. Fifty or so people sat on the Chippendale chairs, murmuring quietly—elegantly dressed women in small hats with flowers, nets, and feathers, most men in kilts. The happy 99.9 percent of her had been glad to shake the hand of every single one of them as they had arrived and smile so much her face ached.

The happy 99.9 percent of her rejoiced in being the maid of honor, making sure all went according to Karin's German standards: perfectly and by the minute. Which was good because Rogene was the responsible one. The one who had basically raised her brother, David, from the time she was twelve years old, despite living with their aunt and uncle.

David was talking to one of Karin's relatives sitting in the front row. The fabric of his suit stretched across his broad shoulders. He was close to being accepted into Northwestern and was likely to get a football scholarship. Good Lord, when did he start looking so much like Dad?

Rogene's eyes prickled.

That was the 0.1 percent talking.

To distract herself, she turned back to the table and placed the silver candleholder by the quaich.

The 0.1 percent reminded her that she couldn't rely on people. That people could disappear at any moment. That they could die. That people wouldn't take care of her when she needed them the most.

That she was so much better off on her own.

She took the vase that held a gorgeous bouquet of thistle, white roses, and freesias and placed it in the center of the table. As she removed a rose from the side of the bouquet and put it into the center, the unhappy 0.1 percent of her wondered if she'd ever have a bouquet like this at her own wedding. Probably not. She couldn't imagine getting married. How did others manage to be happy and in love and trust another human being?

As she turned the vase a little, she went completely still.

The bouquet!

She whirled around to the arched exit, her heart slamming in her chest.

"What is it, Rory?" Anusua, her colleague from Oxford University, asked. She stood at the entrance to the hall, ready to greet newly arriving guests. Short and full-figured, she looked stunning in a similar lilac dress to Rogene's.

"The bouquet..." Rogene grabbed her hair, likely messing up the intricately woven braids and the chic updo that felt like bread crust under her fingers. She felt naked in the long, mermaid-style, lilac dress with low cleavage. Rogene's usual wardrobe included elegant blouses and turtlenecks with suit pants or black jeans, which made her look like a professor before she even was one. "I forgot to pick up the bouquet."

"Oh, bollocks," Anusua muttered, abandoning her post. "Let me fetch it. What's the address?"

Anusua was an Indian Brit, and definitely more accustomed to driving on the "wrong" side of the street. But Rogene was the maid of honor, and if Anusua made a mistake, Karin would be crushed. There was also the bagpipe player who was due to arrive any minute...

"Come on, Rory," Anusua said. "Give me the car key."

Anusua was right, Rogene could delegate, be part of a team.

But the 0.1 percent stopped her.

David walked towards them and opened the beautiful, massive door under the arched entryway for an old lady to pass through. Too bad the door was only a replica made in the grand restoration of the castle in the 1920s, the historian within Rogene thought distantly.

"Everything okay?" David asked.

He was so handsome in his suit, his dirty-blond hair cut in a simple, classic style that made him look older than he was.

Or, maybe, it was because he'd had to grow up sooner than he should have, especially with her abandoning him in Chicago for her doctoral program at Oxford.

"All good," Rogene said, her voice tense.

"You aren't going to let me help, are you?" Anusua said softly. "You know you *can* rely on people to give you a hand."

Anusua sighed and walked to the old lady who had just come

in, no doubt to see if she needed any help. David patted Rogene on the shoulder. "What was that about?"

"I need to go get the bouquet, but the bagpipe player still isn't here."

"Let me get the bouquet. You deal with the bagpiper."

"Is your permit even valid here?"

If he misread the name of a street while driving the car on the other side of the road, she'd need to deal with a lost teenager in a foreign country. His face darkened. He knew she was thinking of his dyslexia, not his driver's license.

"Okay," he said. "Go. I can deal with the bagpiper."

She sighed. That was the lesser evil, even though she did hate to leave the responsibility to anyone but herself.

"I'll be right back. Thanks, Dave."

She opened the arched door into the damp, freezing air of the Scottish Highlands and hurried down the old stone stairwell into the courtyard. Harsh wind blew in her face as she passed through the gatehouse with the raised portcullis and onto the long bridge that connected the island to the mainland. She barely glanced at a couple of tourists who roamed around the shape of the medieval tower back on the island.

Rogene's heels clacked against the bridge as she ran towards the parking area. Damn it, she hadn't taken her bolero, and it was so windy—probably because of three lochs that met here. Her lungs ached for air, and a needle pierced her side, reminding her that she should really get more exercise, not spend all her time in archives and libraries working on her PhD.

But her current discomfort didn't matter. She couldn't let her best friend down on her wedding day. She was already walking on a thin ice by refusing to let other people help with her research. There were two problems with that. One, her thesis supervisor was pissed off. Two, she had a bold topic, and she had no proof for it yet.

Panting, she got into the car. After three and a half years in the UK, she was used to driving on the other side of the road, and quickly navigated to Inverinate, which was ten minutes away. Luckily, there were no problems on her way, and she quickly picked up the bouquet and drove back to the castle.

When she was back in the courtyard of Eilean Donan, she saw Karin on the small landing in front of the arched entrance into the Banqueting Hall. Wind played with the long locks of her blond hair that cascaded down her back. A wreath of white heather circled her head. She was such a beautiful bride. One hand was on her flat, corseted belly, the other on her mom's shoulder. David watched her, looking as if he'd swallowed a frog.

Rogene's legs growing cold, she waved with the bouquet as she climbed the stone stairs, careful not to slip on the smooth surface. "It's here! Don't you worry, everything's all right."

Karin glared at her. "All right?"

Rogene swallowed as she kept climbing. Usually, Karin was sweet, but she was now definitely in bridezilla mode.

When Rogene stood in front of Karin, she handed her the bouquet and plastered a happy smile on her face. "Did the bagpipe player arrive?"

Karin paled as her eyes widened at David. "Did he?"

"Yes, he's already inside," David said.

Karin sighed. Her eyes glistened, and Rogene knew her best friend was on the verge of tears. "Do I look horrible?" Karin asked.

Rogene gasped. "What? No! You look amazing. Where is this coming from?"

"Even with this makeup?"

"What do you mean?" Narrowing her eyes, Rogene studied Karin. This looked like her usual evening makeup. Oh...shoot!

Karin sniffled. "The makeup woman never showed up."

"Doesn't matter," Rogene said. "You look beautiful and Nigel's going to be over the moon. Are you ready?"

Karin exchanged a glance with her mom, then took a deep, steadying breath and nodded. "Yes." She smiled. "I am."

"Okay. Let's go."

She opened the door and nodded to the bagpipe guy, who began playing. Nigel, who stood tall and handsome in his kilt, watched the door like a hawk. When Karin appeared, his face lit up, and Karin beamed as she met his gaze.

The couple lit candles and said their vows, which were beautiful and very Scottish. They drank from the silver quaichs, and finally signed the marriage license—or the marriage schedule, as they called it over here.

There were photos, and more bagpipe music, and cheers and broad smiles. The couple looked happy, and as enamored with each other as they could be.

After the ceremony, everyone descended into the Billeting Room on the ground floor for the champagne reception. As the waiters carried trays with drinks around, Rogene felt like she could finally take a breather. Her stomach squeezing in nervous spasms from the adrenaline that hadn't stopped racing through her veins yet, she took her bolero and her clutch and went out onto one of the curtain walls facing north.

David stood on the circular wall around the Great Well, leaning on the parapet with his elbows.

Rogene knew something was wrong and made her way up to him. His eyes were on the island, which was covered with grass, a few bushes and small trees. A group of four people walked down the pebble-covered path that stretched from left to right.

Rogene couldn't see any sign of the curtain walls that she'd seen on archaeological maps of the islands. There were supposed to be three towers that had been raised here in the first phase of construction, in the thirteenth to fourteenth centuries, and the castle where the wedding took place must have only had the keep building.

David's profile was stern, his gray eyes fixed forward.

"Is everything okay?" she asked.

"I almost ruined Karin's wedding." He swallowed hard as he met her eyes, a muscle in his jaw flexing.

"Don't say that," she said.

"It's my fault. The makeup artist's car broke. Her phone was dead, and she came here. I gave her the address of Karin's hotel..."

"Good."

"Not good. I said 51 Dornie Street..."

The address was 15 Dornie Street. Rogene felt the blood leave her face. He sometimes reversed the numbers or the letters in a word and read things like "left" instead of "felt."

"Karin was upset because of me," he muttered.

Rogene searched for David's hand to squeeze it like she had when he was younger. A dyslexic born to professor parents, and with his older sister receiving a scholarship to do a PhD at Oxford, he'd always felt inferior. That was part of the reason he'd gone into sports and was now a football team captain.

"It wasn't your fault," she said.

He scoffed and shook his head. "Who else's?"

"Mine. I should have never left you. I should have sent Anusua to get the bouquet."

He sighed and lowered his head, looking at his shoes. "Whatever. It wouldn't change a thing about me. My only hope for a good future is a football scholarship, and it's still up in the air. I'm the black sheep in a family of geniuses, and you know it. Mom and Dad were professors. You will be, too, one day."

She wasn't so sure about that. The date of her thesis defense was fast approaching and she still didn't have any tangible proof of her mom's outrageous hypothesis that Robert the Bruce had come to Eilean Donan in 1307 on his way to surrender but something or someone had changed his mind.

"David, come on. You're not a black sheep."

"Stop," he said and pulled away. "I don't want anyone's pity."

He pushed himself off the banister and strode into the castle.

"David!" Rogene called.

Guilt weighed in her chest. He was upset, and she couldn't just abandon him, not again.

She went after him, fighting against the icy wind, her heels clacking against the stones. She hurried down to the ground floor, hoping he had gone back into the Billeting Room where the reception was taking place, but he wasn't among the guests. Maybe he'd gone into the kitchens? She turned, trying to think of the best route to get there when she heard steps against stone. The tiny foyer had only three doors, two of which led to the Banqueting Hall.

Could he have gone through the third one? Wrought iron hardware held together the planks of massive wood under the arched pathway. A barrier with a red rope guarded the entrance, but that wouldn't stop an upset teenager. She thought she heard footsteps descending.

There were no museum workers present. She went around the barrier, opened the door, and flicked the switch. Lights came on, illuminating stone steps leading down.

"David!" she called as she made her way down the stairs into the grave-like coldness of the basement.

Downstairs was a surprisingly large space illuminated by electrical lamps. Tables and chairs covered with protective sheets stood along the rough stone walls. The chilly air smelled like wet stone, earth, and mold. Light didn't quite reach the very far end of the hall where she noticed a massive door in the shadows.

"David, where are you?" she called.

Only her echo answered, jumping off the ancient, vaulted ceiling. Looking around, she remembered an old legend claiming the castle's name didn't originate from a sixth-century saint, but from a colony of otters that had inhabited the island. Supposedly, the King of the Otters was buried beneath the foundations of the castle. Cu-Donn meant an otter, or a brown dog, but it was also very likely that a Pictish tribe might have been called this. There had been, after all, an Iron Age fortress here before, which had burned to the ground.

Suddenly, Rogene felt like a little girl again, like the first time Mom had gotten her fascinated with history. They had been on a trip in Stirling, and Mom had told her a ghost story, and then the real story behind it. Life would never be the same for Rogene.

She wished she could spend more time here, but she needed to find David. The reception would be over soon, and the wedding party would head to the hotel for dinner. Huddling in her bolero, she walked towards the dark door.

"David?" she called.

The echo of her heels was loud and felt foreign here, as though she could wake up the ghosts of Bronze and Iron Age people, the Picts, and generations of Mackenzies and MacRaes. She could almost feel their eyes on her.

With a shaking hand, she pushed the cold wood of the door and it opened with a gnash. The scent of wet earth and mold breathed on her from the pitch darkness. Was it even safe to be here?

She stepped in.

For a moment, she had the weirdest sense she had left the world as she knew it and stepped into another one. She also had the sense that someone was there.

"David? Hello?"

The echo greeted her back.

She searched with her left hand against the rough wall and found a switch. A single electric bulb suspended from an arched ceiling illuminated the space, which resembled a dungeon, minus the iron grating and torture instruments. A pile of boulders and rocks rose to her right. Steel columns supported the ceiling.

Rogene shivered and huddled into her bolero.

To her left and straight ahead, the walls of rough stone and mortar were whole. Curious, she walked farther into the room, her heels sinking into the packed-earth floor. She held the edges of the bolero closed over her chest, but the wet cold crept into the marrow of her bones. Her knees shook, but she couldn't say if it was from cold or from excitement.

With her eyes on the pile of stones, she approached it and

went completely still. Among rubble, dirt, and sand, a carving on a flat rock caught her attention, and something else...

A handprint?

She gasped and her echo gasped with her. Sinking to her knees, she began clearing the rock. When the carving and the handprint were clearly visible, she tasted dust on her tongue. She realized she was touching her mouth with her dirty hand.

Light-headed, she felt the ground shift. Gently, she brushed the carving with her palm, every indent distinct against her fingers. There were three wavy lines and then a straight line and a handprint, just like the footprint on the inauguration stone of the Kings of Dál Riata in Argyll.

"Wow..." she whispered.

"Do ye ken what that is?" a woman said behind her.

Rogene jerked, lost her balance, and fell right on her behind. A woman in a green hooded cloak stood a few steps away from her.

Rogene sighed out. "Jesus Christ, you gave me a heart attack."

The woman came closer and stretched her hand out. When Rogene accepted her hand, the woman pulled her to stand up.

"Sorry," the woman said with a Scottish burr. "I didna mean to frighten ye. I always forget ye humans get so startled."

Ye humans? She must be the castle worker and had probably gotten a bit too into her role or something.

"I'm probably not supposed to be here," Rogene said.

"'Tis all right," the woman said. "I dinna mind. My name is Sìneag, by the way. And ye are?"

"Rogene Wakeley."

"Well, Rogene, ye found a fascinating stone." Her eyes sparkled in the yellow semidarkness.

Rogene distantly wondered why a castle worker didn't scold her for being in a prohibited area. Perhaps Sìneag was a bit more chill about the rules...and maybe this basement wasn't as dangerous as it looked.

Sìneag lowered her hood, and Rogene marveled at her pretty pale face and beautiful red hair that cascaded in soft waves down her shoulders.

"'Tis a Pictish carving that opens a tunnel through time," Sìneag said.

A tunnel through time? Rogene frowned.

"I've never heard of a time-travel myth," she said. "Are you sure?"

"Oh, aye." She nodded. "Very sure. The three waves are the river of time, and this line is the tunnel through it. A druid carved it."

Rogene bent down and studied the lines and the curves. "Hm. It does look ancient. Picts, huh? So, between sixth and eighth centuries, probably."

"Aye. That druid believed ye can fall through time and find the person ye're truly destined to be with. The one person ye love. Do ye ken?"

Now Sìneag was clearly inventing things. Picts didn't have written language, so they had no way of leaving such messages. The only tiny accounts of them came from the Romans and Christian monks, who wrote chronicles that were concerned with battles and wars. Not myths of romantic love.

"One romantic druid, huh?" she mumbled, not wanting to confront the woman.

"Aye. He was. This stone has always caused curiosity. When clan Mackenzie owned the castle in the fourteenth century, a certain Angus Mackenzie wondered what this carving could mean."

Rogene glanced sharply at Sìneag. "Angus Mackenzie?"

"Aye."

"The one who married Euphemia of Ross?"

"The very same."

"Their marriage produced Paul Mackenzie, who famously saved the life of King Robert III. Did Angus Mackenzie have something to do with this rock? Did he leave some information about this myth?"

Sineag laughed. "Nae he didna. But he is the man for ye."

Rogene stared at her in disbelief. Then gave out a loud laugh. "For me?"

"Aye, dearie. Look." She looked down at the rock and Rogene followed her gaze.

The carved lines glowed.

Rogene shook her head, not believing her eyes. The three lines of the river glowed blue, and the straight line through it glowed brown. Blinking, she sank to her knees by the rock and looked at it from different angles. What could glow like that? Puzzled, she ran her finger along the blue line, and a buzz went through her. Her heart accelerated. What the hell was that?

She looked at the handprint and had an inexplicable urge to put her own palm into it. Had the Kings of Dál Riata had a similar impulse to step into the footprint? Something called to her, and she just had to press her hand against this rock.

As though, if she did, everything would be all right in the world.

Blood pulsing in her hand, she pressed her palm into the print.

A shiver went through her. The sensation of being sucked in and swallowed consumed her. She felt as if she were falling into emptiness, hand, then head down, as nausea rose in her throat. She screamed, terror washing through her in a cold, paralyzing rush.

And then she became darkness...

Keep reading HIGHLANDER'S DESIRE.

ALSO BY MARIAH STONE

MARIAH'S TIME TRAVEL ROMANCE SERIES

- Called by a Highlander
- Called by a Viking
- Called by a Pirate
- Fated

MARIAH'S REGENCY ROMANCE SERIES

- Dukes and Secrets

VIEW ALL OF MARIAH'S BOOKS IN READING ORDER

Scan the QR code for the complete list of Mariah's ebooks, paperbacks, and audiobooks in reading order.

GET A FREE MARIAH STONE BOOK!

Join Mariah's mailing list to be the first to know of new releases, free books, special prices, and other author giveaways.

freehistoricalromancebooks.com

ENJOY THE BOOK? YOU CAN MAKE A DIFFERENCE!

Please, leave your honest review for the book.
As much as I'd love to, I don't have financial capacity like New York publishers to run ads in the newspaper or put posters in subway.

But I have something much, much more powerful!

Committed and loyal readers

If you enjoyed the book, I'd be so grateful if you could spend five minutes leaving a review on the book's Amazon page.

Thank you very much!

SCOTTISH SLANG

aye – yes
   bairn - baby
   bastart - bastard
   bonnie - pretty, beautiful.
   canna- can not
   couldna – couldn't
   didna- didn't ("Ah didna do that!")
   dinna- don't ("Dinna do that!")
   doesna – doesn't
   fash - fuss, worry ("Dinna fash yerself.")
   feck - fuck
   hasna – has not
   havna - have not
   hadna – had not
   innit? - Isn't it?
   isna- Is not
   ken - to know
   kent - knew
   lad - boy
   lass - girl
   marrit – married

SCOTTISH SLANG

nae – no or not
shite - faeces
the morn - tomorrow
the morn's morn - tomorrow morning
uisge-beatha (uisge for short) – Scottish Gaelic for water or life / aquavitae, the distilled drink, predecessor of whiskey
verra – very
wasna - was not
wee - small
wilna - will not
wouldna - would not
ye - you
yer – your (also yerself)

ABOUT MARIAH STONE

Mariah Stone is a bestselling author of time travel romance novels, including her popular Called by a Highlander series and her hot Viking, Pirate, and Regency novels. With nearly one million books sold, Mariah writes about strong modern-day women falling in love with their soulmates across time. Her books are available worldwide in multiple languages in e-book, print, and audio.

Subscribe to Mariah's newsletter for a free time travel book today at mariahstone.com!

- facebook.com/mariahstoneauthor
- instagram.com/mariahstoneauthor
- bookbub.com/authors/mariah-stone
- pinterest.com/mariahstoneauthor
- amazon.com/Mariah-Stone/e/B07JVW28PJ

Printed in Great Britain
by Amazon